Edward Sylvester Ellis

The Life and Deeds of Admiral Dewey, the Hero of Manila Bay

For our boys and girls

Edward Sylvester Ellis

The Life and Deeds of Admiral Dewey, the Hero of Manila Bay
For our boys and girls

ISBN/EAN: 9783337214043

Printed in Europe, USA, Canada, Australia, Japan

Cover: Foto ©Raphael Reischuk / pixelio.de

More available books at **www.hansebooks.com**

THE LIFE AND DEEDS

OF

ADMIRAL DEWEY
The Hero of Manila Bay

FOR OUR BOYS AND GIRLS

Telling in Simple Language of Admiral Dewey's Ancestry, and Early Life,
His School Days, Life at the Naval Academy, Brilliant Career in the
Civil War, Services in the Navy Department, Various
Commands on the White Squadron

His World-Famed Victory at Manila
AND
Glorious Reception Upon His Return to America

By EDWARD S. ELLIS, A. M.
The Noted Writer for Young People

SUPERBLY ILLUSTRATED WITH EIGHT-COLOR LITHOGRAPHS, AND
BEAUTIFUL HALF-TONE ENGRAVINGS

INTRODUCTION.

THERE are giants who salute one another across the gloom of the centuries. They are majestic figures towering above the myriads clustering at their feet, and limned against the eternal background, their heroic forms will stand out distinct in all their impressive grandeur, as the ages, throbbing with human endeavor, sweep past. Other giants will rise and take their places in the immortal group, and the world will do them homage.

It is only within modern times that the Sailor has become the equal brother of the Soldier. Alexander, Cæsar, Hannibal, Charlemagne, Washington, Napoleon and Wellington, were all leaders of armies of greater or less magnitude, but Nelson, Farragut and Dewey climbed to their mighty pedestals during the present century, and the last of the peerless trio, at its very close. Henceforward, as Mahan shows, the struggle for supremacy between warring nations must take place on the sea and the Sailor promises to pass beyond his brother Soldier in the race for glory.

How true that the career of all whom the world calls great is rarely or never foreshadowed by their youth. Who would have dared to prophesy the wonderful future of Grant, Sherman, Sheridan, Nelson, Farragut or Dewey while they were still boys? If circumstances favored the development of their genius, it is none the less true that their genius was simply awaiting its opportunity. And being true of them, it must be equally true of thousands of others who are at this hour living uneventful lives, and who will pass to their rest, without their friends or probably themselves suspecting the powers lying latent within them, because the crisis will never arise to call them forth; but if the need is for a leader, Washington or Grant steps forward; if for comrades to the leader, Greene, Wayne, Sullivan and Putnam, or Thomas, Sherman, Sheridan, Farragut, Porter and a host of compatriots appear. When they passed from the stage of action, and the cry was heard again, it was answered by Dewey, Sampson, Schley, Watson and the commanders in the field.

It is an impressive truth we repeat that this transcendent ability is never absent or lacking among the American people. We have hosts fully measuring up to every requirement, and who, when weighed in the balance will never be found wanting. In the career of no man is this fact more strikingly shown than in that of Admiral George Dewey, who rising from the ranks of the "common people," has reached, almost at a single bound, the highest pinnacle of fame and won the everlasting gratitude of his countrymen. It is a comforting assurance indeed that no matter how immense the demands that may be laid upon us in the future, we have a plenitude of brain, of brawn, of courage, of skill and of genius fully to meet and surmount them all. From the loins of the Anglo-Saxon spring in a human sense the saviours of the world, and our hearts glow with gratitude at the consciousness that among all nations, peoples, climes and ages none has been so favored of heaven as ours.

TABLE OF CONTENTS

CHAPTER I

Ancestry and Boyhood of Admiral Dewey

Thor.—The Illustrious Lineage of Admiral Dewey.—His Birth and Boyhood.—
Dewey at School.—An Unmitigatedly Bad Boy.—His Bout With His Teacher.—
His Conquest.—The Beneficial Result to Dewey.

HAVE you ever heard of Asa-Thor, more generally known as Thor? He was a wonderful being, if the accounts of him are true. Think of one who lived in a palace containing 540 halls, who was monarch of all the forces of the air, who directed the meteors as they whizzed through space, and held full mastery of the winds and storms, who launched the lightning and controlled the earth-quaking thunder and was therefore the greatest "boss" of which there is any record. I am quite sure that not all of you, when thinking of the fifth day in the week, have noted that "Thor's day" was named in honor of this same Thor, but such is the fact.

Enough has been said to make it clear that Thor was one of the creations of mythology. It was to him the Saxons and Danes prayed, when they wanted favorable weather, and the Scandinavian mythology claimed that he was a son of Odin, the Supreme God, and Freya his wife. His stupendous palace was called Thrudwanger and it was there his invincible warriors gathered after battle and were received in fitting state by the great, red-bearded god who must have been a terrible fellow, for it is said that when the other gods got into trouble, they called on Thor to help them out, and he was generally quite willing to do so. He was fond of war, and made ten pins of those gods who had the presumption to combat his awful will. All that Thor had to do was to get within reach of those fellows when with one whack from his hammer he struck them down.

The hammers used by Thor were very accommodating, for, after being hurled with resistless power, they unerringly executed their mission and then whisked back into his hand again. If we could make such weapons in these days, what a good thing it would be for us and what a bad thing for our victims! Naturally the sign of Thor's hammer was a sacred emblem among the sturdy old Teutons.

Now what has all this to do with Admiral George Dewey the conqueror of Manila, and the hero of the Spanish-American War? Have patience and you shall learn.

THE LINEAGE OF ADMIRAL DEWEY.

Some of the mightiest monarchs that ever reigned have laid claim to being the descendants of Thor. There must have been a tremendous tapering off as the line ran down the centuries, but that could well be and still retain a good deal of the majestic power and genius that lifted those rulers above the ordinary human beings. For instance, there was Hugues Capet, the founder of the third or Capetian dynasty in France, who died in A.D. 996, and who was succeeded by thirteen kings in succession before the close of the dynasty, when the sceptre was wrenched from their grasp by Philip VI. of Valois and transferred to his own race.

Then there were Alfred the Great of England and Anne of Russia, who like Capet insisted that they came in a direct line from Thor. There were still others of less renown, and among them were the unquestioned ancestors of the sturdy son of New England, whose name just now is in everybody's mouth. So you see, provided all these accounts are reliable, George Dewey is a decendant of the marvelous Thor of Scandinavian mythology.

AMERICAN PRIDE OF DECENT.

We care very little for ancestry in this country. We prefer to take a man as we find him, without regard to who his parents or grandparents were. While the lineage of Dewey is of the very best, there have been instances in this country where it was risky to climb too high among the branches of the family tree, for there was no saying what one would reach. The witty poet, John G. Saxe, once expressed this danger in the following lines:

> " Of all the notable things on earth,
> The queerest one is the pride of birth
>   Among our fierce Democracy;
> A bridge across a hundred years,
> Without a prop to save from sneers,
> Not even a couple of rotten *peers*,
> A thing for laughter fleers and jeers
>   Is American aristocracy.

Depend upon it, my snobbish friend,
Your family thread you can't ascend
Without good reason to apprehend
You'll find it waxed at the further end
    By some plebeian vocation ;
Or worse than that your boasted line
May end in a loop of stronger twine
    That plagued some worthy relation."

THE FATHER OF DEWEY.

Some of the admiring biographers of Admiral Dewey have carefully traced his descent back through the centuries to the dim personalities that figure creditably upon the pages of history, but let it suffice to say that the first Dewey, who came to America, arrived in 1633, and settled at Dorchester, Massachusetts, and his name was Thomas. Following down the line of good men and true, we come to Julius Yemans Dewey, who was born in Berlin, Vermont, August 22, 1801. By his first wife (he was married three times), he had a daughter and three sons. The youngest was Mary, and the three sons were Charles, Edward and GEORGE DEWEY, who was born at Montpelier, December 26, 1837.

The head of this family was a physician, who practiced for a number of years in Montpelier, and then turned his attention to life insurance, in which he became very successful. His home was a roomy, old-fashioned colonial building that stood on State Street, and the family was widely noted for its generous and graceful hospitality, its culture and its social position. There was none in the State held in higher regard. Dr. Dewey was a most worthy man in every respect and was the founder of the principal Episcopal church in Montpelier. He was devout and of spotless integrity, and when he passed away, at the age of 76 years, there was none whose death was more widely regretted.

DEWEY'S BOYHOOD.

Now, there are precious few youths whose early history is of special interest. There is a striking similarity in the early years of all American boys, and to attempt to give every detail of Dewey's childhood would be to publish a mass of dull stuff that never rose above and failed to reach the stirring level of that which through many less distinguished men than he passed in their early youth.

Suppose we should tell of his roaming through the New England woods, hunting for squirrels or game birds? You have probably had the same experience yourselves, and many of you can recall a more stirring one, especially if you had lived in the Southwest, where graver dangers threatened.

It may be entertaining to read of young Dewey's excellence as a swimmer, for he excelled at that accomplishment, but I doubt whether you would admit that he exceeded you, when you were of his age. He certainly did not equal Benedict Arnold, who was fond of seizing the paddles of a big waterwheel and holding fast, while he was carried under and above the rushing torrent to the intense fright of his youthful audience. As a horseman, young George Washington surpassed the boy Dewey, as have hundreds of Texans and cowboys, of whom it has been said that they were born in the saddle.

Still less interesting would be the story of George Dewey's earliest boyhood, when he shed tears over that mournful ballad of the little sailor boy, whose mother was dead, and who was found begging on the streets by his father—

> " 'What, my Willie!' he cried. 'My poor little boy,
>   At last I've returned from the war,
> Thy sorrows shall cease, nor shall grief more annoy
>   The poor little child of a tar.' "

The fact that young Dewey used to sob over this touching recital was no proof of his future greatness, for what little boy or girl would not have done the same when the mournful tale was repeated, with proper solemnity and well-placed inflection?

This tendency to magnify trifles in the life of those who became famous has been humorously shown by a newspaper writer who said of young Dewey:

"At five months he could put a sailor's noose in his bib strings, and his nurse noticed with surprise that no matter how hard she rocked him he never showed signs of seasickness. This surprised her all the more, because the first words he uttered were, 'Heave yo!' When he yelled it was usually on the high C, and his first attempt at walking—although erroneously attributed to bow-legs—was really a clever imitation of the rolling gait of a seasoned navigator."

ADMIRAL GEORGE DEWEY

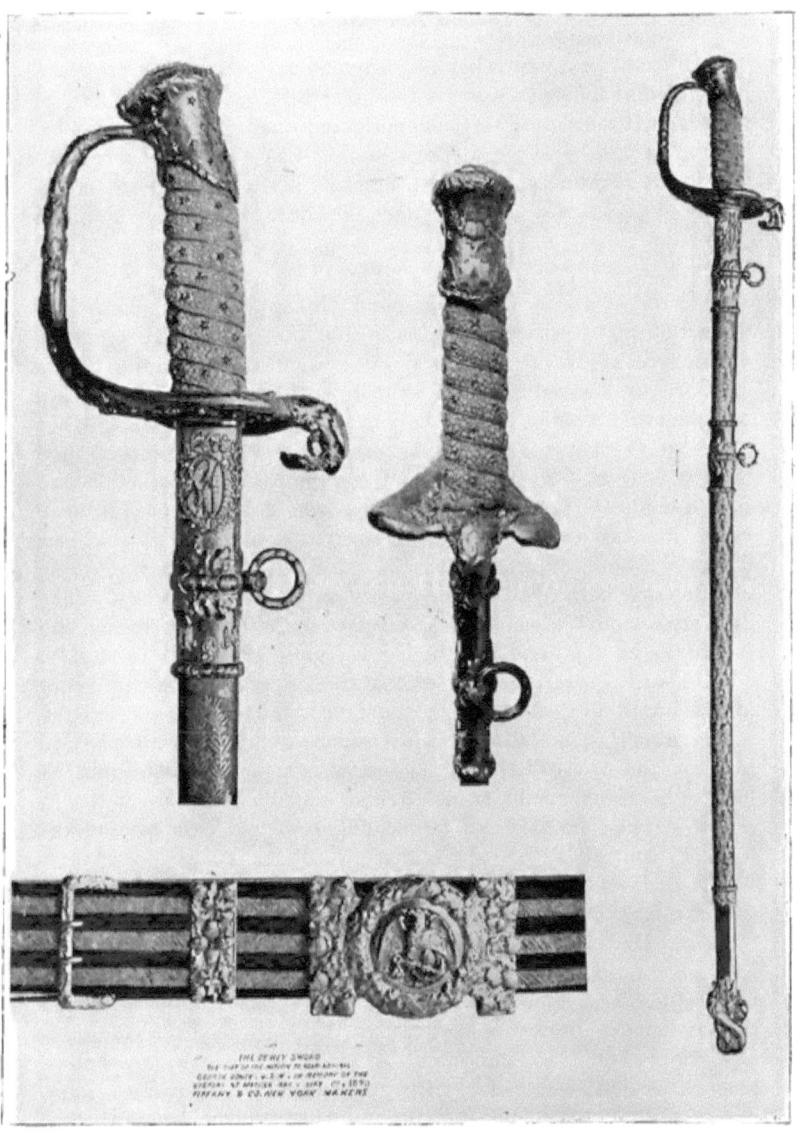

THE ADMIRAL DEWEY SWORD

The Nation's Gift: the Most Beautiful Sword in the History of Our Times.

It would be a vast relief to many people if the statement could be made that George Dewey was a good boy, but he was nothing of the sort. If there ever was an unmitigatedly bad youngster, it was he. When angered he swore, and at school he was not only disobedient, but openly rebellious. In short, he badly needed a good trouncing, and I am glad to say that just when he needed it most he got it to perfection.

DEWEY A BAD BOY.

There is a good deal of sound philosophy in the Scriptural injunction that to spare the rod is to spoil the child. The tendency of late years is to run to "moral suasion," many maintaining that a stubborn or disobedient child should never be subjected to physical punishment. This is undoubtedly true in the majority of cases, but it is none the less true that occasions sometimes arise when a merited chastisement has checked the youth on the road to destruction and turned him into the right path. As one who taught school for many years, I assert that no lad ever received a punishment which he deserved that he did not esteem the teacher more highly for having unflinchingly performed an unpleasant duty. It used to be a saying in a large school in which I was engaged : "Whip a boy to-day, and to-morrow he will bring you the biggest apple he can buy or steal."

This, of course, pre-supposes that the corporal punishment is not inflicted until all gentler means have failed. There are great hulking bullies among country boys, who respect nothing except physical prowess, and who will render an instructor's life a burden. until he has conquered them by sheer strength and superior skill, and such conquest must be made, or the school itself will pass beyond the teacher's control.

Now there is a big difference between simply a "bad" boy and one who is mean, sneaking and treacherous. It could never be said of young Dewey that he had any of the latter traits, but, overflowing with animal life, sturdy, active and strong, and with a disposition to be troublesome, he made no effort to restrain those propensities, and thus at times he became a nuisance that woefully needed abating.

Major Zenas K. Pangborn, of Jersey City, is widely known throughout that State and in many others as an editor of fine ability, and as not only a brilliant, forceful and witty speaker, but as the terror of stenographers.   Of all the orators to which I have listened, I never heard one who could talk with so much rapidity, and he has said that he never yet met the man who could keep up with him in a verbal race.

Like many of our famous men, Mr. Pangborn spent a number of years when comparatively young in teaching, and in the course of time he drifted to Vermont and was hired to conduct the school in which young George Dewey was a pupil.   Pangborn is not a large man, but he is strong and as active as a cat, and he learned of the reputation of that particular school for "carrying out" its teachers. More than one had given up in disgust and gone elsewhere to escape the stormy experience that had been theirs when in charge of the Montpelier educational institution.   The new teacher, therefore, knew what to expect, and he prepared for it.

A SCHOOL REBELLION HEADED BY DEWEY.

While walking to the schoolhouse, he saw a boy perched in the branches of a tree, his pockets filled with stones, which he was hurling with exasperating accuracy at all who came within range.   He was impartial in his attentions, and the smaller boys served equally well with the bigger ones for targets.   The indignant teacher shouted to young Dewey to cease throwing stones, as he could permit nothing of the kind.   Dewey stopped long enough to peer down among the branches and to reply to his instructor with a suggestion that he should go to a warmer place than can be found on this planet.   The gentleman felt like climbing the tree and yanking the young scapegrace down by the nape of his neck, but he restrained his temper and moved on.

Instead of waiting for hostilities to open on the side of the teacher, Dewey gathered a number of companions and boldly attacked him, first with snowballs and then with fists.   The result may be described as a drawn battle, and the question remained unsettled until the following day.   Encouraged by their partial success, Dewey and his wicked companions notified the instructor, that they had decided to give him a good licking, and then Dewey himself opened the attack.

It should be stated just here (and the statement is made with

the utmost respect to Mr. Pangborn) that nature had given him an
advantage beyond his alertness of movement and his strength. He
is cross-eyed, so that his assailants could never tell from his counte-
nance where he was looking, or where his next blow would land.
Dewey's futile drive was answered by the swish of a rawhide, which
descended so rapidly that his legs, shoulders and head felt as if they
were encased with blistering rings of fire. The other boys rallied to
their champion's help, and, dropping the rawhide, the teacher caught
up a big stick from the pile that served as fuel for the old-fashioned
stove, and which was fully a yard in length, and the lithe, sinewy
instructor gave an excellent imitation of a policeman running amuck
with his night-stick.

DEWEY CATCHES A TARTAR.

Bang! bang! went the club with an aim that never missed, and
every boy who served as a target was tumbled sprawling on the floor.
Instantly, attempting to leap to his feet again, he was battered back
by another thump on his head or shoulders and each was suggestive
of the kick of a horse. As ringleader of the rebels, Dewey was
given chief attention, and he received more thumps in those few
minutes than ever fell to his lot before or since.

The beauty of it all was that, after Mr. Pangborn had felled the
rascals, he found there was just enough of them to keep him comfort-
ably busy. All he had to do was to watch, and, whenever he saw a
head rising, hit it, by which means he maintained the "general level"
of the whole line, the performance suggesting a farmer threshing grain
with the flail that was so common in the days of our grandfathers.

Thus you see the affair had reached that point where the teacher
had all the fun to himself. So long as the rebels were kept on the
floor, they could do nothing in the way of attack, and, when one of
them, more soundly belabored than the others, attempted to crawl
away, he was followed by another bang from the club that made him
howl with pain.

Now, there could be but one issue to this rebellion, which was
really settled the moment the heavy stick began whirling about the
head of the athletic teacher, and descended with crushing effect upon
every rebel within reach. The whole party was soundly whipped,

and young Dewey had received the severest punishment of all, as he certainly deserved.

Like his companions in rebellion, Dewey slunk to his seat, cowed and was as meek as a lamb. It seemed to him that he had stopped about a hundred blows from the club, whose circlings were so swift that the eye could hardly follow them, and he was aching from head to foot. One fact was impressed upon his mind too firmly to be displaced : the attempt to whip the new teacher was a failure, and, all things considered, it would not pay to repeat the attempt.

THE HAPPY ENDING OF IT ALL.

George Dewey (and it is to be hoped the same was true of his companions) did some hard thinking, while poring over his lessons and waiting for his aches and pains to wear themselves out. He knew he had not received one whit more than he richly merited, and he respected and liked the man who chastised him. His after conduct was another illustration of the truth already stated—any boy who is justly punished blesses in his heart the hand that administers the punishment.

It is to the credit of young Dewey that he felt not a particle of resentment. As he looked furtively up at the undersized instructor, camly attending to his duties, the man assumed the proportions of a giant in his eyes, and he knew he was one of the best friends in all the world to him.

Mr. Pangborn was a little uneasy over the possible indignation of the father of Dewey, for the boy was badly battered and the teacher decided to walk home with him and explain to the parent the cause of his son's appearance. Dr. Dewey listened attentively and then said :

"I thank you, Mr. Pangborn, for punishing George as he deserved ; possibly however," he added with grim humor, "a little more medicine would have been beneficial to him."

Years later, when Dewey had grown to manhood and was fairly started on his brilliant career, he took the hand of his old instructor, and with a deep earnestness said :

"I thank you from the bottom of my heart for what you did to me when I was such a bad boy, for I believe that but for you in all probability I should have ended my days in the State prison."

CHAPTER II

At the Naval Academy—First Years in the Navy

The Sporting of a Good Negro Minstrel.—Dewey's First Cruise.—His Appointment
to the Naval Academy at Annapolis.—His Graduation.—Cruise in the Mediterranean and Appointment to a Lieutenancy on the *Mississippi*.—The Capture of
New Orleans.—Dewey's Daring and Coolness.

ENOUGH has been told of young George Dewey to show that
he was a genuine American boy, full of mischievous propensities, always ready to fight for his rights, inclined to get into
trouble, when really there was no necessity for it, active, abounding
with animal spirits and life, and with not the least inclination to be of
the "goody goody" sort. While still a boy, he was received into
the Protestant Episcopal Church, and though as a youth his example
may not always have been edifying, yet as he grew in years, he became more thoughtful and conscientious, and has always lived con-
sistently the profession of faith he took upon himself when a boy.

The cottage where he was born is still standing, it has been
removed from its original site and is now opposite the old fashioned
State House. Directly back of it ran the Onion River, which was a
constant source of delight and enjoyment to him. It was in its current that he learned to become a fine swimmer, and many a happy
hour was spent in pattering along its bank, barefooted and hunting
for the best place to woo the finny inhabitants from the water. Between him and his sister Mary, two years younger, there has always
been a tender affection, and she was his constant companion, gladly
carrying the angle worms or bait for him and as happy as he when
he landed a flopping fish on the bank between them.

NEGRO MINSTRELSY.

Among the many amusements of which young Dewey was fond
were performances in imitation of "negro minstrels." That kind of
entertainments was much more popular before the Civil War than afterward. With the passing of human slavery the romance of the sugar

cane and the cotton field departed, and we see no such organizations of the old time minstrels that were so well liked when our colored brother was a slave on a southern plantation.

The Dewey barn was the hall in which George and his young friends gave these shows, and among the interested spectators and listeners was his more thoughtful sister Mary, who preferred to sit far at the rear and quietly enjoy the fun made by the happy boisterous youngsters. George was stage manager, business manager and the star and life of the entertainment, quite content to glance from the stage now and then, in the midst of the hurly-burly and catch the encouraging smile on the face of his appreciative sister.

But on one occasion, George was stumped by finding that his leading lady, a miss of ten years, was absent. It is not known whether she resorted to the fashionable excuse of professionals that she was the victim of a sudden cold or indisposition, or whether she was pouting for an increased "salary," but she was elsewhere and the particular skit could not go on without herself or her understudy.

"My gracious, Mary!" he exclaimed; "you must take her place."

"But, brother, I don't know all the part," she protested.

"That doesn't make any difference; when you get stuck I'll fire off the pistol."

She held back for a time, but finally yielded. George watched her closely, and by blazing away at the awkward hitches, he smoothed over everything, and Mary did so well that the wonder is her ambition was not fired to attempt greater efforts. Her tastes, however, did not lie in that direction. There is nothing more pleasing to a lot of youngsters than the smoke and banging of firearms and the explosions within the barn became so frequent that some of the timid neighbors protested, and Dr. Dewey vetoed the whole business, thereby possibly nipping in the bud the blossoming of one of the greatest of negro minstrels.

DEWEY'S FIRST CRUISE.

All admirals of the seas must of necessity make their first cruise, and George Dewey's was made when he was eleven years old. One day, he and a playmate set off in the Doctor's gig, bent on having a

good time, and you may be sure they were not disappointed. Their
ostensible errand was to bring the cows home, but when they reached
Dog River, a tributary of the Winooski, it was so high from recent
rains as to be unfordable.

"It won't do, George," said his companion; "we must turn
back."

"Not a bit of it," replied the young admiral, striking the horse
so smart a blow, that, snuffing with fear, he stepped into the muddy
current and began gingerly feeling his way toward the opposite bank.
Five minutes later he was vigorously swimming, and the gig was
bobbing about like a cork. The top of the carriage swung free and
sailed away toward Lake Champlain. Dewey laughed and felt not
the least fear. It was all jolly fun to him, though his companion was
pale with fright.

"Let's grab hold of the harness," said Dewey; "the horse will tow
us to land."

The advise was followed, and before long both boys could touch
bottom without losing their balance. Presently they managed to
climb upon the horse's back. The adventure was not without considerable peril, and when at last Master Dewey reached home, he
thought it would be prudent to keep out of sight of his father.
Fortunately, the Doctor was absent attending to his professional
calls, and before he returned, the boy stole off to bed. When, however, his parent returned and learned what had taken place, he
hurried upstairs to "interview" his son. The latter knew what that
rapid step meant and shutting his eyes pretended to be sleeping.

"I hope he won't wake me up," was his thought; "what's the
use of disturbing a fellow when he's all tired out?"

But those professional eyes were not mislead by this pretense.
The parent began at once a severe scolding because of the rashness
of his boy, and there was a prospect that more drastic measures were
at hand, when the lad said:

"I should think, father, you would be thankful I wasn't
drowned."

"So I am, but if this conduct goes on you *will* be drowned,"
replied the parent, soon bidding his boy good night and leaving him
to his meditations.

When fifteen years old, George Dewey entered the Military Academy at Norwich, Vermont. It was excellent for him in every way, for he learned the virtue of obedience and strict discipline. His body was educated at the same time with his mind, which is the true method of training a child. He was an excellent pupil and became proficient in military tactics, so far as they are taught at the "tin soldier" school, as the West Point cadets term every such institution.

The military spirit in young Dewey was roused, but, instead of wishing to enter the Military Academy on the Hudson, his taste lay in the direction of the Naval Academy of Annapolis. He told his father of his wishes, but the parent was displeased. He had not intended that kind of a career for his boy and shook his head. But this did not change his son's tastes, and the doctor, being much of a philosopher, finally said that if George had really set his heart upon the naval profession, he would not only withdraw his objection, but would do what he could to secure an appointment to Annapolis for him.

The happy youngster told his good fortune to one of his school-mates, George Spalding, and to his dismay learned that Spalding had the same purpose in view, and was seeking the appointment. More than that, he secured it, much to the disgust of young Dewey, who was keenly disappointed, though he was made an alternate. All that saved him from being left high and dry was the intervention of a stern mother who sat down so heavily upon the project of her boy, Master George Spalding, that he gave it up, and turning his thoughts to theology, is at this writing a prominent clergyman in the interior of the State of New York.

AT THE NAVAL ACADEMY.

Dewew entered the Naval Academy at Annapolis September 23, 1854, when he was 17 years old. He was slim and active, with piercing black eyes, as full of mischief as ever, but well aware that there could be no outlet for his propensities in that centre of rigid discipline. The fact did not affect his high sense of honor nor the consciousness of his own rights. It was said of him that he was ready any moment to study or to fight, and he was as good at one as the other.

BATTLE OF MANILA, MAY 1, 1898

BATTLE OF MOBILE BAY, AUGUST 5TH, 1864

The above illustration represents the critical moment when it appeared as if the Flagship *Hartford* would be blown out of the water by the Ram *Tennessee*. Admiral Farragut leaped into the rigging and calmly awaited the results. Young Lieutenant Dewey fought in this battle, and it was under this renowned Commander that the future Admiral learned lessons of naval warfare, heroism and bravery

It will be noted that the period spent by young Dewey at Annapolis was one of intense political excitement throughout the country. The slavery and secession agitation had stirred turbulent passions to the exploding point, and thousands of thoughtful men saw that the black clouds would never be swept from the darkening sky until they had first been drained of their awful tempest of blood and the land filled with mourning and desolation.

In the national colleges, at West Point and at Annapolis, the line between the students and cadets from the respective sections was sharply drawn. There were wrangles and fights typical of the deadly meeting afterward on the battlefield, and in no place was the feeling more bitter than at Annapolis. The fiery spirit of Cadet Dewey could be confidently counted on to get him into trouble, for no Southerner was quicker to resent an insult than he. When called a "Yankee," he was rather pleased than otherwise, but when the Southerner, who had selected him as the most prominent Northern representative, called him a "doughface," Dewey knocked him down. In an instant the incensed cadet was on his feet, and the two went at it like a couple of tigers, while their partisans cheered them on. At the end of a few minutes the fight ended with Dewey the victor.

This was not the end of the unpleasant business, for a few days later an inkstand was viciously hurled at Dewey and missed his head by barely an inch. The Southerner who threw it did not deny the act, but proceeded to mix it up with Dewey, who pummeled him more severely than he had punished his friend. The hot blood of the victim was up, and he sent Dewey a challenge to mortal combat, which was promptly accepted by the equally hot-tempered Northerner.

There was no French business about this affair. Each youth meant to do his best to kill his opponent when they met on the so-called field of honor, for the duel was to be with pistols at short range. Seconds were chosen, and the ground paced off, when a number of cadets, knowing the meeting was certain to result in the death of one or both of the combatants, hurriedly notified the officers stationed at Annapolis, who stopped the duel. This incident is a key to what may be called one side of George Dewey. He never sought a hostile meeting with his fellows, nor did he avoid one. He resented the domineering, offensive manner of those around him, and refused to submit to it.   More than all, he was American to the core and considered any insult or slight to the flag of his country unpardonable. He stood ready and eager to risk his life in defence of his own rights or to aid any one oppressively treated.

The North and South are such firm friends now that those whose memories do not reach back to 1861–65 find it hard to understand the fierce passions that arrayed the sections against each other. Harder is it to understand why the South ever *did* array herself thus, and almost as hard to comprehend how more than one leader, both on sea and land, who afterward became famous under the banner of the Union, hesitated as to the side on which to cast his lot.   Such was the fact, and it is easy to believe that they thanked their stars many a time afterward for the decision they reached by them.

Among these doubters was never a Green Mountain boy.   Not for an instant did the naval cadet, George Dewey, hesitate as to his duty in the tremendous conflict that was drawing nearer with every day.   When on the threshold of the Naval Academy and about to enter it for the first time, he would have promptly turned aside and rushed to the defense of his country, had she needed him.   Fortunately for that country his help was not required until the young Hercules was armed and equipped *cap-a-pie.*

DEWEY'S GRADUATION.

Dewey was graduated with the class of 1858, which numbered fourteen, and in which his rank was five. This was a creditable standing, and better than he expected to attain.   He was ordered to the steam frigate *Wabash* for a cruise in the Mediterranean. The frigate was under the command of Captain Barron, of Virginia, who, when the Civil War broke out, cast his lot with the Southern Confederacy. He was an excellent officer, and took no pains to conceal his sentiments, as was the case with the midshipmen under him. Dewey was respectful, obedient and conscientious in the performance of duty, but no one who was ever associated with him could have any excuse for mistaking his views of patriotism, or indeed on any question.

The two years' cruise gave him many interesting glimpses of foreign lands and peoples.   At Jerusalem he obtained a handsome cane made from olive wood, which he sent as a present to his grandfather, much to the old gentleman's delight, and kept by him until his death a few years later.

Dewey returned to Annapolis to be examined for his commission and led all his class, his final rating being three, an honorable rank which pleased his friends and relatives, when he went home for a brief vacation. It was a happy reunion, sobered by the truth apparent to every one, that the country was on the verge of the most tremendous conflict of modern times. It would be unreasonable to think that the fiery young Lieutenant of twenty-three, in whose veins every drop of blood tingled with patriotic fervor, did not feel the throbbing of ambition. He knew his beloved land would soon need the help of every loyal son; the fighting would be long and of the most furious nature; the chaff would be winnowed from the wheat, and every man would have to prove the stuff of which he was made. Fortunate in one respect were the young officers and privates of 1861, for to them was given the golden opportunity that comes only once in a century. Those who were worthy would win the laurel, and those who were unworthy must fall by the wayside. In homely words the occasion was to be one that was to make or break those who aspired to service in behalf of their country.

DEWEY AS LIEUTENANT

George Dewey was at Montpelier, quietly enjoying the companionship of his loved ones, when the news was flashed through the country that the disunionists had begun the bombardment of Fort Sumter. What an uprising followed! From the Gulf States to the pine woods of Maine, from the Atlantic to the Pacific, the land was swept by the hurricane of war. Those who had held back, hesitated and faltered no longer. The Northern sentiment crystallized into resistless patriotism and the effect in the South was the same. Men who had clamored for sustaining the Union did not become silent, but shouted for disunion and were the most blatant of secessionists. North and South at last faced each other in battle array and the terrific problem was to be fought out to its bloody end.

One week after the momentous news reached Montpelier, Dewey received his commission as Lieutenant and was ordered to the steam sloop *Mississippi* attached to the Western Gulf Squadron, she being the only side-wheeler of the fleet. Melancthon Smith was her Captain and Dewey her First Lieutenant. The peerless Farragut raised his flag over this group of vessels in February, 1862, and began his preparations for the capture of New Orleans, the Queen City of the South, its chief metropolis and one of the most elaborately fortified places in the Confederacy.

Among the primal steps in the War for the Union was the opening of the Mississippi. That accomplished, the Confederacy would be split in twain and the immense Southwest, from which the main supply of beeves and cattle were obtained, would be hewn off. The beginning of this enormous task must be the capture of New Orleans.

As will be remembered, the *Hartford* was the flagship of Farragut. When he took command of the expedition it was believed there were nineteen feet of water on the bar, which was sufficient to allow such ships as the *Hartford* and *Brooklyn* to cross readily, while the heavier frigates that drew twenty-two feet of water could be worked over by relieving them of their guns, coal and heavy stores. Examination, however, revealed that the water was only fifteen feet deep, and the hope of getting the *Wabash* and *Colorado* over was abandoned, while there was grave doubt of working the *Mississippi* and *Pensacola* across. By the hardest kind of work, however, both were gotten over, but after taking everything possible out of the *Mississippi* that could lighten her, it required eight days to force her above the bar. This unavoidable tardiness was a bad thing for the expedition, since it gave the enemy plenty of time in which to make their preparations as thorough as possible.

THE CAPTURE OF NEW ORLEANS.

The defenses of New Orleans could not have been more formidable. Some ninety miles below the city, on the right bank, stood Fort Jackson, a modern fort in every respect, armed with sixty-seven heavy guns and a powerful garrison under the command of a former United States Navy Officer. On the opposite bank, and a little above, was Fort St. Philip, with forty-nine pieces, also well officered and garrisoned. In addition there was a strong fleet of gunboats and ironclads ready to attack any Union craft that tried to force its way up the river.

Far more dangerous than all this fleet was the *Louisiana*, sheathed in iron and rapidly approaching completion, while a second ironclad, the *Manassas*, was fully as formidable. While the early ironclads were crude and clumsy affairs, compared with the modern warships they proved themselves terrific engines of destruction, and more than once played woeful havoc with the modern walls of the Union fleets. Still other vessels of similar make were in course of construction, while there were a large number of wooden gunboats, manned by brave officers and crews.

It would be supposed that the Confederate defenses could not have been made stronger, but in addition to what has been named, an immense raft of cypress logs had been swung across the river under the guns of the forts. The logs were forty feet long, all large, placed a yard apart so as to permit drift-wood to pass between, and were held together by strong iron cables, while thirty huge anchors kept the structure in place in mid-stream. A heavy freshet having swept a third of the raft away, the gap was filled by eight schooners chained together, with their masts dragging astern so as to entangle the screws of passing steamers. Flatboats were filled with resinous pine knots, ready to be fired at a moments warning and sent down among the Union vessels. From this description some idea of Captain Farragut's stupendous task may be formed.

The fleet of twenty-four vessels and twenty schooners steamed up to a point three miles below Fort Jackson, on the 16th of April, 1862. The work was of the most difficult and dangerous nature, but about the middle of the forenoon on the 18th, the mortar schooners began hurling their thirteen inch shells from their place of conceal-ment over the intervening wooded land toward the fort. The bombardment continued for several days and nights. During its continuance, careful reconnoissance established the fact that the channel of the river was clear and the way open for the great task Captain Farragut had laid out for himself.

From what has been stated, it will be understood that to attempt to run by the forts must prove one of the most perilous acts conceiv-able. Indeed many of the officers of the fleet strenuously opposed it, believing success utterly impossible, and, it is to be added in favor of this view, that tradition and history supported it.

That, however, made no difference to the grim Farragut. His resolution when he took command of the expedition was to run past the batteries. He steadily worked toward that end, and, everything at last being in readiness, the night of the 23d of April was fixed upon for the attempt.

The story of the ascent of the *Mississippi*, of the furious struggle and the final Union triumph is one of the most thrilling in all history. Farragut and his gallant sailors were not fighting Spaniards, but Americans like themselves. The Confederates were commanded by skilful officers and they were as brave as the Unionists. This is not the place to repeat the account of that amazing achievement of Farragut, but rather to show the part taken in it by his great pupil, Lieutenant George Dewey, of the *Mississippi*.

Farragut arranged that the fleet should start up the river in single file, so as to clear the obstructions and avoid fouling one another. They were in three divisions and the *Mississippi* third place in the first division, being preceded by the *Cayuga* and *Pensacola*. The moment this line came within range, the Confederates opened a tremendous fire, from every gun that could reach the vessels.

A TERRIFIC BATTLE.

The *Mississippi* and *Pensacola* deliberately slowed up when opposite the forts, in order to draw their fire and the better to deliver their own, hoping also to save the smaller vessels, so far as possible, from injury. During this fearful struggle, the ships were so close to the forts that the jeers and curses of the combatants were heard as they exchanged compliments. The *Mississippi* was hit repeatedly, her rigging torn, her mizzen mast mangled, while eight shot went clean through her as if she were so much pasteboard.

In the midst of the awful hurly-burly, when in the gloom lit up by the bonfires on shore, by the flaming guns in fort and vessels, ships were being sunk and scores of men killed and wounded, the formidable Confederate ram *Manassas* plunged from the smoke and charged upon the *Mississippi* like a runaway locomotive. Before the Union vessel could dodge, she received a terrific blow on the port quarter which gouged out a hole seven feet long and six inches wide. A little more force and the *Mississippi* would have gone to the bot tom, but shaking off her assailant, she headed up stream, and wounded and bleeding as she was, crippled one of the enemy with a broadside, and then steamed above the range of the forts.

Amidst the furious fighting, the ram *Manassas* returned at full speed eager for her work of destruction. The *Mississippi* crowded on every ounce of steam and lunged for the monster, but the latter sheered to one side, plunged ashore and the crew scrambled to land and skurried off into the woods. The *Mississippi* came closer and opened a fire that did not cease until the *Manassas* was riddled like a sieve.

At 1 o'clock on the afternoon of April 25th the Union fleet anchored off New Orleans. The inhabitants were in a frenzy of rage over the passage of the forts and the destruction of their fleet but there was no help for them, when Farragut demanded the surrender of the city which was made on the 29th, Forts St. Philip and Jackson having submitted the day before. Among the Federal vessels thirty-seven had been killed and one hundred and forty-seven wounded. The loss on the enemy's ships is not accurately known, but no doubt it equalled that of the Unionists. The Confederate land forces had twelve killed and forty wounded.

It will be admitted that George Dewey's first battle was one to be remembered. In the midst of the frightful tumult and swirl he was calm and self-possessed as he coolly kept his place on the high bridge of the *Mississippi*. Chief Engineer Baird, U. S. N., gives this vivid picture of Lieutenant Dewey in the battle of New Orleans:

DEWEY'S COOLNESS AND DARING.

" I can see him now in the red and yellow glare flung from the cannon-mouths. It was like some terrible thunder-storm with almost incessant lightning. For an instant all would be dark and Dewey unseen. Then the forts would belch forth, and there he was away up in the midst of it, the flames from the guns almost touching him, and the big shot and shell passing near enough to him to blow him over with their breath, while he held firmly to the bridge rail. Every time the dark came back I felt sure that we would never see Dewey again. But at the next flash there he stood. His hat was blown off and his eyes were aflame. But he gave his orders with the air of a man in thorough command of himself. He took in everything. He saw a point of advantage and seized it at once. And when from around the hull of the *Pensacola* the rebel ram darted, Dewey like a flash saw what was best to be done, and as he put his knowledge into words the head of the *Mississippi* fell off, and as the ram came up alongside the entire starboard broadside plunged a mass of iron shot and shell through her armor, and she began to sink. Her crew ran her ashore and escaped, A boat's crew from our ship went on board thinking to extinguish the flames which our broadside had started and capture her. But she was too far gone. Dewey took us all through the fight, and in a manner which won the warmest praise, not only of all on board, but of Farragut himself. He was cool from first to last, and after we had passed the fort and reached safety and he came down from the bridge his face was black with smoke, but there wasn't a drop of perspiration on his brow."

THE DEWEY HOMESTEAD AT MONTPELIER, VT.

In this house the future Admiral was born, December 26, 1837. Within its walls, along the little river that ran back of it, and in the barn and grounds near by, the scenes of his adventurous boyhood are laid.

WASHINGTON CO. GRAMMAR SCHOOLHOUSE, MONTPELIER, VT.

George Dewey was a "sassy," obstinate schoolboy, and in this house, Mr. Pangborn, his teacher, gave him a severe thrashing, which the Admiral still treasures as an important part of his education.

ADMIRAL DEWEY AT THE AGE OF 30 YEARS

This picture was made in October, 1867, about the time (then)
Lieutenant-Commander Dewey married Miss Goodwin

WIFE OF ADMIRAL DEWEY

Miss Susie Goodwin was the daughter of Governor Goodwin, of New Hampshire. Married George Dewey,
October 24, 1867. Died December, 1872.

CHAPTER III

Dewey Under Admiral Farragut

The Early History of the "Mississippi".—Farragut's Attempt to Run the Batteries of Port Hudson.—A Disastrous Failure.—Loss of the "Mississippi".—Gallant Action of Lieutenant Dewey.—At the Siege of Port Hudson.—Executive Officer of the "Agawam".—A Poor Investment by Dewey.

THE steamer *Mississippi* gained a unique distinction because she was the real training ship of Admiral George Dewey. Aside from that, her career possesses a peculiar interest of its own, which entitles it to further reference.

THE "MISSISSIPPI" IN THE MEXICAN WAR.

She first came into notice at the opening of the Mexican War, when she formed part of the American squadron lying off Point Isabel on the Gulf. Through the soft sunshiny air of May 8, 1846, Captain David Conner, commander of the fleet, and his officers and seamen heard the faint booming of cannon from the inland town of Palo Alto, making known that the war between the United States and Mexico had begun. Not knowing whether his countrymen had won or been defeated, Captain Conner landed a number of seamen and marines to protect the supplies at Point Isabel. But Palo Alto and Resaca de la Palma were brilliant victories, and the stores were never in danger.

Captain Conner was ordered to maintain a rigid blockade of all the Mexican ports on the Gulf of Mexico, for which purpose he was furnished with three 44-gun frigates, the side-wheel steamer *Mississippi* of ten guns, five 20-gun sloops of war, five 10-gun brigs, and the 9-gun screw steamer *Princeton.* These vessels were scattered along the whole Mexican Gulf coast, and most of them saw brisk fighting, the *Mississippi* taking part in several important expeditions. In July, 1847, yellow fever broke out among the crew and she was sent to Pensacola, but was soon in service again, and gallantly assisted in the capture of Vera Cruz and later of Tuspan.

Down to the middle of the present century the wonderful empire of Japan, whose enterprising people have well won the name of the "Yankees of the East," was closed to the rest of the world, but the development of California, the growing commerce with China, and the increase in whale-fishing led Congress in 1851 to send an expedition to Japan. It was under the command of Captain Matthew C. Perry, who sailed from Norfolk November 24, 1852, on the *Mississippi*, the same steamer that he had commanded during the Mexican War. He reached Hong Kong early in the following April, and appeared off Japan on the 8th of July.

THE "MISSISSIPPI" THE FLAGSHIP OF THE EXPEDITION TO JAPAN.

Although going thither with pacific intentions, Captain Perry expected trouble with the Japanese, and was prepared for it. He was ordered to leave Japanese waters at once, but refused, and after long and delicate negotiations a treaty was concluded with the Japanese Government by which several ports were opened to commerce with our country. Captain Perry's work received the high praise it deserved, for he had accomplished a seemingly impossible task, without the shedding of a drop of blood.

Naturally, when the Civil War broke out, the *Mississippi* was one of the first steamers to be placed in active service. It has already been shown that Lieutenant George Dewey began a very lively experience and a marvelously brilliant career upon her decks, and it now remains to complete the history of the steamer, which is far less pleasant than we could wish it to be.

THE "MISSISSIPPI" AT PORT HUDSON.

You have learned of the fine service rendered by the *Mississippi* in the capture of New Orleans, and the partial opening of the great river, but the gigantic work was still incomplete. Vicksburg held the Father of Waters firmly sealed at that point, and it remained for General Grant to enforce the surrender of that stronghold, which did not take place until July 4, 1863. Almost equally impregnable were the powerful batteries at Port Hudson, Louisiana, and it was necessary to reduce them in order to command the Mississippi from New Orleans to Vicksburg.

There was a good deal of indecisive fighting above Vicksburg, in which the Unionists met with some severe losses. Farragut was busy with his command in the Gulf, but he chafed at the stubbornness with which the Confederates held the Mississippi closed at the points named, and determined to break through the formidable gates that had been locked so long. About the middle of March, 1863, he arrived with his fleet below Port Hudson, and made ready to run the terrible gantlet and join the forces above that point.

The bravest man might well recoil from the ordeal, for the bluff at Port Hudson is a hundred feet high and the batteries on their crest, included two 10-inch and two 8-inch columbiads, two 42-pounders, two 32-pounders, three 24-pounders and eight rifled guns. The plunging fire from these pieces was enough to sink the most powerful war vessel that ever floated.

Captain Farragut did not shrink, however, from the tremendous task. He might well believe that after his exploit in running the forts, batteries, obstructions and fire rafts below New Orleans, he was warranted in undertaking the work that now confronted him.

In order to make the passage, he formed his vessels in pairs, each of the heavier ones taking a gunboat on its port side, the only exception being the *Mississippi*, still under the command of Melancthon Smith with George Dewey as First Lieutenant.

It lacked about an hour of midnight, March 14, when the fleet cautiously approached the batteries. Including the *Mississippi*, the warships were eight in number. As they came within range, the batteries opened and the ships replied with their bow guns and the howitzers in their tops. The Confederates, in continual expectation of this attempt, had piles of wood ready to be lighted and they were now set on fire, blazing up and throwing their vivid glare far across the river. The atmosphere was so damp that the smoke gradually settled over the water, and so deepened the gloom that the line of the advancing ships was thrown into confusion.

The *Hartford*, the flagship, being in advance, was able to push through the volume of her own smoke and thus keep comparatively free, but the heavy vapor enveloped the vessels behind her and added to the confusion. Just as the *Hartford* entered the bend, the swift current swung her bow around and swept her toward the shore

directly under the guns of a battery.   Her stern touched, but with
the help of her consort, she drew free and headed up the river again.
She afforded another instance of her proverbial good luck by passing
beyond range of the enemy's batteries, with the loss of only one man
killed and two wounded.

The *Richmond* following next, was struck by a plunging shot that
entered her berth deck, and, crashing into the engine room, knocked
the lever of the safety valve askew, throwing it open and releasing so
much steam that the pressure quickly sank so low that the craft could
not resist the current, even with the help of her consort and was
forced to drop out of battle.   In order to do this she had to pass the
enemy's batteries again, besides running the risk of being struck by
her friends.   By the time she had drifted beyond range, she had
eighteen men killed and wounded.

The *Kineo* coming soon after was disabled by a shot which
struck her rudder, and the *Monongahela* ran aground.   The *Kineo*
swung loose from her consort and a little distance below also ran
aground, and remained fast a half hour before the *Kineo*, which had
managed to work free, was able to tow her beyond danger.   Resuming her advance, the *Monongahela's* machinery was injured and she,
like the *Kineo* drifted helplessly out of action with the loss of six
killed and twenty wounded.

END OF THE "MISSISSIPPI."

Now came the *Mississippi*, which was the last of the line.   She
always conducted herself gallantly and safely passed all the batteries,
but while under full speed, she ran aground with such force that
there was no possibility of getting her off again.   She tugged and
steamed and pulled and backed, but at the end of half an hour, was
as inextricably fast as at first.   The enemy, quick to perceive her
plight, kept up a galling fire, until Captain Smith saw that the only
hope for his men was to abandon her.

Accordingly, he gave orders to spike the port battery and throw
the guns overboard, but the fire of the enemy became so hot that he
stopped the work and made haste to get his men out of the doomed
ship.   Unwilling that the *Mississippi* should fall into the hands of the
Confederates, he made preparations to destroy her, while the sick and

wounded were lowered into the boats and taken ashore, and the men at the starboard battery coolly kept at work aiming at every flash of the enemy's guns. The small arms were flung overboard, the engine was wrecked and finally the ship was set on fire in the forward store-room, but a curious incident checked the destruction for a few minutes. Several shots passed through the hull below the waterline and the inrushing water extinguished the flames. She was then fired in four different places aft, the men waiting until the blaze had progressed so far that her doom was certain. The last men to leave the ship were Captain Smith and Lieutenant Dewey.

The *Mississippi* was now wrapped in flames from stem to stern, and, being relieved of much of her dead weight floated free and drifted down stream, becoming an element of danger to the other Union vessels which were liable to be set on fire by her, but providentially she passed all in safety and some two hours later blew up, having suffered a loss of twenty-five killed and a greater number wounded. Such was the fate of the *Mississippi*. When the ship's company were mustered after the action, sixty-four were missing out of a total of two hundred and ninety-seven. It is worth noting that the *Missouri*, the sister of the *Mississippi* was destroyed by fire twenty years previous at Gibraltar.

It has been said that when the crew were told to save themselves, Lieutenant Dewey and Captain Smith were the last to leave the flaming ship. The young officer was as cool and collected as he has always been since that time in the face of danger, but he was thinking of others beside himself. He needed no boat in which to make his way ashore, for he was too powerful a swimmer to feel any alarm, when he finally plunged overboard and struck out for land.

A GALLANT ACT BY LIEUTENANT DEWEY.

He had taken a few strokes, when he saw a poor fellow making desperate but futile efforts to save himself, for one of his arms had been rendered useless by a shot. A strong effort carried Dewey to his side and he seized the man as he was sinking.

"You will soon be all right," said the Lieutenant cheeringly; "let me support you till we find something better."

A spar was drifting near and Dewey headed for that, swimming smoothly and evenly, with his companion too exhausted to resist or make a dangerous struggle. When the piece of wood was reached, the young officer placed the strong arm of the sailor over it and asked :

" Are you sure you can manage it now, my good fellow ?

" No trouble at all," replied the grateful sailor ; " all I've got to do is to hang on, and it's easy enough to do that."

" Hang on then and I'll tow you.'

And in due time, Lieutenant Dewey brought his charge safely to shore. Undoubtedly the latter owed his life to the young officer, who had more excuse to pass him by than had those who preceded him, since their danger was less than his own.

ADMIRAL PORTER.

All know that the bull-dog siege of Vicksburg by General Grant resulted in the surrender of that formidable post on the 4th of July, 1863, the prisoners thus captured numbering fully twenty thousand, while the victory itself was one of the most important of the whole war. Occurring at the same time as the decisive triumph of Gettysburg, the success of the Union arms, on the whole, was so great, that it may be said the doom of the Southern Confederacy was sealed during those fateful days in early July.

AT THE SIEGE OF PORT HUDSON.

The fall of Vicksburg rendered Port Hudson untenable, and it surrendered five days after the fall of the more important position. Previous to this, however, the siege of Port Hudson was vigorously pushed and there was a good deal of hard fighting in front of the stronghold, without any important advantage being gained. Undoubtedly it would have been captured in time, but the loss of life must have been heavy.

While the siege was in progress, the *Monongahela* arrived, under Commander Abner Read, and was fired upon by a masked battery of field pieces, which killed two and wounded four men. Among the latter was Commander Read, who lived but a short time. He was succeeded by Lieutenant Dewey, who handled the vessel and crew with admirable skill. But for the surrender which took place two days later, he would have given a most excellent account of himself. Admiral Porter was assigned to the command of the Mississippi, now fully opened throughout its entire length, while Farragut gave his attention to enforcing the blockade of the coast.

According to Admiral Dewey's views, he was one of the luckiest officers of the Civil War, since it was continually his fortune to get into the thickest of the fight, no matter where it happened to be. At the beginning of 1864 he was transferred to the North Atlantic Squadron, and assigned to the gunboat *Agawam*, of which he became executive officer. The *Agawam* was an unarmored side-wheeler, carrying eight guns, and therefore could not be considered a very formidable vessel.

AN AMUSING INCIDENT.

Clark Fisher is at this writing one of the most prominent citizens of Trenton, New Jersey, where he was born and spent his boyhood. He is a highly educated gentleman, who entered the naval service early in the war as chief engineer. About the same time, his younger brother Otis became a lieutenant in the army. He made a brilliant beginning, and, had his life been spared, must have reached a high command, but he was shot dead while gallantly fighting with his regiment in Virginia.

Clark was chief engineer of the *Agawam*, when Dewey became executive officer of the gunboat. The two, alike in many traits, were attracted to each other and soon became intimate. The *Agawam* was assisting General Grant in his operations in the vicinity of City Point and Petersburg and had a warm time of it. The craft was almost continuously under fire, and was kept darting here and there to escape the torpedoes, which the Confederates had an unpleasant way of releasing up the river and allowing to float down among the Union vessels. Fisher says that Dewey was recognized by every one as without a superior in the service. He was alert, active, tireless, cool, self-possessed, and a fine disciplinarian, but with all his intrepidity never rash, and, though ready at all times to assume any risk, did not do so needlessly.

Fisher tells an amusing anecdote of his association with Dewey. Having obtained a furlough, the engineer decided to make a visit to his friends in the North, and lost no time in packing his trunk. While busily engaged in doing so, Dewey came up, and, with his hands in his pockets, silently watched his friend.

"He was always a reticent sort of fellow," says Fisher, "even when with his most intimate friends, and he hadn't talked long before I knew that he wanted to say something that he hated to, so I finally asked him why he didn't drive straight at the mark. I told him that I knew he was simply beating around the bush, and suggested that we had been good friends enough for him to speak right out and let me know exactly what he wanted.

"'Well, Fisher,' said he, 'you know I don't like to trouble anybody, but I do want you to do me a favor if you will when you get North."

"'Now,' said I, 'what is it; old man?'

"'You see, Fisher,' said he, 'a fellow corked up here like a mouse in a trap hasn't much use for money, and I have saved a little. It has been rattling around in my trunk for sevral months doing nobody any good, and I want to get it to my father; he might invest it for me, and when I need it, it may amount to something. I thought that it might not be too much trouble for you to take it to the old gentleman while you are up in his neighborhood. I'd mail it, but you know that under the present circumstances it would probably never reach him.'

"'Probably not,' I answered; 'and if I can get it to him I shall be very glad to do so.'

"Dewey pulled a roll of money out of his pocket and counted it. 'There's four hundred dollars, even,' said he; 'it isn't much, but it will come in handy if a fellow is ever laid up.'

DR. JULIUS YEMANS DEWEY
Father of the Admiral. At the age of seventy years.

HON. CHARLES DEWEY
The Admiral's oldest brother. The family consisted of
Charles, Edward, George, and one sister, Mary,
born in the order named.

CAPTAIN EDWARD DEWEY

Second son of Dr. Dewey. Next older than the Admiral

MRS. MARY P. GREELEY

The Admiral's only sister, his boon companion in childhood, and constant friend and correspondent throughout manhood.

"He handed me the money and I tucked it away in an inside pocket of my coat, along with some money of my own. The next day I started for home. On the way our train was held up by a band of guerrillas. I tried to escape, but one of the thieves caught me by the coat tails. The coat that he had hold of was a trifle loose for me, and I slipped out of it, leaving it in the hands of the guerrilla, jumped for the bushes, and made my escape. The fellow sent a bullet after me, but he was probably too astonished to take good aim. When I reached a point where I felt that I was safe, I sat down and thought the situation over. It occurred to me for the first time then that Dewey's money had gone with the coat. I regretted it, of course, but I didn't feel like going back and making an effort to get it. My own money went along with it. The money was never invested for Dewey, but I guess he has managed to get along pretty well without."

CHAPTER IV.
Meritorious Service in the Civil War

Blockade-running by the Confederates.—Wilmington, N. C., Their Principal Port —
The First Attempt to Capture It.—Its Fall.—Tactical Skill of Dewey.—His Promotion.—His Transfer to the "Kearsarge".—Dewey as a Seaman.—His Exquisite Taste in His Attire.

IT is curious that many histories of the great Civil War give less
attention to the capture of Fort Fisher than its importance
deserves. It may be that this is because it occurred so near the
final campaign when the attention of the country was directed to the
operations of Grant in front of Petersburg and the march of Sherman from Atlanta to the sea.

BLOCKADE—RUNNING.

Although the Nationals had an immense number of vessels with
which to enforce the blockade, it would have been impossible to make
it rigidly effective had the fleets been doubled. Along the thousands
of miles of Gulf and seacoast were innumerable bays and sinuous
inlets, with which the Confederates were intimately familiar, and
which bristled with torpedoes and were protected by strong forts.
Blockade-running was risky, but when successful yielded so enormous
profits that the business was a resistless temptation to hundreds of
daring captains and officers, many of whom were foreigners. It is said
that the owner of a vessel, after making a single round trip, taking out
cotton and bringing back the supplies sorely needed by the Confederacy, could afford to have his vessel sunk by the blockaders and would
still be ahead. Two trips and then failure brought him a handsome
profit, while one or two additional successes made him independent
for life.

As the war progressed, Wilmington, North Carolina, became the
most important port for the blockade-runners. In that city the days
and hours of the departure of the steamers and the cost of passage
to the Bahamas or England were advertised. Ladies and children
went aboard the boats with little or no misgiving, for they were regu-

(54)

lar, though it was not quite so certain as to the hour they would reach port on their return. Thus as regards Wilmington, the blockade was so ineffective that it was virtually no blockade at all.

Of course this state of affairs could not exist without good reason. when as many as forty vessels tried to enforce the blockade. In the first place, the two widely separated entrances offered the best chances in the world for the swift steamers, which were handled with great skill by officers and crews. The southern entrance to Cape Fear River was guarded by Fort Caswell and the northern by Fort Fisher. There were no earthworks on the Atlantic coast more powerful than those of Fort Fisher, and the most expert engineers had exhausted their art in making them impregnable.

FORT FISHER.

For instance, the fort mounted forty-four guns, the parapets were twenty-five feet thick and twenty feet high, with the traversers ten feet higher and of the same thickness. Nevertheless, the port of Wilmington could not be closed until this fort was reduced and the national authorities determined to reduce it.

A land and naval expedition was fitted out under the command of Rear-Admiral David D. Porter and General Benjamin F. Butler, and the fleet brought together at Hampton Roads, numbered 150 vessels. This was in the latter part of 1864, and Lieutenant Dewey, who had been transferred to the *Colorado*, was delighted to take part in the attack. Butler was one of the few political generals who managed to retain their commands throughout the war, but his many blunders proved his incompetency and was a lesson to the Government itself, which, truth to say, it regularly forgets whenever the time for politicians arrives to exert their " pull."

Butler was the brilliant originator of the mine in front of Petersburg, on the previous July, which resulted in the loss of several thousand of our own troops without materially hurting the enemy. Something of the same nature was now tried, when the old steamer *Louisiana* was filled with powder which it was intended to explode under the walls of Fort Fisher. The officers and men were eleven in number, and, of course, were volunteers, for the risk was too great for any regular detail. On the night of December 23, the powder ship steamed boldly to within four hundred yards of the fort, when her anchor was dropped, the fuses were lighted and the men rowed away. Reaching the steamer that had brought them in, the vessel hastily put to sea and was a dozen miles away when the explosion took place.

It was like the vomiting of a volcano's crater and as a display of fireworks was worth going a long way to witness. No doubt the garrison of the fort enjoyed the sight, as they could well afford to do, since it did no harm to them.

FIRST ATTACK ON FORT FISHER.

Just as the wintry morning was breaking, the next day, the fleet stood in for the attack. The first gun was fired a short time before noon, and for several hours one of the most terrific cannonades that ever took place on this continent, shook the land and sea. The fort was hidden under an appalling storm of exploding shells, which opened immense pits in the earthworks, burst two service magazines and burned a number of buildings ; but when the bombardment ceased the fort itself had received no material injury, nor had the fleet been much harmed.

The following day, Christmas, the cannonade was renewed and three thousand men were landed under the protection of the fire. General Butler made a close inspection of the enemy's works and decided they could not be carried. Fire was opened again at its conclusion, the fleet retired, having suffered a loss of twenty killed and sixty-three wounded, that of the Confederates being six killed and fifty-two wounded, while several of their guns were disabled.

The failure of the expedition was a great disappointment to the Government. General Butler, with the expertness of a lawyer, rather than that of a soldier, explained that the capture of the fort was impossible, but the military authorities were not satisfied, and determined upon a second attempt to be made the following month. This expedition sailed on January 12th and 13th, the troops being under the command of General Alfred H. Terry, while among the vessels engaged was the *Colorado*, Commodore Henry K. Thatcher, with Lieutenant George Dewey as his assistant.

The tremendous cannonade of December was repeated, six thousand men having been previously landed. The bombardment began on the afternoon of January 13th, most of the fleet retiring at night, though the ironclads kept up a desultory fire until morning, when the terrific cannonade was renewed. The day passed and late in the afternoon, General Terry arranged with Porter for a combined land and naval attack to be made on the following morning. Under the cover of light gunboats, 1600 sailors and 400 marines were landed, the attacking column lying concealed under the sloping bank of the river.

Between 3 and 4 o'clock in the afternoon, the fire ceased, in order to give the troops an opportunity to charge. The land forces dashed to the left flank of the fort, and the naval column advanced across the open beach, where they had no protection whatever. They were in three divisions and were met with so murderous a fire, that after the loss of 82 killed and 269 wounded, they were driven back.

THE WOUNDING OF BOB EVANS.

Among the desperately wounded was Ensign "Bob" Evans, who was almost smothered under a pile of dead and dying, unable to help himself or do anything more than barely move his shattered leg. When at last he came under the hands of the surgeon, he was told that nothing but the amputation of his limb could save his life. Anticipating something of the kind, Evans had provided himself with a revolver and swore that at the first attempt to cut off his leg, he would shoot the surgeon. Even then as a young man, he was known as one whom it was not safe to trifle with, and the leg remained, which explains how "Bob" Evans is compelled to limp when he walks.

But, although the naval force was repulsed, it was not so with the troops under General Terry. They met with a desperate resistance, and the fight was of the most furious nature, but the Unionists prevailed and Fort Fisher was compelled to surrender. It so happened that the news of its fall was received by the committee listening to General Butler, at the very moment he was demonstrating that the fort was impregnable. The news was somewhat embarrassing, but the adroit lawyer smiled and accepted it with the best grace possible.

4 D.D.

The *Colorado* conducted herself gallantly in this memorable affair, but being a wooden vessel, she was in the second circle of attacking boats. While the fight was going on, and it was apparent everything was coming right, Admiral Porter signalled to Thatcher, in command on the *Colorado* to close in and silence a portion of the enemy's works. The ship had been roughly handled and was so battered that a number of the officers remonstrated, believing that if the order was executed, the *Colorado* would be sunk, but Dewey, like a flash, saw that the movement was the very best one to make under the circumstances.

DEWEY'S TACTICAL SKILL.

"It is the safest position we can take," he remarked; "and it will not require more than fifteen minutes." It was this quick perception of the situation that proved not only his bravery but his extraordinary tactical knowledge, already much superior to that of his associates. The command was promptly obeyed, and one of the leading journals, commenting upon it, pronounced it the most beautiful duel of the whole war.

When victory was won and the firing had ceased, Admiral Porter met Commodore Thatcher and congratulated him upon the fine precision and effectiveness of the move he had made.

"It was not *my* move," promptly replied Thatcher; "but Lieutenant Dewey's; he is the one to be thanked."

DEWEY'S FIRST PROMOTION.

Nevertheless, it was that movement which made Thatcher acting Rear-Admiral, though the real credit belonged to his brilliant Lieutenant. Thatcher was a generous as well as a just man, and when he was ordered to Mobile Bay, to relieve Farragut, he strongly recommended Dewey for his fleet captain. It would have been only a fair recognition of Dewey's genius, but it must be remembered that he was a very young man, and his appointment would probably have caused jealousy. Be that as it may, the promotion was not made, and it is hardly to be supposed that young Dewey expected it. He was content to serve his country, wherever and whenever she needed him, and left others to wrangle over the question of promotion. However,

his Government did not forget his service and two months after the
capture of Fort Fisher, he was commissioned as Lieutenant-Commander.

Hardly less gratifying than his promotion was his transfer to the
Kearsarge, which had covered herself with glory a few months before
by sending the rebel *Alabama* to the bottom of the ocean in the
famous fight off Cherbourg, France. That superb sloop of war
deserved a better fate than that which overtook her, when on the
night of February 2, 1894, she was wrecked off Roncador Reef, and
totally destroyed.

A MODEL OFFICER.

When the war closed, as it did shortly after Dewey's promotion,
he was transferred to the steam frigate *Colorado*, the flagship of the
European squadron. It is superfluous to add that in every respect he
was a model officer. No one could be kinder than he, nor at the same
time a stricter disciplinarian. He detested drunkenness, and abhorred
lying. Knowing the weakness of "an old salt," he was willing to regard
him with charity when he took a drop too much, and, if the sailor had
enough sense frankly to own his fault, he need have little fear of
severe punishment ; but woe betide him, if he tried to escape by lying.
Fixing those piercing black eyes upon the stammering culprit, Dewey
seemed to look him through, and his face became a thundercloud
when he penetrated the flimsy falsehood.

" You tell me you overstayed your time on shore," he said in his
biting tones to a petty officer, " because you were ill. You are lying ;
you were drunk ; you show it in your appearance ; if you had told
me the truth, I would have forgiven you ; I don't punish you for getting drunk, but give you ten days in irons for lying ; remember that.
I know you to be a good seaman, and a good seaman has no excuse
for lying."

DEWEY'S SEAMANSHIP.

Mr. Charles E. Rand, who served under Dewey in the Civil War,
gives this tribute to his bravery and skill :

" I remember when I was with Admiral Dewey on the flagship
Colorado ; he was then Lieutenant-Commander and executive officer.
Once during a terrific gale, we were off the Bay of Biscay, oftentimes

a nasty place, too, and the command was given to save the ship. The old *Colorado* could not move faster than eight knots an hour, and we were on a lee shore.   I tell you, it looked bad for us.

"At the height of the storm the Admiral took the bridge, relieving Dewey, and the order was given to set sails to help us out to sea. We fellows had to hustle into the riggings, and just to encourage us Dewey himself mounted the ladder, and in less time than I can tell it, was on the yard unfurling sail.   It was an exciting scene, and a dangerous situation, but in a short time we were clear of the coast, and safe from wreck on one of the rockiest shores I know of."

It has often been remarked of Admiral Dewey that he is an exquisite in dress, and it cannot be questioned that in personal attire his taste is faultless, but it would be wrong to refer to him as a fop. He is nothing of the sort, his cleanliness and attractive person being simply a type of his cleanliness of mind and character.   Some of the bravest fighters that ever lived have been dandies in dress, but it did not prevent their being "dandies," in the common acceptation of the word, when it came to striking sturdy blows for their country.

FORWARD DECK OF THE "OREGON." PHOTOGRAPHED THE MORNING OF HER ARRIVAL

SOLDIERS LEAVING THE UNITED STATES FOR THE PHILIPPINES ON BOARD THE TRANSPORT, "SARATOGA."

CHAPTER V

Services in the Navy Department

At the Portsmouth Navy Yard.—"Fighting Governor" Goodwin.—Marriage of Commander Dewey to Miss Susan B. Goodwin.—Her Death.—His Varied Duties.—A Narrow Escape from Death.—A Visit to His Old Home.—Dewey's Tact and Firmness.—Chief of the Bureau of Equipment and Recruiting.—His Faultless Taste in Dress.—As a Club Man.—Incidents Illustrating the Truth That the Most Momentous Consequences Often Flow from Insignificant Causes.—Dewey's Appointment to the Command of the Asiatic Squadron.

EARLY in 1867, Lieutenant-Commander Dewey was ordered home from the European station and assigned to duty at the Kittery Navy Yard, at Portsmouth, New Hampshire. He was still a young man, faultless in dress, a Chesterfield in manners, courteous to every one, no matter what his station in life, held in the highest esteem by those who had served under him, and a man in whom his native State felt a special pride, for everything in his career justified this feeling toward him.

And here he was, thirty years old, handsome, distinguished, with a fine reputation for bravery and skill, and a young bachelor. It may be said that he had been too busy serving his country to give attention to the gentler sex, but that he was not insensible to its charms was proven by what took place, while he was on duty at the navy yard at Portsmouth.

NEW HAMPSHIRE'S WAR GOVERNOR.

One of the most widely known and respected of New Hampshire's citizens was Governor Ichabod Goodwin, a Jackson Democrat, and consequently, no matter how bitter his feeling against Abolitionists and Republicans, a lover of the Union in every fibre of his being. When Fort Sumter was fired upon, he boiled over with indignation. It has been said that he seriously meditated shouldering a musket and hurrying southward with the hosts that were marshaling in all the northern States, in order to punish the traitors that had dared to fire on the Stars and Stripes.

But had the old gentleman followed his first patriotic impulse, he would have rendered far less service to the Union than he was able to do in his official position and with the wealth that was at his command. The legislative bodies elsewhere were vigorous in their action, but the law-makers of New Hampshire could not be prompt enough to satisfy the impatience of its war governor. When President Lincoln's call for volunteers was issued the law-making body of the Granite State was not in session. That made no difference to Governor Goodwin, who shoved his hands deep into his capacious pockets and paid all the expenses of fitting out a regiment of volunteers.

"When the State gets ready, it will repay me," he remarked; "and if it never gets ready, it is all the same."

It need hardly be said that the rock-ribbed State did her whole duty and fully reimbursed the lusty patriot. With her meagre population, she furnished 33,937 soldiers to the Union, and in the numerous battles in which they took part they fought with gallantry, and hundreds of lives were laid on the altar of patriotism, willing tributes of their love for the best Government on earth.

The chief executives of the Northern States, many of whom were politically opposed to the Administration, were loyal and energetic in their support of all measures for prosecuting the war, and are still referred to as "war governors." None was more popular than Governor Goodwin, who was often called the "Fighting Governor." Streets were named in his honor, and we believe that one of the most active locomotives that draws the trains from Portsmouth to other points along the shore is the "Governor Goodwin," built fully a generation ago.

Commander Dewey was a welcome visitor at the homes of the most cultured and exclusive families of Portsmouth, and it was not long before he was captivated by Miss Susan B. Goodwin, daughter of the Governor, and one of the most cultured of her sex.

DEWEY'S MARRIAGE.

It would be supposed that so attractive a personality as Commander Dewey would have had nothing to fear in approaching this new species of "engagement," but he found a rival in his way,—no less a person than an older officer, Commander Rhind, whose tribute

had already been recorded. They were both too thorough gentlemen
to allow the rivalry to become anything but a friendly one, though it
was none the less earnest because of that. We are inclined to think
the younger would have won in the end, though there can be no certainty of it, since a great advantage came to Dewey, when his old
comrade received orders which compelled him to sail away, thus leaving the field clear for the younger suitor.

There was something in the nature of Dewey that pleased the
bluff old War Governor. He liked a brave man, and he knew Dewey
was just that sort of man.

"He may be a little headlong and reckless at times," remarked
the Governor, "but hang it, I like him. It is such as he that are
sure to be heard of if they're given half a chance."

Of course the whole thing depended upon her who had the
privilege of saying "yes" or "no," when the all-important question
was submitted to her. Suffice it to say that her gentle answer was
in the affirmative, and so they were married. In the fine old' homestead still standing on one of the cool, shaded streets of Portsmouth,
the wedding took place, and was followed by a reception that is
recalled with pleasure by the surviving guests who were present.

A SEVERE BLOW.

Soon after his marriage, Dewey was assigned to the Naval
Academy at Annapolis, where he remained for two years, when he
was given command of the *Narragansett*, and on April 13, 1872, was
advanced to the rank of Commander. When everything was so prom-
ising, however, and his happiness was perfect, the greatest affliction
of his life came to him. A son, named George Goodwin, was born
at Newport, December 23, and five days later the mother died. The
grief of the stricken husband was deep, and all sympathized with him,
but none could drive away the sorrow that could be softened only
by the slow passage of years. The son, as he grew older, showed no
disposition to follow in the footsteps of his illustrious father, but after
his graduation from Princeton College engaged in business in New
York, which at present is his home.

As commander of the *Narragansett*, Dewey sailed for the Pacific
coast, where for three years he was engaged in making surveys. The

duty was a quiet one, though preferable to staying on shore, but he was recalled to Washington, during the Centennial year, and made Lighthouse Inspector, and soon Secretary of the Lighthouse Board The work was important, and Dewey's thoroughness, brightness, quick grasp of matters and unvarying courtesy made him one of the most popular as well as one of the most useful members. In 1882-83 he commanded the *Juniata*, on the Asiatic squadron, and became Captain in September, 1884, when he was placed in charge of the *Dolphin*, one of the four vessels that formed the famous "White Squadron." The advance squadron, as it has also been called, was composed of the *Atlanta*, the *Boston*, the *Chicago* and the *Dolphin*, because of whose initials they were often referred to as the "A, B, C, D," of the navy. The last named was launched in 1884, and, although designed simply as a despatch boat, she carried an efficient armament, and made the voyage round the world.

A NARROW ESCAPE FROM DEATH.

While in command of the *Juniata*, Dewey was stricken with what threatened to prove a fatal illness, and was compelled to stop at Malta to receive medical treatment. He was in a bad way, and his peculiar disease was beyond the skill of his own physicians. If his life was to be saved, it could be through only the utmost skill of the most skilful of surgeons.

Fortunately for him and our country he found them at Malta in the persons of two eminent English practitioners, under whose hands he passed through one of the most difficult operations known to surgery, consisting in the removal of a portion of his liver. As has been aptly remarked, one discovery made by the surgeons was that he was not "white livered," though everybody knew that before.

Admiral Dewey's gratitude to these gentlemen was profound, for he felt that under heaven he owed his life to them. He has often referred to that ordeal and always with deep emotion, though he has been heard to add :

"I never meet a Maltese cat without feeling peculiarly drawn toward her."

Soon after his promotion to a captaincy in the navy, Dewey paid a visit to his old home in Montpelier. By that time, his fame had

become such that some of his townsmen stood a little in awe of him, but it required only a few minutes to discover that he was the same genial, whole-souled neighbor as when he left them to play his part in the great Civil War. None could be more pleased than he to meet his old acquaintances and to talk over with them the incidents of his childhood, when as he freely admitted, he well deserved the name of being the worst boy in town. Though he was grown into a sturdy man, sobered by the stirring scenes through which he had passed, and in all of which he had been a prominent actor, he had not lost, as he can never lose, the pleasure in his memories of boyhood.

What touched him and caused a feeling of sadness, was that most of the children whom he met showed a certain degree of timidity, as if they saw a great gulf between him and them. No man loves children more than Admiral Dewey, in which respect it may be noted that he resembles Farragut, who once donned his Admiral's uniform and paraded before a little girl, becauce she had expressed the wish to see how the great war captain looked in his fighting rig.

Dewey formed the habit of sauntering from his own grounds into those of the State House, just across the way, where on pleasant days a number of children were sure to be frolicking, and inviting them over to his house, when he grouped them around him and told his stories of the strange lands he had visited. To please the boys, he pictured the stirring battles that had taken place before they were born, but of which they had read and heard from their parents. They sat with open mouths and staring eyes, swallowing every word of his graphic description, and looked with wonder upon the man who had gone through them all and lived to tell about it. You will hear to-day many of those tales repeated by those whose good fortune it was to listen to them from the distinguished narrator.

DEWEY AND THE STUBBORN YEOMAN.

As an instance of the tact and firmness of Dewey in the management of his men, the following anecdote is told of him while in command of the *Dolphin* in New York harbor :

A paymaster's yeoman was very sensitive as to his sphere of duties, and when he received a command from the First Lieutenant, refused to obey, because, as he claimed, the work demanded of him

was outside his line of service.   The Lieutenant insisted otherwise
and sharply repeated the order, but was met with another refusal.
Finding it impossible to make him obey, the Lieutenant reported the
matter to Commander Dewey.

The latter strolled out on deck, as if the question was a trifling
one, and halting in front of the recalcitrant fixed his piercing black
eyes on him.   He did not speak for a minute or so, but looked
steadily at him, much to the fellow's discomfort.   Finally he said :

"What is this I hear ? Do you refuse to obey your Lieutenant ?"

" He has ordered me, sir, to do something that is out of my line
of duty," replied the sullen yeoman.

" Are you aware that what you are doing is mutiny?   When you
entered the service, you swore to obey your superior officers."

" I am ready to do so, sir, in all proper things."

" And who is to be the judge of proper orders ?" demanded
Dewey ; " discipline would be impossible if the question were left to
the men themselves.   I expect you to obey without another word."

The commander stood quiet and expectant, but the stubborn
man was immovable.   Dewey had said all he had to say, and knew
better than to bandy any more words with the incipient mutineer.
Turning to the corporal he quietly told him to call the guard.   They
appeared and the yeoman was stood on the further side of the deck.

" Now load," added Dewey in the same low but distinct voice,
and the order was obeyed with regulation promptness, the yeoman
beginning to look and feel more uncomfortable.   He had been
expecting an argument, a violent outbreak perhaps and a chance to
bluster, but there was something very disturbing in the cool delibera-
tion of the commander.   He hardly expected to be shot offhand for
his disobedience, but there was enough uncertainty about the intentions of his superior to add to his uneasiness.

Dewey took out his watch, and in the same even smooth voice
as before, but with the manner of one in deadly earnest said :

" Now, my man, I'll give you five minutes in which to obey
orders."

Holding the timepiece in hand, he waited until the sixty seconds
were ticked off when he called the fact.   For a brief while the yeoman
did not move, but his growing uneasiness was evident to all.

" Two minutes—three minutes—four minutes—"

That was enough. The mutineer could stand it no longer, and moved off with more briskness than he had ever shown. Some time later, when the flurry was over, he announced a discovery to his friends.

" It ain't safe to fool with the old man."

A MERITED SNUB.

Dewey's next command was the *Pensacola*, the flagship of the European squadron, and it need not be added that he displayed the same characteristics in every station of responsibility to which he was called. When at Malta, toward which city, as will be under stood, he felt a strong partiality, a number of his sailors were given shore leave. Jack Tar, after weeks and months of hard work and close confinement on board ship is pretty certain to become boisterous and often unruly when given the freedom of the port. Being with his own friends among strangers, for whom he cares nothing, and with no feeling of restraint, he may be counted upon to start a first-class row just so soon as he has had time to swallow a few glasses of grog.

Nothing delights him more than a fight, and he cares little with whom it occurs. If the crew of a German, Dutch, Russian or Spanish ship happens to be on shore at the same time, in quest of similar amusement, the result of a meeting between the parties can hardly be imagined. If none of these is present and a company of English sailors heave in sight, they serve very well as a substitute, but it is a fact worth noting that English and American sailors as a rule are friendly toward each other. If the two nationalities are the only ones in sight they will pitch in to each other and make things lively, but it is really in the nature of a friendly bout. They are simply in quest of fun, and when one tar sends another sprawling there is no viciousness in the blow. He will help him to his feet, and, after explaining matters, proceed to knock him down again, unless the other gets in his work first, as is quite likely to be the case.

But let a company of British or American sailors be assailed by a party belonging to another nation ; let the defenders be outnumbered and get the worst of it, and if they are Americans, let a

number of English Jacks heave in sight, or let the reverse be the fact.
No one could ask a more beautiful and emphatic demonstration of
the superiority of the Anglo-Saxon race over all others than that
which is sure to follow with the vim and effectiveness of a western
cyclone.

In the instance we have in mind, Dewey's sailors from the
Pensacola were in an unusually hilarious mood and created so great a
rumpus that the armed police determined to arrest the whole party.
The sailors, however, managed to elude them and get back to ship.
The outrage was so flagrant that the captain of the port came out to
the *Pensacola* in high dudgeon the next morning, and, asking to see
Captain Dewey, laid his complaint before him.

"I am very sorry to hear this," replied the officer, "and hope the
offenders will be punished ; what can I do to aid you ?"

"The conduct of your men was shameful; they caused a riot
and you can help me teach them better."

"Be good enough to show me in what way," said Dewey, with
the same courtesy that he showed to every one.

The visitor became angry, and said hotly :

"It is your place, sir, to parade your crew before me that the
rioters may be pointed out ; I will attend to the rest."

The black eyes flashed.   Pointing to the Stars and Stripes floating aloft Captain Dewey replied in the same even voice, whose
earnestness could not be mistaken :

"You are standing upon American territory, sir, and I'll parade
my men for no foreigner on earth. I have the honor to bid you
good day, sir."

DEWEY'S SERVICE IN WASHINGTON.

Long before this, our Government had learned that Captain
Dewey was not only an officer of rare courage and skill, but that he
possessed a genius for what may be called "little things." In other
words, he was patient, thorough, quick to comprehend the most
difficult problems and subjects, and was never satisfied until he had
gotten to the bottom of all questions submitted to him. Since there
was no important strictly naval matter to engage his attention, he was
appointed, in 1888, chief of the bureau of equipment and recruiting.

FRONT VIEW OF THE "OLYMPIA"

On this bridge Commodore Dewey stood when he gave the famous command: "You may fire, Captain Gridley, when ready." The great guns in the forward turret did masterly execution on May 1st, 1898.

IN THE FIGHTING TOP

This appointment carried with it the rank of Commodore, though eight years passed before the honor was formally conferred upon Dewey.

His administration of the bureau added to his popularity and raised him higher in the opinion of those whose opinion was intelligent or of value. No one could come into his presence without the knowledge that he was holding an interview with a born gentleman. It was impossible for him to be discourteous, or knowingly to wound the feelings of the humblest individual. Unhappily this cannot be said of all officials in Washington, and the fact regarding Dewey therefore is the more worthy of record.

Commodore Dewey was chief of the bureau of equipment for four years, and in 1893, was once more made a member of the lighthouse board. His commission as Commodore was handed him February 28, 1896, and shortly after he was made President of the Board of Inspection and Survey.

DEWEY AS A CLUB MAN.

During his residence in Washington, he acquired the reputation of being the best dressed man in the service, and the remark was made of him that the creases of his trousers were as clearly defined as his views on naval duties. This characteristic, to which we have referred elsewhere, has distinguished him through life, and doubtless is so "confirmed" that it will remain to the end.

The Commodore was a popular club man in the national capital, courteous and considerate in his intercourse with every one, yet he was never a leader in the club for he is not talkative or forward, preferring to remain in the background and listen to the conversation in which none is more competent than himself to take part. His quarters were modest but furnished and cared for with the exquisite taste that always showed in his personal attire and appearance.

All history, ancient and modern, is crowded with illustrations of the fact that the most momentous and far-reaching events often turn upon incidents so trifling of themselves that they attracted no notice at the time of their occurrence. Without referring to those of other nations, let us recall a few that are connected with our own country and are of comparatively recent date.

Suppose, for instance, when young George Washington was making his memorable journey through the wilderness with Christopher Gist the guide, and was knocked from their raft into the ice-gorged river, he had been so hampered by his heavy boots and clothing as to drown, what would have been the subsequent history of the United States? At Braddock's massacre an Indian fired eight or ten times at Washington and his clothing was punctured by several bullets, while men fell dead all round him. Suppose one of those bullets had swerved a little in its direction and killed him, who would have been left to lead the Continentals through the long years of suffering and battle to final triumph? None, for the Revolution was one of the few instances in which the fate of the country and the struggle itself was wrapped up in one man. Had Washington fallen at any time during the first part of the war, the resistance would have ceased and our independence, though sure to come in the end, would have been postponed for many years.

THE IMPORTANCE OF WASHINGTON'S LIFE.

By and by, matters began to go wrong, and when the winter of 1776, approached most of the patriots who had been ardent and hopeful lost heart. Those were the days that tried men's souls, and few beside Washington himself maintained their faith. Even he saw that if something was not quickly done to raise the drooping hopes of his countrymen, the resistance must be given up and submission made to England.

So he planned the battle of Trenton. With his 2,500 picked soldiers and officers, he crossed the icy Delaware through the storm of sleet and bitter cold, eight miles above the town, into which the ragged patriots marched with bleeding feet to surprise the 1,500 Hessians, and unless they could be surprised there was slight hope of victory.

Now, it so happened that a malignant Tory saw the campfires burning on the banks of the Delaware, and the American soldiers forcing their way in their flatboats to the Jersey side. Reading the meaning of the movement, he sprang upon his horse and galloped at headlong speed through the sleet to Trenton, where he arrived hours before Washington could appear.

He knew that the headquarters of Colonel Rall, the Hessian commander, were at the house of Abraham Hunt, the leading merchant of Trenton, and, riding straight thither, the Tory knocked on the door and handed a note to the negro servant, with word that it was of the utmost impórtance and must be given to Colonel Rall without a moment's delay.

WHAT FOLLOWED A GAME AT CARDS.

This was done, but the Hessian and merchant were drinking toddy, smoking their pipes and were deep in a game of cards. Rall impatiently shoved the note into his pocket, remarking that he would read it at the conclusion of the hand he was playing. But when the hand was played, he forgot the note and the game went on, until he was startled by the booming of cannon and the rattle of musketry at the head of the town, showing that Washington and his patriots had arrived. When he recalled the note in his pocket, Colonel Rall lay dying from the wound received a short time before in trying to rally his Hessians against the impetuous attack of the Americans.

Now, suppose that Tory miscreant had reached Abraham Hunt's door a few minutes sooner or later, when one of the men was dealing instead of playing his hand. The note would have been read, as would have been the case had it not been forgotten by the sodden brain of the officer. Rall was a good soldier, and he would have made such preparation for the American attack that it is quite likely the patriots would have been defeated, though, of course, this cannot be known with certainty. At any rate, the decisive blow that raised the hopes of the despairing patriots would have been ineffective, and one shudders to recall the probable effects upon the cause of independence itself. It may not be doubted that Colonel Rall lost the battle of Trenton and his own life because of the trifling incident related.

THE POWER OF A SINGLE VOTE.

In 1844, a man in the backwoods of Indiana was placed on trial on the charge of murder. He was defended by a lawyer named David Kelso, who secured his acquittal. Some time later, Kelso was nominated for the State Senate, and the man whose life he had saved lay ill at home. Nevertheless, he showed his gratitude by commanding that he should be bundled into a carriage and driven two miles to the polls, where he voted for Kelso, and that single vote elected him, though his client who cast it died from the consequences of his exposure.

It was the duty of the State Senate to choose a United States Senator. Kelso bolted the Democratic caucus and carried a friend with him, as a result of which the vote was tied for weeks. Finally Kelso nominated Edward A. Hannigan, and declared that if he was not elected he and his friend would support the Whig candidate, who opposed a war with Mexico. Kelso's threat brought about the election of Hannigan who took his seat in the United States Senate. Immediately came the wrangle over the admission of Texas. The candidate who would have been elected United States Senator, but for the defection of Kelso, had announced that he would vote against bringing Texas into the Union. Hannigan voted for the measure and his single vote made Texas a State, and the making of her a State brought on the war with Mexico. Thus the solitary vote of a dying man in the wilds of Indiana, caused the war with our neighboring Republic and the acquisition of an immense area of territory by the United States. While it may be the conflict would have occurred later, it is none the less true that the little incident related was fraught with most momentous conse uences.

THE RESULT OF A MAN'S VANITY.

When the war was impending, a secret agent was sent to Cuba where Santa Anna was undergoing a penalty of exile, with the purpose of bribing that wily old scoundrel to betray his country. It was known that the fickle Mexicans were likely to call him from exile and place him at the head of military affairs, and it was known too that a round sum of money would make a traitor of him. The plan was to land Santa Anna in Mexico, where the army was certain to declare in his favor, and he would thus be enabled to make his treason successful. All that was necessary was to conduct the business with prudence and secrecy.

· It so happened, however, that the naval officer sent on this mission had a handsome new uniform of which he was quite vain. Instead of attiring himself in civilian dress, he wore his uniform, and, 'anding at Havana was driven to the home of Santa Anna. The ,ublicity of his act drew suspicion to him, for of course the Mexican General was under surveillance. Had he accepted the proposed offer and attempted to carry it out, his treachery would have been so apparent that he would have been shot. So Santa Anna declined the proposal, the certain penalty of which was more than he was willing to face, and the bargain, which might have ended the Mexican War before it was fairly on foot, was never consummated, through the vanity of a young naval officer regarding his uniform, though it may be noted that the conscienceless Santa Anna did try afterward to betray his country to the American arms.

OTHER TRIFLING INCIDENTS THAT PRODUCED FAR REACHING CONSEQUENCES.

When the great Civil War was about to break forth, General Robert E. Lee spent hours in prayer and distressing debate with himself, as to whether he should join the Southern Confederacy or remain loyal to the Union. You all know the decision he finally reached, but suppose his doubts had ended in a contrary decision, what a tremendous effect it would have had upon the four bloody years that followed! Had not Virginia seceded, the rebellion would have been so hopeless that it could not have lasted more than a few weeks. The Union would have been restored with slavery intact, and the appalling struggle would have come later, with perhaps more woeful consequences, for that it had to come was ordered of heaven.

We could multiply instances showing that the most tremendous results have flowed from the slightest causes, but it is unnecessary, and you can doubtless recall incidents as striking as those I have enumerated.

As illustrative of the perversity of fate or ill-luck, as it may be termed, all must sympathize with Admiral Sampson. At the breaking out of our war with Spain, it was universally believed that he had no superior as a naval officer in the American navy. He possessed the full confidence of the Government and of his country. His previous career justified this confidence, and it cannot be doubted that had the opportunity offered, he would have shown himself one of the best of our naval commanders. He arranged the blockade of

5 D.D.

the Spanish fleet in Santiago, and the plan of battle whenever the ships dared to poke their noses outside the harbor. Days and weeks passed, and the strict watch was maintained, until finally on that sunshiny July morning, Admiral Cervera and the rest of his commanders made their dash, with the result that every Spanish vessel was captured or destroyed.

And it so happened that on that eventful morning Admiral Sampson was a few miles down the coast, holding a conference with General Shafter. Had he been with his fleet, he would have been heralded as one of the greatest heroes of the war ; but he was absent and the glory passed him by. People do not accept what men might have done, but what they did, as the criterion by which to judge them, and so it has come about that an unseemly wrangle has raged between the partisans of Sampson and Schley, and the fame and honor that might have gone to each will never be fully accorded to either.

Now, when war was declared between Spain and the United States, every officer and soldier, on land and sea, was eager to get into the fight. Where was the fighting most likely to be ? Naturally all eyes turned to Cuba, but the greatest anxiety was felt over the Spanish fleets. It was known that they included many first-class modern ships, all well armed and equipped, and we remember the general uneasiness as to their probable action. There was alarm everywhere. Fortifications were hastily thrown up along the coast ; the forts were manned and armed ; new ships were bought ; auxiliary cruisers prepared ; the seaboard cities were put in the best possible condition for defence, and in short everything was done to repair the unpreparedness of the country for a war with a foreign power, for whenever war breaks upon the United States, she is never prepared for it.

Who of us suspected that the most terrific and effective blow would be struck thousands of miles away on the other side of the world ? And who dreamed that this amazing blow would be delivered by Commodore George Dewey ? But no man can penetrate the plans of an over-ruling Providence, and the agents of such designs often fail to understand them until the end is attained.

During the hot, enervating summer of 1897, Dewey found his health was failing. Close devotion to his duties began to tell upon his naturally rugged frame, and he did not need a physician to remind him that the best thing to do was to go upon a cruise. Accordingly he made application for such orders and it was granted.

DEWEY APPOINTED TO THE COMMAND OF THE ASIATIC SQUADRON.

Matters were becoming strained between our country and Spain, though many people believed the trouble would be adjusted without war. In view, however, of the contingency, Dewey did not fancy being sent into Asiatic waters, with slight prospect of fighting. He preferred the Atlantic, where there was promise of measuring strength with the best fleets of our enemy, in a battle that would recall his stirring experience in the Civil War.

But the clouds grew thicker and more threatening, and he accepted the command of the Asiatic squadron. Theodore Roosevelt, fiery, impetuous and patriotic, was Assistant Secretary of the Navy, and he knew the worth of Dewey. He insisted upon his appointment, but one of the Naval Board objected.

" He is a fop, a dude, a dandy."

" You will find him a dandy of a fighter ; he knows his business ; he is level-headed and will make no blunders."

" You seem interested in him ? "

" I am, and so will you and the rest of the country be before long. It doesn't make any difference what kind of clothes he wears ; he's our man."

One fact helped Roosevelt in securing the appointment for Dewey. Roosevelt was so headstrong and impetuous in his war sentiments, that the board had refused to do many things advocated by him, and they now felt inclined to make some concession. Consequently Dewey was appointed, though it cannot be said he was pleased with his field of duty.

On the night of November 27, 1897, the Metropolitan Club in Arlington gave a farewell dinner to Commodore Dewey, where bright and witty speeches were made, toasts drank and the best wishes extended to the guest. During the course of the evening, Colonel Archibald Hopkins, Clerk of the Court of Claims, read the following clever lines :

"Fill all your glasses full to-night;
    The wind is off the shore;
And be it feast or be it fight,
    We pledge the Commodore.

"Through days of storm, through days of calm,
    On broad Pacific seas;
At anchor off the isles of Palm,
    Or with the Japanese;

"Ashore, afloat, on deck, below,
    Or where our bulldogs roar;
To back a friend or breast a foe
    We pledge the Commodore.

"We know our honor'll be unstained
    Where'e'r his pennant flies;
Our rights respected and maintained,
    Whatever power defies.

"And when he takes the homeward tack
    Beneath an Admiral's flag,
We'll hail the day that brings him back
    And have another jag."

When the news came from Manila, making known the marvelous
work of Commodore Dewey on May 1, 1898, Colonel Hopkins was
inspired to add the following stanzas:

"Along the far Philippine coast,
    Where flew the flag of Spain,
Our Commodore to-day can boast
    ' 'Twill never fly again.'

"And up from all our hills and vales,
    From city, town, and shore,
A mighty shout the welkin hails:
    'Well done, brave Commodore!'

"Now let your Admiral's pennant fly;
    You've won it like a man,
Where heroes love to fight and die,
    Right in the battle's van."

SOME OF THE MEN WHO STOOD BEHIND THE GUNS AT MANILA

GUN PRACTICE ON THE "BALTIMORE," MANILA BAY, DURING THE BLOCKADE

CHAPTER VI

In Asiatic Waters—Beginning of the War With Spain

Opening of the War With Spain.—Dewey In Asiatic Waters.—Preparations for Attacking the Spanish Fleet.—The Respective Fleets.—The City of Manila.—Its Defences.—Why the American Gunners Are So Much the Superior of the Spanish.

THE United States having determined upon forcible intervention in Cuba, where the horrible cruelties of Spain shocked the world, history began making and continued to make with a rush. No sublimer instance of the self-restraint of a people is recorded in history than that of the American nation, when it became known that the battleship *Maine* had been blown up in the harbor of Havana, with an appalling loss of life among the brave officers and sailors. While every one felt morally certain that this crime of the century had been committed by Spaniards (though undoubtedly without the sanction of the home government), all were willing to await the verdict of the Court of Inquiry. This verdict left no doubt that the destruction of the splendid battleship was the work of miscreants, for whom no adequate punishment could ever be provided, and ten times the number of volunteers called for by the President could have been had for the simple asking.

WAR DECLARED BETWEEN SPAIN AND THE UNITED STATES.

The Queen Regent of Spain declared war against the United States on the 24th of April, and our Government replied that war had existed since the 21st, on which day our Minister at Madrid was given his passports. Preparations were hurried and thus the memorable struggle began.

Our account of the life and services of Admiral Dewey requires our attention to that magnificent group of islands, known under the name of the Philippines, a full account of which is given in the latter part of this work.

It has been shown that the retention of Dewey in the Asiatic waters was directly due to Assistant Secretary of War Roosevelt. The *Olympia*, the flagship of Dewey, was ordered to return to San Francisco, but the following confidential despatch was sent to Dewey on the 25th of February :

"Order the squadron, except *Monocacy*, to Hong Kong. Keep full of coal. In the event of a declaration of war with Spain your duty will be to see that the Spanish squadron does not leave the Asiatic coast, and then offensive operations in Philippine Islands. Keep *Olympia* until further orders."

Well aware of the important work thus outlined, and which was likely to be required of Dewey, no pains was spared by the Navy Department in keeping him supplied with coal, ammunition and stores. Express trains were hurried at the highest speed across the continent, carrying the indispensable ammunition, which was placed on the warship *Mohican* at San Francisco, and the vessel steamed away for Honolulu. At the latter port, the ammunition was transferred to the *Baltimore*, which was crammed full with the explosives. She was also filled to her utmost capacity with coal, and then the cruiser headed for Yokohama, 5,000 miles distant, from which port she was to go to Hong Kong, where Dewey was awaiting the supplies. The voyage was completed without incident, and it need not be said how welcome the cargo proved to the brave Commodore and his men.

READY FOR THE FRAY.

Everything being in readiness, Dewey paused for instructions from Washington. He was not held long in suspense. The throbbing wire that carried the news for thousands of miles under many oceans of the declaration of war carried also orders for him to capture or destroy the formidable Spanish fleet that was known to be in Manila waters. Almost immediately came another message making known that Great Britain had issued a proclamation of neutrality. This compelled Dewey to leave Hong Kong with his squadron within twenty-four hours after receiving the word in accordance with the terms of England's neutrality. The Commodore steamed to Mirs Bay, a Chinese port only a short distance away, where by the 27th of April his preparations were completed and he set sail for Manila.

In the latter portion of this work will be found a full description of the Philippines, of Manila and the surrounding bay and country, so that only sufficient reference is made here to follow the incidents of one of the most famous naval battles of modern times. Dewey's ships and equipments were:

THE AMERICAN FLEET.

Olympia—First-class protected cruiser (flagship), 5,500 tons. Speed, 21.7 knots. Complement, 450. Armor, protected deck, 2 inches to 4 3-4 inches. Guns, main battery, four 8-inch, ten 5-inch, rapid-fire; secondary battery, rapid-fire, fourteen 6-pound, seven 1-pound, four Gatlings, one field gun and five torpedo tubes. Captain Charles V. Gridley.

Baltimore—Protected cruiser, 4,400 tons. Speed, 20.1 knots. Complement, 386. Armor, 2 1-2 inches to 4 inches. Guns, main battery, four 8-inch, six 6-inch, slow-fire; secondary battery, rapid-fire, four 6-pound, two 3-pound, two 1-pound, four 37 MM. Hotchkiss, two Colts, one field gun and five torpedo tubes. Captain Nehemiah M. Dyer.

Raleigh—Protected cruiser, 3,183 tons. Speed, 19 knots. Armor, 1 inch to 2 1-2 inches. Guns, one 6-inch, rapid-fire, ten 5-inch; secondary battery, eight 6-pounders, four 1-pounders, and two machine guns. Complement, 320. Captain Joseph B. Coghlan.

Boston—Protected cruiser, 3,189 tons. Speed, 15.6 knots. Complement, 270. Armor, 1 1-2 inch deck. Guns, main battery, two 8-inch and six 6-inch rifles; secondary battery, rapid-fire, two 6-pounders and two 3-pounders. Captain Frank Wildes.

Petrel—Fourth-rate cruiser, 890 tons. Speed, 13.7 knots. Guns, four 6-inch, two 3-pounder rapid-fire, one 1-pounder, and four machine guns. Commander Edward P. Wood.

Concord—Gunboat, 1,700 tons. Speed, 16.8 knots. Armor, 3-8 inch deck. Guns, main battery, six 6-inch rifles. Commander Asa Walker,

Hugh McCulloch—Revenue cutter, light battery of rapid-fire guns.

Zafiro—Auxiliary cruiser; supply vessel.

Although the Spanish fleet was known to be somewhere in the neighborhood of Manila, there was no certainty as to its precise location.   Dewey believed it was at anchor in Manila Bay, defiantly awaiting attack, and he determined to hunt for it at that place.   That he was right in his theory was speedily proven by the events themselves.

THE SPANISH FLEET.

This fleet under the command of Admiral Montojo was as follows :

Reina Maria Cristina—Steel cruiser (flagship).   Built in 1887, iron, 3,520 tons, 14 to 17.5 knots, according to draught, and a main battery of six 6.2-inch rifles.

Castilla—Steel cruiser, built in 1881, wood, 3,342 tons, 14 knots, and four 5.9-inch Krupps and two 4.7-inch Krupps in her main battery.

Isla de Cuba—Cruiser. } Each 1,030 tons, speed 14 knots, crew
Isla de Luzon—Cruiser. } 200 men, battery four 4.7 inch, four 6-pounder and two 3-pounder guns.

Velasco—Small cruiser, built in 1881, iron, 1,139 tons, and three 6-inch Armstrongs in her main battery.

Don Juan de Austria—Small cruiser, completed in 1887, iron, 1,152 tons, 13 to 14 knots, and four 4.7-inch rifles in her main battery.

Don Antonio de Ulloa—Small cruiser, iron, 1,152 tons.   Four 4.7-inch Hontoria guns ; two 2.7-inch, two quick-firing ; two 1.5-inch ; five muzzle loaders.

Gunboats *Paragua, Callao, Samar, Pampagna* and *Arayat*, built 1881-6, steel, 137 tons, 10 knots, and each mounting two quick-firing guns.

Gunboats *Mariveles* and *Mindoro*, built in 1886 and 1885, iron, 142 tons, 10 knots, each mounting one 2.7-inch rifle and four machine guns.

Gunboat *Manileno*, built in 1887, wood, 142 tons, 9 knots, and mounting three 3.5-inch rifles.

Gunboats *El Cano* and *General Lezo*, built in 1885, iron, 528 tons, 10 to nearly 12 knots, and each mounting three 3.5-inch rifles.

Gunboat *Marquis Del Duero*, built in 1875, iron, 500 tons, 10 knots, and mounting one 6.2-inch and two 4.7-inch rifles.

It must not be supposed that the Spanish fleet was unaware of the danger of an attack from the Americans.   General Augustin, the

Governor-General, had issued the following proclamation, which is so striking an example of Spanish bombast and so called chivalry that it is worthy of preservation :

A CHARACTERISTIC PROCLAMATION.

" The North American people, composed of all the social excrescences, have exhausted our patience and provoked war with perfidious machinations, acts of treachery and outrages against the law of nations and international conventions.

" A squadron, manned by foreigners and possessing neither instructions nor discipline, is preparing to come to this archipelago with the ruffianly intention of robbing us of all that means life, honor and liberty.

" The aggressors shall not profane the tombs of your fathers, shall not gratify their lustful passion at the cost of your wives and daughters, shall not cover you with dishonor, shall not appropriate the property your industry has accumulated as provision against old age, and shall not perpetrate any of the crimes inspired by their wickedness and covetousness, because your valor and patriotism will suffice to punish this miserable people, that, claiming to be civilized and cultivated, have exterminated the unhappy natives of North America, instead of bringing them to a life of civilization and progress."

A comparison of the Spanish and American fleets shows that the latter was superior in guns and calibre ; but the advantage was greatly outweighed, from the Spanish view, by the shore batteries and the mines and torpedoes in the bay itself. The war proved, as indeed it had been proven before, that between armored ships and shore batteries, the gain is overwhelmingly on the side of the latter.

THE CITY OF MANILA.

The city of Manila, with its quarter of a million population, is on the western coast of the Luzon, the principal island of the Philippines, and has long been the capital of the group and Spain's centre of trade in the far East. Standing on a land-locked sea, it faces a sheet of water large enough to allow all the navies of the world to ride at anchor It is a modern city, with a venerable university, fine buildings, a grand cathedral, the residence of the Governor-General, has street cars, electric lights, and has an immense trade in tobacco, sugar, coffee, hemp, rice, cocoa, cotton, cordage and the various products of a semi-tropical country.

The entrance to Manila Bay is seven miles wide and contains several islands, the largest of which are Corregidor and Caballo, with the city twenty-six miles to the northeast. These islands divide the entrance into two channels, known as the Boca Grande, five miles wide, and Boca Chico, two miles across.

The fortified portion of Manila is the older or official section, lying to the south, but the modern city north of the Pasig river, was without any fortifications, until war became imminent, when the Spanish authorities mounted a number of guns and strengthened the shore batteries, the chief attention being given to those at Cavite, which is a suburb standing on a promontory, and some ten miles nearer the entrance to the bay than the city of Manila itself.

This brief description of the important metropolis shows how capable it was of making a strong defence against the most powerful fleets. Had it been in the possession of Americans it would have been quickly made impregnable. The bay would have been so mined that any ironclad attempting to force an entrance would have been sunk, before she could pass either of the islands guarding the mouth of the bay. During our civil war, the harbor of Charleston, where nature had done less than at Manila, was so fortified by means of mines, torpedoes and forts, that the most formidable efforts of the Unionists, backed by limitless resources, came to naught. All that ingenuity and science could do to force an entrance was repeatedly tried, but in vain, and, as is well known, Charleston never fell until the closing days of the war, when it was assailed at the rear by Sherman's army advancing from Atlanta.

Decrepit, corrupt and inefficient as is Spain, she would have been blind had she not seen the danger that threatened her chief city in the Philippines, and criminally negligent had she neglected the precautions dictated by ordinary prudence. She sank mines in the entrance and torpedoes were strung across both channels. The absurd self-confidence with which she contemplated an attack by the American squadron has been shown in the grandiloquent proclamation of

Manila's Governor-General. It may be said that she felt secure and probably in her self-complacency had a mild pity for the American "pigs," as she was fond of calling us, who were rash enough to think they had a chance of success against these defences.

Many persons have been mystified to understand how it was that in every conflict between the American and Spanish ships, the power of the latter crumbled to pieces. It cannot be denied that the Spanish soldier is a brave and dangerous fighter. The battles around Santiago proved this, and the sailors on the ships taken individually, were as courageous as those of any nation. Moreover, it cannot be said that the officers lacked in ability, and, furthermore, as in the case of Admiral Cervera, they were provided with the best types of modern battleship. Why then did they make so miserable a showing when brought face to face with our own vessels?

WHY AMERICANS SURPASS ALL NATIONS IN MARKSMANSHIP.

The explanation is simple. It lies not only in the inherent difference between the respective "men behind the guns," but in the opposite methods of training. The war of 1812 proved, that in markmanship our countrymen not only have no superior anywhere in the world, they have no equals. Their natural aptitude was trained to the highest point of efficiency, by continual and intelligent practice. No doubt when we heard, during the serene days of peace that a battleship spent twenty thousand dollars in a few hours' practice at the guns, it sounded extravagant. The fact that every missile fired by some of the enormous pieces cost Uncle Sam $2,500, made it seem a wicked waste to indulge in the sport of firing those thunderous guns, whose recoil was terrific enough to sink an old-fashioned battleship, and when this thing went on for days at a time, not by one ship, but by scores of ships, some of us were aghast. The United States is a rich nation, but even she could not afford thus to hurl thousands upon thousands of dollars into the deep, merely for the purpose of affording amusement to men who were proud of their skill in gunnery, but the results showed our error. No expense is too great that helps strengthen the power of a ship, squadron or fleet.

This truth is so self-evident that even Spain was accustomed to make large appropriations for the purpose, but in her case, the officers took the money, made a pretence of gun practice, and then divided the funds among themselves. They looked upon them as a part of the regular "tip" to which they were entitled. This system has prevailed for generations throughout all the military, naval and civil divisions of the kingdom. The service is honey-combed with corruption from the highest to the lowest position. Weyler only imitated the Governor-Generals that had preceded him in the Philippines and in Cuba, when he became a millionaire in a brief time, and, as I have stated in another work, the filibustering expeditions from this country to Cuba, before the late war never could have attained one-half their success, but for the treachery of the officials whose duty it was to suppress them. Every such official had his price, and when it is added that in many instances this price was quite insignificant, enough has been said to explain one of the most potent causes of Spain's weakness and decay.

As has been stated, Manila Bay and its entrance had been mined and laid with torpedoes, after the Spanish fashion. Commodore George Dewey knew all this as well as the Spaniards themselves. Moreover, he knew the location of all these fearful defenses, for he was not the man to rush headlong into danger ; but as he steamed from Mirs Bay it is not improbable that in the light of this knowledge, he recalled the exclamation of his great teacher Farragut, when advancing to the attack of Mobile, which was : "D—— the torpedoes ! "

CAPTAIN COGHLAN AT THE WHEEL OF THE "RALEIGH"

The above photograph on board his ship was taken in the Spring of 1899, as the returned cruiser lay at anchor in the Delaware River, Philadelphia. It was the *Raleigh* that fired the first shot at the battle of Manila in reply to the batteries of Corregidor Island, shortly before midnight, April 30, 1898.

CHAPTER VII

The Great Battle of Manila Bay

Panic in Manila.—Arrival of Commodore Dewey.—Consternation in Manila.—The Great Battle.—Wonderful Markmanship of the Americans.—Commodore Dewey's Coolness and Intrepidity—One of the Most Remarkable Battles in Naval Annals.

ONE of the strangest things in this world is the manner in which news sometimes travels and spreads. The tidings of some important treaty between the chiefs of an Indian tribe and our Government is often known hundreds of miles away among the lodges of the red men within an hour or so of the signing of the treaty. Of course the news is telegraphed by means of signal fires, but that fact hardly removes the singularity of it all, while in some instances, even the method referred to, fails fully to account for the swift passage of tidings.

THE PANIC IN MANILA.

When Commodore Dewey sailed from Hong Kong, a cable carried the information to Manila, where the authorities used every possible effort to keep the matter a secret, but it was impossible, and in a short time every one in the city knew that the American fleet was on its way to attack the city. A panic followed. Hundreds of those who had the means took refuge, with such valuables as they could carry, on the merchant vessels in the harbor, and breathed a prayer of thankfulness when the vessels sailed away. The majority, however, stayed behind. They heard the confident boastings of the army and navy officers around them, who rejoiced at the prospect of sticking so many American "pigs" that knew no better than to rush to their own slaughter ; but these vaporings did not relieve the dread of the people. They knew something of the fighting qualities of the barbarians on the other side of the world, and they knew something, too, of the qualities of their bombastic countrymen and their masters. Hence their panic.

A little mental calculation showed that the American fleet would be due at Manila by Saturday evening. Admiral Montojo's fleet cruised back and forth around the entrance to the bay, waiting for a chance to pounce upon the audacious " pigs " as soon as they showed themselves. On the afternoon of Saturday, the fleet was lined up at Cavite, seven miles from the city, where a long line of earthworks had been thrown up, and every preparation made by the Spanish engineers to defend the arsenal, dry dock and naval workshops. It must be remembered, too, that the fort on Corregidor Island, the battery on Caballo, the works to the north and south, the mines in the channel and the torpedoes were all in readiness. Due warning had been given of the coming of the enemy, ample time was afforded for preparation, and it would seem that the self-confidence of the Spaniards was fully warranted.

ARRIVAL OF DEWEY.

Meanwhile, Commodore Dewey was steaming swiftly for Manila, and just as the dusk of evening was closing over the ocean, he sighted Corregidor Island. He knew the place was strongly fortified, but that fact did not change his purpose of forcing his way past it to the city. Pressing forward, he soon had a full moon to aid him. As he drew nearer, all lights in the squadron were put out, and the crews were stationed at their guns. The flagship led the impressive procession, and was followed by the *Baltimore*, the *Raleigh*, the *Petrel*, the *Concord* and the *Boston*, all advancing like so many vast phantoms across the heaving waters.

The night wore on, for a good many miles remained to be passed before Manila Bay would be reached. It was well beyond midnight, when a flash suddenly lit up the gloom on Corregidor Island, a thunderous boom rolled over the waters, and an immense shot screeched over the *Olympia* and *Raleigh*, quickly followed by a second which splashed in the water astern. The first shot on our side was fired by the *Raleigh*, the *Concord* and *Boston* joining, and the shells appeared to drop inside the shore battery, which quickly ceased firing.

Perhaps the consternation created in Manila by these shots may be partly imagined. The people had been on edge for hours; in fact, ever since they knew the American fleet was approaching. Here it was, thundering at their doors. Men, white-faced and trembling, ran panting through the streets, women rushed to the shelter of the churches, children screamed and the panic was intensified by the rumors that the natives to the rear of the city were massing to rush in and massacre the inhabitants. The panic spread to the soldiers, who began to think that if caught thus between two fires, even Spanish intrepidity would not save them.

When the morning sun of May 1, 1898, appeared in the hot horizon, it showed all sides of the harbor lined with thousands of spectators, terrified by the sight of the American ships drawn up in line of battle, scarcely ten miles distant in the bay. Standing on the deck of the *Olympia*, Commodore Dewey through his glasses sighted the Spanish fleet off Cavite, with the flag of Admiral Montojo flying from the *Reina Christina*, the *Castilla* lying a short distance in front, while to seaward were the *Don Juan de Austria*, *Don Antonio de Ulloa*, *Isla de Cuba*, *Isla de Luzon*, *Quiros*, *Marquis del Duero* and the *General Lezo*.

A GREAT NAVAL BATTLE.

Promptly and majestically the American ships advanced to the attack. Passing in front of Manila, three shore batteries opened with their guns, whose range was easily five miles away. The only reply was from the *Concord*, which answered with two shells. Shortly afterward, as the squadron drew near Cavite, two mines of prodigious power were exploded a little way in front of the *Olympia*. Immense columns of water flew high in air, but the flagship neither faltered nor swerved in her course. Recalling the incident already referred to of Admiral Farragut in Mobile Bay, Commodore Dewey signalled to the other ships to pay no attention to the torpedoes.

A few minutes later, the great battle of Manila opened. The Spanish batteries on shore and the war vessels began firing at the same time. Amid the thunder and roar some one hoarsely shouted, " Remember the *Maine*!" and the cry, slipping between the deafening discharges of the cannon, was caught up and repeated by hundreds of throats. The men seemed to feel that the hour had come for avenging that crime and all were eager for the opportunity.

Still the grand *Olympia* led the way. As before, when the battle opened, it was the good fortune of Dewey to be in the hottest of it

Cool, self-contained, alert and grasping every point and possibility in his field of vision, the Commodore, clad in a white duck uniform and a golf cap, issued his orders, as if directing the maneuvering of his ships in the harbor of some friendly nation.

Seeing that everything was in readiness, he turned to his executive officer and uttered these words, which are destined to immortality:

"You may fire, Gridley, as soon as you are ready!"

Immediately, a series of sharp, crackling reports split the air, followed by earth-shaking roars, and a vast mass of smoke, pierced here and there by crimson tongues of flame, rolled over the bay and traveled round the ships. In a naval battle, as is well known, the vessels keep continually in motion so as to disconcert the aim of the enemy. It was a grandly thrilling scene, as the American vessels slowly circled about, with their sides aflame, the air pulsating with the tremendous discharges, and the murderous shells crashing into the hulls and rigging of the Spanish ships.

The battle began about seven o'clock in the morning and the people on shore, failing to understand the maneuvering, allowed their hopes to persuade them that the Americans were suffering defeat. At the end of half an hour came a lull. A breeze sweeping across the bay, wafted the smoke aside, and the terrified spectators then saw that Admiral Montojo's flagship was in flames. She was burning fiercely when Commodore Dewey signalled to his vessels to withdraw. This action again filled the spectators with hope, and the news was cabled to breathless Madrid, nearly ten thousand miles away, that the Americans had been hopelessly beaten. As may be supposed, the information threw the Spanish capital into spasms of delight, for no one doubted its truth. As one of the leading officials expressed it, "I can scarcely restrain my joyful emotions."

But Commodore Dewey had retired only to replenish his ammunition. He was disturbed by a report that the supply was short, but happily it proved a mistake, and, ever mindful of the comfort of his men, he ordered them to breakfast and rest. One grim old tar when the order was repeated exclaimed:

"To —— with breakfast! let's first finish the Spaniards!"

Meanwhile, Admiral Montojo transferred his flag from the burning *Reina Cristina* to the *Isla de Cuba* and between ten and eleven

)ck, the American squadron again moved forward to the attack.
:e more the flames spouted from the iron sides, the deafening
· shook the air, and the bursting shells, aimed with unerring
:ty, crashed into the ships of the enemy, tearing great yawning
s, killing scores and spreading death and destruction on every hand.

OVERWHELMING DEFEAT OF THE SPANIARDS.

Then it was that the results of the native skill of our country-
ι, supplemented by long practice, even though costly, proved how
l it paid, considered as a simple "investment." The second flag-
ι was soon set on fire and something in the nature of a panic
:ad through the Spanish fleet. All was confusion, for it had
ɔme apparent that the ships were doomed beyond hope. War is
rrible thing, and its horrors were now seen in all their fulness.
·m the blazing, splintered and mangled ships, came wild shrieks
:gony and the sight of the crimson decks, slippery with blood and
·wn with writhing or motionless and torn forms, would have filled
stoutest soul with terror. Quoting from an eyewitness :

"The Americans now pressed their advantage, and poured a
vy fire into the sinking ships. At this juncture the *Don Juan de*
stria became the center of interest. She had been in the very
ιt of the battle, and had received perhaps more of the American
ts than any other. Admiral Montojo, on the burning *Cuba*, threw
his arms with a gesture of despair as a heavy roar came from the
stria, and part of her deck flew up in the air, taking with it scores
dead and dying and mangled. A shot had set off one of her
ʒazines. She was ruined and sinking. Her crew refused to leave
. Weeping, cursing, praying, firing madly and blindly, they went
ʌn with her. As the *Don Juan* went down, the *Castilla* burst into
ιes. The remainder of the Spanish fleet now turned and fled
ʌn the long narrow isle behind Cavite. Several of the gunboats
e run ashore, while others fled up a small creek and were grounded
re."

The batteries of Cavite were silenced and cheers rang from the
ks of the victorious American vessels. A great battle had been
ght between ironclads, and the victory was with the Americans.
d not the least wonderful feature of it all was that while the
― 6 D.D.

Spaniards had lost a thousand in killed and wounded, there was not a single American slain !

In truth it is impossible to understand this amazing fact, for, it has been truly said, that if the Spanish gunners had shut their eyes and fired at random, it would seem that some of their shots, guided by the laws of blind chance, must have taken effect *somewhere*, and killed a number of their enemies, who took no means of sheltering themselves beyond the screen provided by their vessels.

The terrific outburst and uproar was followed by a Sabbath calm. The conquering fleet rested off the humbled city which was at its mercy, silent, grim and mighty, and able at the word of a single man to lay the metropolis in ruins. Would Manila invite its own destruction by a refusal to surrender ?

By and by, the British consul came out to the *Olympia* with a request to Commodore Dewey not to bombard Manila. He replied that the matter rested with Manila itself. He would not harm the city provided the Spaniards surrendered all their torpedoes, guns and the control of the cable and telegraph wires. If that were refused, he would open the bombardment at daylight the next morning.

When this notice was received by Captain-General Augustin he indignantly refused, whereupon Dewey, without any more parleying, made his preparations to carry out his threat. The course of the Spanish leader is the more idiotic when the appalling results of the late battle were before his eyes. Eleven warships had been destroyed or sunk, besides the thousand men killed and wounded, but to the honor of the Spaniards be it recorded that in no instance did they strike their flag. When they went down it was with colors flying. Knowing all this, it may be supposed that the Spanish commander was merely bluffing. Be that as it may, he reconsidered his refusal and thus saved Manila from the horrors of bombardment.

THE CONDUCT OF DEWEY DURING THE BATTLE.

It is interesting to note all that pertains to the personality of Admiral Dewey in the battle which proved him one of the greatest sea captains in naval history. The following account is from Lieutenant Charles G. Calkins, who was the navigator of the *Olympia* during the battle :

" I had known Admiral Dewey for thirty years, and I cannot say
his demeanor that morning was greatly different from what it
ys is. ˙ Always he impresses one as a man who knows himself,
knows what he has to do, and who means to do it. Such was
1iral Dewey then. He was cool, alert, intense, and for the most
silent. He observed closely the movements of the fleet from
light compass platform where we stood.

" Much has been made about the attire of the Admiral that morn-
A popular monthly pictured him in a long frock coat twining
it his legs. Another magazine hastened to correct this by describ-
Admiral Dewey as wearing shoulder straps, gold lace on his sleeves,
three-inch stripes on his trousers. Some of these latter items
correct for the occasion of full dress, but as a matter of fact the
1iral mounts them once or twice a year. At the battle of Manila
/ore a white duck uniform and a golf cap.

" His manner did not noticeably change all through that morning.
showed the strain, perhaps, but very slightly. It was, however,
e like a stroll than one ᵇf the battles of history. The shots did
come near enough to worry us, or when they did come near
1gh we were too busy to pay them much attention. People who
pretty busy have no time to heed trifles.

" The nearest that Admiral Dewey came to swearing during all
engagement was when we were coming out of the battle for the
1 time, I think. I remarked to the Admiral : ' It's damnable that
1ave not done them more damage.'

" ' I think it is damnable, lieutenant,' he replied, with quiet
hasis.

" I'm afraid I'm responsible for all the swearing that Admiral
/ey did that day, although I know that he is capable of using
ng language where it is absolutely necessary."

CHAPTER VIII

The Nation's Acknowledgment of Dewey's Service

The News from Manila.—First Official Report—Thanks of the Government—Account of the Battle by Consul Williams—Prompt Acknowledgment of Dewey's Services by Congress—Official Action of the Government of the United States Regarding the Reports—Dewey Made Rear-Admiral.

ONE of the acts of Commodore Dewey was to cut the cable in Manila Bay. He explained that this was done to prevent the enemy sending to or receiving any messages from Madrid and the outside world, though, as has been shown, the news of a bogus victory was telegraphed to the Spanish capital. Such it is said was the explanation of Dewey, but there is a general suspicion that his real purpose was to shut off communication with Washington. There have been so many instances of attempts by our Government to direct campaigns, hundreds of miles distant, followed by disastrous consequences, that one of the greatest dreads of a military or naval commander is that he, though on the ground and knowing the situation as no one else can know it, may be interfered with and hampered, and therefore one cannot help smiling and commending the precaution taken by the Commodore.

FIRST OFFICIAL REPORT OF COMMODORE DEWEY.

It followed, therefore, that a week passed before the official news reached this country, since the only communication between Dewey and the United States was by way of Hong Kong, which is 630 miles from Manila. The *McCulloch* was instantly dispatched to Hong Kong with reports to the Navy Department, and the boat reached that port on the 7th of May, from which point the first official despatch was forwarded to Secretary Long in the following words:

"MANILA, May 1st.—The squadron arrived at Manila at daybreak this morning. Immediately engaged the enemy and destroyed the following Spanish vessels :.*Reina Cristina, Castilla, Ulloa, Isla de Cuba, General Lezo,* the *Duero, Correo, Velasco, Mindanao,* one transport, and the water battery at Cavite. The squadron is uninjured, and only a few men were slightly wounded. The only means of telegraphing is to the American consul at Hong Kong. I shall communicate with him.   DEWEY."

The second despatch was :

"CAVITE, May 4th.—I have taken possession of naval station at Cavite, on Philippine Islands. Have destroyed fortifications at bay entrance, paralleling garrison. I control bay completely, and can take city at any time. The squadron in excellent health and spirits. Spanish loss not fully known, but very heavy. One hundred and fifty killed, including captain of *Reina Cristina.* I am assisting in protecting Spanish sick and wounded. Two hundred and fifty-six wounded in hospitals within our lines. Much excitement at Manila. Will protect foreign residents.   DEWEY."

REPLY OF SECRETARY LONG.

The news, as may well be supposed, caused rejoicing in the United States, and Secretary Long replied :

" DEWEY, Manila :   WASHINGTON, May 7, 1898.

" The President, in the name of the American people thanks you and your officers and men for your splendid achievement and overwhelming victory.

" In recognition he has appointed you Acting Rear-Admiral, and will recommend a vote of thanks to you by Congress.   LONG."

CONSUL WILLIAMS' REPORT OF THE BATTLE.

There have been many graphic descriptions of this battle, but none is superior to that made to the State Department by Oscar F. Williams, United States Consul at Manila, which is appended :

" CONSUL OF THE UNITED STATES,
      " BAY OF MANILA, PHILIPPINE ISLANDS,
                                       " May 4, 1898.
" The Hon. Judge Day, Assistant Secretary of State, Washington, D. C.
      " SIR: I have the honor to briefly report to you concerning the

battle of Manila Bay, fought on May 1, 1898. Heeding your mandate, and by repeated request of Commodore George Dewey, of the United States Asiatic Squadron, I left Manila on Saturday, April 23d, and on Wednesday, April 27th, at about one o'clock, P.M., boarded the flagship *Olympia* in Mirs Bay, near Hong Kong. After meeting the Commodore and his captains and commanders in council, the Commodore at once ordered his fleet to start at 2 P.M. for Manila Bay. On Saturday, April 30th, Subig Bay was reconnoitered because of reported hiding of Spanish fleet in its inner harbor ; but no fleet being there found, the Commodore proceeded at once to the south channel entrance to Manila Bay, and while by many reports mines, torpedoes and land defenses obstructed entrance, yet the flagship led the van, and between 10 P.M., April 30th, and 2 A.M., May 1st, our fleet of six warships, one despatch boat and two coal-laden transports, passed all channel dangers unharmed despite shots from forts, and at 2 A.M. were all safe on the broad expanse of Manila Bay.

"After my departure, April 23d, and by drawing fire, to save Manila if possible, all Spanish warships went to their strongly fortified naval station at Cavite, where the inner harbor gave refuge and where potential support could be had from several forts and well-equipped batteries, which extended several miles right and left from Port Cavite.

"At about 5.30 A.M., Sunday, May 1st, the Spanish guns opened fire, at both the Manila breakwater battery and at Cavite, from fleet and forts. With magnificent coolness and order, but with the greatest promptness, our fleet, in battle array, headed by the flagship, answered the Spanish attack, and for about two and a half hours a most terrific fire ensued.

"The method of our operations could not have shown greater system, our guns greater effectiveness, or our officers and crews greater bravery, and while Spanish resistance was stubborn and the bravery of Spanish forces such as to challenge admiration, yet they were outclassed, weighed in the balance of war against the methods, training, aim and bravery shown on our decks, and after less than three hours' perilous and intense combat one of Spain's warships was sinking, two others were burning, and all others, with land defenses, had severely suffered, when our squadron, with no harm done to its ships, retired for breakfast.

"At about ten o'clock, A.M., Commodore Dewey renewed the battle, and with effects most fatal with each evolution. No better evidence of Spanish bravery need be sought than that, after the castigation of our first engagement, her ships and forts should again answer our fire. But Spanish efforts were futile; ship after ship and battery after battery went to destruction before the onslaught of American energy and training, and an hour and a half, of our second engagement wrought the annihilation of the Spanish fleet and forts, with several hundred Spanish killed and wounded, and millions in value of their government's property destroyed, while amazing, almost unbelievable, as it seems, not a ship or a gun of our fleet had been disabled, and, except on the *Baltimore*, not a man had been hurt. One of the crew of the *Baltimore* had a leg fractured by slipping, and another was hurt in the ankle in a similar manner, while four received slight flesh wounds from splinters thrown by a six-inch projectile, which pierced the starboard side of the cruiser.

"But in the battle of Manila Bay the United States squadron of six warships totally destroyed the Spanish fleet of eight warships, many forts and batteries, and accomplished this work without the loss of a man. History has only contrasts. There is no couplet to form a comparison. The only finish fight between the modern warships of civilized nations has proved the prowess of American naval men and methods, and the glory is a legacy for the whole people. Our crews are all hoarse from cheering, and while we suffer for cough drops and throat doctors, we have no use for liniment or surgeons.

"To every ship, officer and crew all praise be given. As Victoria was answered years ago, ' Your majesty, there is no second,' so may I report to your department as to our warships conquering the Spanish fleet in the battle of Manila Bay, there is no first, ' there is no second.' The cool bravery and efficiency of the Commodore were echoed by every captain and commander, and down through the lines by every officer and man, and naval history of the dawning century will be rich if it furnishes to the world so glorious a display of intelligent command and successful service as must be placed to the credit of the United States Asiatic squadron under date of May 1, 1898.

"It was my lot to stand on the bridge on the *Baltimore* by the side of Captain Dwyer during the first engagement, and to be called to the flagship *Olympia* by the Commodore, at whose side on the bridge I stood during the second engagement, and when the clouds roll by and I have again a settled habitation, it will be my honor and pleasure to transmit a report showing the scene somewhat in detail, and for which commanders promise data. Meanwhile, our Commodore will officially inform you of events which will rival in American history the exploits of Paul Jones.

"I have the honor to be, sir, your most obedient servant,

OSCAR F. WILLIAMS,

" United States Consul Manila."

PROMPT ACKNOWLEDGMENT OF DEWEY'S SERVICES BY CONGRESS.

Prompt as was Commodore Dewey in making known his victory to his government, the news reached Europe still earlier, and on May 2d, Representative Grout, of Vermont, introduced the following resolutions in the House:

" *Resolved*, That the thanks of Congress are due and are hereby tendered to Commodore George Dewey and the officers and seamen of the Asiatic Squadron, by him commanded, for the heroism and skill displayed by them in the total destruction of the Spanish fleet in the harbor of Manila, and the capture of the city and the planting of the American flag in the capital of the Philippines."

In no part of the United States was the pride and delight greater than in the South, as was shown by the introduction on the same day of the resolution of Representative Livingston of Georgia:

" *Resolved*, That the thanks of Congress be and they are hereby tendered to Commodore George Dewey, commanding the Asiatic squadron, for the eminent skill and valor exhibited by him and his squadron in the recent engagement resulting in his glorious victory over and the destruction of the Spanish fleet at Manila."

The United States cannot be justly accused of ingratitude to her patriotic sons, who risk their lives in her defense. She has proven this by the millions of dollars she ungrudgingly gives to the disabled veterans of the War of the Union, and to the families of those who perish on the field of battle. Hardly was the official report of Admiral Dewey received, when President McKinley sent the following message to Congress:

" To the Congress of the United States :

"On the 24th of April I directed the Secretary of the Navy to telegraph orders to Commodore George Dewey, of the United States Navy, commanding the Asiatic squadron, then lying in the port of Hong Kong, to proceed forthwith to the Philippine Islands, there to commence operations and engage the assembled Spanish fleet. Promptly obeying that order, the United States squadron, consisting of the flagship *Olympia*, *Baltimore*, *Raleigh*, *Boston*, *Concord*, and *Petrel*, with the revenue cutter *McCulloch* as an auxiliary despatch boat, entered the harbor of Manila at daybreak on the 1st of May, and immediately engaged the entire Spanish fleet of eleven ships, which were under the protection of the fire of the land forts. After a stubborn fight, in which the enemy suffered great loss, their vessels were destroyed or completely disabled, and the water battery at Cavite silenced. Of our brave officers and men not one was lost, and only eight injured, and those slightly. All of our ships escaped serious damage.

"By the 4th of May Commodore Dewey had taken possession of the naval station at Cavite, destroying the fortifications there and at the entrance of the bay, and patroling their garrisons. The waters of the bay are under his complete control. He has established hospitals within the American lines, where 250 of the Spanish sick and wounded are assisted and protected. The magnitude of this victory can hardly be measured by the ordinary standards of naval warfare. Outweighing any material advantage is the moral effect of this initial success. At this unsurpassed achievement the great heart of our nation throbs, not with boasting or with greed of conquest, but with deep gratitude that this triumph has come in a just cause, and that by the grace of God an effective step has thus been taken toward the attainment of the wished-for peace.

"To those whose skill, courage and devotion have won the fight, to the gallant commander and the brave officers and men who aided him, our country owes an incalculable debt. Feeling as our people feel, and speaking in their name, I sent a message to Commodore Dewey, thanking him and his officers and men for their splendid achievements and overwhelming victory, and informing him that I had appointed him an Acting Rear-Admiral.

" I now recommend that, following our national precedents, and expressing the fervent gratitue of every patriotic heart, the thanks of Congress be given Acting Rear-Admiral George Dewey, of the United States Navy, for highly distinguished conduct in conflict with the enemy, and to the officers and men under his command for their gallantry in the destruction of the enemy's fleet and the capture of the enemy's fortifications in the Bay of Manila.

" WILLIAM McKINLEY.

" Executive Mansion, May 9, 1898."

CONGRESSIONAL JOINT RESOLUTION.

Upon the conclusion of the reading of this message, Mr. Hale, of Maine, Chairman of the Committee on Naval Affairs, reported the following joint resolution :

"*Resolved, etc.,* That, in pursuance of the recommendation of the President, made in accordance with the provisions of section 1508 of the Revised Statutes, the thanks of Congress and of the American people are hereby tendered to Commodore George Dewey, U. S. N., Commander-in-Chief of the United States naval force of the Asiatic squadron, for highly distinguished conduct in conflict with the enemy, as displayed by him in the destruction of the Spanish fleet and batteries in the harbor of Manila, Philippine Islands, May 1, 1898.

" Section 2. That the thanks of Congress and the American people are hereby extended, through Commodore Dewey, to the officers and men under his command for the gallantry and skill exhibited by them on that occasion.

" Section 3. *Be it further resolved,* That the President of the United States be requested to cause this resolution to be communicated to Commodore Dewey, and through him to the officers and men under his command.

THE ACTION OF THE PRESIDENT VALIDATED.

Following this joint resolution, Mr. Hale introduced a bill, increasing the number of Rear-Admirals of the United States to seven, and validating any promotion to that rank made or to be made, based on the thanks of Congress. This, as Mr. Hale explained was to validate President McKinley's promotion of Commodore Dewey to the rank of Rear-Admiral. Not a vote was recorded in opposition to the bill. In favor of the joint resolution, Representative Boutelle of Maine, used these words :

" This is a case without exception, and I deem it without a parallel, without a precedent in the history of any war. It is unnecessary that I should add any word of commendation. The whole grand story has been so much better told by the thunder of Dewey's guns in Manila Bay, that I ask the House unanimously and by acclamation to pass this resolution tendering the thanks of the Congress and the American people to the gallant Commodore and the splendid officers and men under his command by achieving for American arms one of the most marvelously brilliant victories in the annals of naval warfare."

CHAPTER IX

Growth and Development of the World's Navies

The Eras in Naval Architecture.—Abuses on Board.—English Supremacy on the Seas.
—British Over-Confidence.—Causes of American Superiority.—Birth of the
American Navy.—The Introduction of Steam into the Navy.—The Propeller
Engine.—The New Era Introduced by the "Monitor" and "Merrimac" Fight.—
The Modern Warships.—Views of Admiral Colomb on the Lessons of the
Spanish-American War.

PAUL JONES.

THE battle of Manila Bay, May 1, 1898, was a contest between modern battleships and a striking illustration of the ability of vessels of the most improved pattern in the work of terrific destruction. Doubtless improvements will be made in the future, and some have already resulted as among the lessons of our late war with Spain, but for some years to come the warships of the leading nations will be substantially what they are to-day.

Now, in looking back over the conflicts that have taken place between different peoples, the periods of naval development may be separated into three grand divisions each accompanied by

distinctive advances. The first reaches from the earliest dawn of
civilization to the invention of gunpowder ; the second from the
latter date to the introduction of armored vessels, and the last in-
cludes the years that have passed since that date.

You will observe that these periods are of widely varying length,
the first covering the long stretch of centuries down to the fifteenth,
the second to our own Civil War, while the last is not yet half acent-
ury in duration.

THE FIRST PERIOD OF NAVAL DEVELOPMENT.

Canoes, small boats and larger ones propelled by oars and sails mark
the first period, when sturdy men ranged their craft side by side, and
fought with the same fury that they displayed on land. Many
ingenious weapons were used, including bows arrows, spears, swords,
targets, pavises, lances and firing barrels. While these weapons and
others were gradually improved, there was none previous to the invention of gunpowder, powerful enough to penetrate the side of a
vessel. This led to a rivalry in the height of the sides of ships, and
castles or towers were built forward and aft from which the fighters
hurled their missiles down upon the decks of their enemies. An old-
fashioned battleship sometimes looked as if it had a church erected
at the bow or stern, and the word "castle," as you have noted, remains
to the present day.

THE SECOND ERA OF NAVAL DEVELOPMENT.

The rearing of these huge structures made the vessels top-heavy
and so unstable that they sometimes capsized in calm water while
maneuvering, thus proving much more dangerous to their friends
than to their enemies. When cannon came into use, the towers were
gradually displaced for the modern stable hulls, but the improvement
in cannon was so slow that the sixteenth century was well on before
the second era of naval architecture was established. The *Sovereign
of the Seas*, built in 1637, was long considered the most powerful and
effective warship in the world. The forecastle was omitted and the
after tower was of slight height. She carried more than a hundred
guns in her three tiers, but they were of nine or ten different calibers,
a fact that proved a serious drawback in the excitement and confu-

sion of battle.   As a consequence the calibers were reduced until the
principal ones were only two in number.

It would be tedious to give a minute description of the numerous
parts and the method of working those old ships.   The nations
learned in the school of experience, until when the Revolution broke
out, many looked upon naval architecture as about as near perfection
as it ever would be.   One improvement made was in the reduction
of the number composing the crews.   It was long the practice to

U. S. MAN-OF-WAR "CHICAGO."

crowd the ships with all the men that promised to be effective in
battle.   Thus it often happened that some of them were really in one
another's way, and the discomfort always was great.   When the voyage was extended, the risk from these unsanitary conditions was
greater than from the guns of the enemy.   Many a time the entire
crew of a ship has been swept away by scurvy, small-pox, yellow
fever or other diseases.   Admiral Charles Stewart, active in the war
with Tripoli and with Great Britain in 1812, once showed me a hand-

some Toledo sword presented to him by the king of Spain, for rescuing a Spanish ship drifting in mid ocean, because every man on board was dead or helpless from yellow fever.

One of the finest exploits of that grand old sailor, Captain David Porter, was that in a cruise of nearly a year and a half in the Pacific in his matchless *Essex*, there was not a death from sickness among his crew of more than three hundred men.

Life on board a man-of-war in the olden days was in striking contrast to what it is in these times. Flogging was common, and officers of brutal temper were merciless in their punishments. One of the most cruel methods of securing seamen was by impressment or by the "press gang" as it was called. A party of sailors were sent ashore and seized the first likely recruit upon whom their eyes fell, forcibly carried him on board their vessel, and compelled him to serve as one of the crew. He might be denied the chance to bid his family good-bye, and they would not see or hear from him for weary months or years. Then perhaps the first news was that he had been slain in battle. The Americans were the first to change this dreadful custom, and in time England followed their example.

In studying the history of our country, we come upon events here and there in which we can feel little or no pride. The fighting of our land forces in the War of 1812 in more than one instance was discreditable, but the exploits of the infant navy were marvelous. Our victories on the sea filled England with amazement and disgust. They could not understand it, for they had finer frigates, that were well manned, and no one can question the courage of the British tar and marine. Why, then, were we so uniformly successful against those veterans of the sea, who were Anglo-Saxons like ourselves?

CAUSE OF THE SUPERIORITY OF AMERICAN NAVAL GUNNERY OVER THAT OF ENGLAND.

E. S. MacClay, in his "History of the Navy," gives as the most potent cause of England's defeats the over-confidence of the British sailors. It grew to be little more than amusement for them to sweep the cowardly Spanish and French from their path, and the saying became common that when France launched a new battleship she was simply adding one to the British navy. England was mistress of the seas, and her reign was so resistless that she imbibed a contempt for her enemies—a contempt that was fully justified until she was brought face to face with her cousins on this side of the Atlantic.

Contemplating our poverty, our few ships and scant material, it was quite natural that she should look upon us as the easiest kind of victims, but she soon had a bitter awakening. Then, too, there were no finer seamen in the world than those trained along our coasts and upon our vessels. They were proud of their calling, and, as has been stated, their natural ingenuity and native skill and the pride they felt in marksmanship made them the superior of any other people on the globe.

Since we have studied a battle of to-day, it will be instructive to glance at the infancy of the American navy, as it was when we first set out to become a nation, and to trace its growth to its present magnificent effectiveness.

You have learned elsewhere of the struggle of the American colonies for independence. The whole number of people in America at that time was less than 3,000,000, but it is only just to England to remember that her population was not much more than double that, and, as the war progressed, she became involved with France, Spain and Holland, so that, though she failed to conquer us, she maintained the reputation of the Anglo-Saxon for bravery and sturdy, persistent stubborn fighting.

FIRST STEPS IN FORMING AN AMERICAN NAVY.

As compared with the British navy, we had none worth naming. While the war broke out early in the year 1775, it was not until autumn that steps were taken toward making a fight on the ocean. One advantage of this state of affairs was with the Americans, for when they should fit out a few cruisers, they would never have to sail far before finding some of the ships of the enemy, while the latter of necessity would have to hunt far and wide to discover the few cruisers flying the Stars and Stripes.

In October, 1775, Congress authorized a committee to fit out two swift sailing vessels, properly armed and provided with crews, who were to make quest for some of the British transports carrying arms and ammunition, of which the Americans stood in sorer need than the British for whom they were intended.

This was the first official step toward the formation of an American navy, and the building of the two ships may be accepted as marking its birth. Most of the naval achievements, however, of the Revolution were accomplished by privateers, and by 1781, all thirteen of the Federal vessels had been either captured or destroyed.

GRADUAL GROWTH OF THE NAVY.

A new navy was created by Congress in 1797 and 1798, when war with France broke out on the ocean. The *Constitution, United States* and *Constellation* were built, and the purchase of other vessels to the number of twenty-four was authorized, but at the outbreak of the War of 1812, we had only twenty

LATEST MODEL OF GATLING FIELD GUN.

vessels as against England's 830. The brilliant victories won by our few cruisers resulted in securing larger Congressional appropriations and a more effective navy was built. It was ordered in 1819, that ships-of-the-line should be named after the States, frigates after American rivers, and sloops-of-war after the chief cities and towns.

When the Civil War broke out, we had but forty-two vessels in commission, and Secretary Toucey, an intense Secessionist, had scattered these all over the globe. With that amazing energy peculiar to Americans, an immense and powerful navy was constructed and played an effective part in the suppression of the rebellion.

7 D.D.

An immense stride forward was taken when steam was introduced into the navy. This was done by the United States in 1813-14, when the *Fulton* was built under the direction of Robert Fulton, who a few years before placed the first successful steamboat on the Hudson. The *Fulton* was a curious craft, with her wheel in the centre, and her battery of twenty 32-pounders, supplemented by a submarine gun intended to fire a hundred-pound shot. The war ending soon after her completion, she was placed in the Brooklyn Navy Yard as a receiving ship, but blew up in 1829, killing a large number of men.

There was strong opposition at first to the introduction of steam in the navy, James K. Paulding, Secretary of the Navy 1838-1841, being a particularly strong opponent. His opposition, however, could not prevent the building in 1841 of the two twin side-wheel steamers *Mississippi* and *Missouri*, to which two others were added six years later.

THE FIRST DIRECT-ACTING PROPELLER ENGINE.

It was clear that it would be a vast advantage to have the machinery and propelling power below the water line, where they were beyond reach of the enemy's shot. The plan was proposed in France, as early as 1823, but curiously enough, the suggestion was not acted upon for a number of years, nor was it favorably regarded for a considerable time in England. The first direct-acting propeller engine ever built, according to MacClay, was the *Robert Field Stockton*, which crossed the Atlantic in 1839, and was used as a tugboat. Commodore Stockton was one of the most prominent officers of the navy, who made a fine record in the War of 1812, and added to it in our war with Mexico. He was a persistent advocate of the new plan, and it was due to his efforts that the first propeller in the United States navy was built and launched in 1844. The Commodore's home was at Princeton and the new vessel was named in honor of that town.

Thus the steam propeller was fairly introduced, and, with the enlarged and improved vessels, our country maintained her place abreast of all other nations, that were on the alert for new and practical ideas respecting warships.

Matters remained thus until the War for the Union had been in progress not quite a year, when suddenly a single engagement brought a complete revolution in naval warfare, and introduced the last grand era in the method of fighting on the water. This was the battle between the *Monitor* and *Merrimac* in Hampton Roads, March 8 and 9, 1862. Both of these vessels, although crudely built, and sluggish and awkward of movement, were genuine ironclads, whose massive hides of metal shed the enormous solid shot and shell, as if they were toy wads fired from pop guns. The days of wooden navies ended and that of ironclads began. Henceforward, all nations clothed their warships in coats of mail, as the warriors of old arrayed themselves against the sword and spear of their assailants.

For years the strife has been between making this armor invulnerable and providing cannon powerful enough to drive their tremendous missiles through it. When it would seem that the

EIGHT-INCH GUN AND CARRIAGE OF THE "BALTIMORE."
(Built at the Washington Navy-Yard, of American Steel.)

Harveyized metal of great thickness would shed any projectile hurled with all possible power against it, the inventive genius of our countrymen would provide the gun to do the trick.

And so invention and improvement have gone on, until it would appear that the nearest point to perfection has been reached; but we know better than to make such a mistake. The wonderful advancements in science render it certain that the near future will witness more marvelous discoveries and achievements than the wildest imagination ever dreamed of. These of necessity will affect national armaments, which some day may reach the point of resistless destructive powers, when nations will shrink from going to war because it will mean mutual annihilation. Thus, even if the Czar of Russia fails to bring all peoples to the point of universal arbitration and peace, the end for which he prays may be attained through the very horrors of war itself.

The battle of Manila was fought between modern warships. Commodore Dewey commanded the best vessels his country could give him, though we had a few battleships which in the point of effectiveness outranked those handled by him.

AN IMPORTANT LESSON TAUGHT BY THE WAR.

It was a great step from the wooden frigates of the Revolution to the magnificent warships of to-day, and perhaps the new century will witness still greater strides forward. As descriptive of the immense, complicated, terrible naval war engine of to-day, with all its appliances of steam, electricity, prodigious ordnance and everything that the ingenuity of man can press into service, note may be taken of the six cruisers whose building was decided upon by the Naval Construction Board in the summer of 1899. Brief as was our war with Spain, it brought its lessons that neither nation can overlook or forget. The most important of these was the fatal risk of using combustible wood in warships, where it is easily reached and ignited by the shells of the enemy. It will be remembered that the battles of Manila and Santiago were hardly under way when many of the Spanish ships broke into flames and this fact hastened the destruction of the vessels. The decision, therefore, is that the minimum amount of wood should be used and that it must first be subjected to chemical process or paint that makes it incombustible.

THE SIX NEW CRUISERS ORDERED IN 1899.

The six fine cruisers referred to are the *Denver*, the *Des Moines*, the *Chattanooga*, the *Galveston*, the *Tacoma* and the *Cleveland*, which were authorized by Congress March 3, 1899. The designs contemplate greatly improved vessels of the *Raleigh* type, heavier in armament and protection, with greater radius of action at a sacrifice of two knots in speed, but with added comfort for the men and almost complete independence of drydocks. Their displacement is almost the same as that of the *Atlanta* class, but they are to have the great advantages over those pioneers of the new navy of higher freeboard and twin screws. Compared with them, they show the marked evolution in warship designing which has taken place in fifteen years, and with the increased use of electricity for auxiliaries, the sheathing of the submerged hull, the substitution .of high-pressure water-tube boilers, and the absence of combustible materials of construction, the new cruisers constitute a distinctly new type in the American Navy, and one that is not surpassed in any ship so far designed abroad. Utility for offensive purposes is the characteristic of the *Denver* class, that object having been kept sharply in view in the design as superior to all other desirable qualifications. The luxurious officers' quarters of early American naval vessels which have astonished foreign officers will be conspicuous by their absence, the naval authorities being satisfied that for a long time in the future American warships will be practically cleared for action at all times and prepared for any emergency.

One of the most remarkable features of the new design is the large displacement adopted, Congress having allowed only for vessels of the *Detroit* class. The Board has added fully 900 tons, and thereby taken the vessels out of the category of gunboats and made them full-fledged seagoing fighting ships.

The act of March 3, 1899, authorized " six protected cruisers of about 2,500 tons trial displacement, to be sheathed and coppered, and to have the highest speed compatible with good cruising quali- ties, great radius of action, and to carry the most powerful ordnance suited to vessels of their class, and to cost, exclusive of armament, not exceeding $1,141,800 each." It was further stipulated that the contracts should be awarded " to the lowest, best, responsible bidder, having in view the best results and most expeditious delivery;" and that not more than two should be built in one yard.

DIMENSIONS AND BATTERY.

The general dimensions of the new ships are as follows :

Full load displacement, tons 3,400
Length, feet 292
Breadth, feet 43
Greatest draught, loaded, feet and inches 16.6
Coal bunker capacity, tons 700
Coal on trial, tons 470
Trial draught, feet and inches 15.6

Trial displacement, tons 3,100
Speed, knots 16½
Horse power 4,500

Battery—Ten 5-inch rifles, eight 6-pounder rifles, two 1-pounder rifles, four machine guns and one field gun.

The remarkable precautions against fire are shown in the require ments that the hull shall be of steel, sheathed and coppered and sub divided into close water-tight compartments. The vessels will be schooner-rigged, and will each carry ten boats, stored away from injury by blasts of the guns. A belt of American corn-pith cellulose will extend the entire length at the water line. No woodwork is to be incorporated in the hull and fittings except such as is absolutely indispensable, and then it must be fireproofed by an approved process. To obviate all possible danger from bunker fires due to spontaneous combustion or other causes, the magazines are to be surrounded in all directions with four inches of air space, which will be well ventilated. Special attention is paid to making all the coal bunkers large for rapidity of coaling and ease of access. All fire mains are to be kept below the water line, and all risers provided with shut-off appliances. Bathrooms for officers, crew and sick will be served with salt as well as fresh water, and 3,000 gallons of fresh water for cooking and drinking will be carried in tanks. There will be storerooms with capacity for four months' provisions and a year's clothing. The blowers for ventilation and forced draught, the ammunition hoists, winches and anchor hoists will be operated by electricity, the only auxiliary steam engines being for the ice machines, steering gear dynamos, distilling plant and machine shop.

The main engines will be of the twin vertical triple-expansion type in separate water-tight compartments, developing 4,500 horsepower. They will get steam from six water-tube boilers aggregating 4,700 horse-power and installed in two air-tight compartments. The weight of the machinery is limited to 405 tons, twenty-two tons of engines will be carried, and there will be forty tons of reserve feed water. The cruisers will have two smokestacks, with their tops seventy feet above the grate. Steam heat will be fitted throughout the hull. For electric light and auxiliaries there will be four generating units weighing not over thirty-five tons.

The constructors are called upon to supply everything except the ordnance and ordnance outfit, the masts and spars, boats and their equipment, furniture, except fixed berths, rigging, anchor and chains, sails, ropes, table linen, hammocks, mess utensils, navigating instruments, lamps, flags, signal outfits and stores of all kinds except electrical stores and tools. The Government always provides these articles.

The battery of these ships shows what faith the experts have in the 5 inch calibre of fifty calibres length, burning smokeless powder. Two of these guns will be mounted on the upper deck, one forward, and the other aft having ranges in all directions. The others will be distributed four on each side on the deck below. The entire battery, with the six and two pounders and machine guns, will weigh ninety-eight tons, and the magazines will be supplied with 153 tons of ammunition, a larger quantity in proportion to the size of the ship than has ever been provided heretofore. In addition there will be three tons of small arms, including 140 rifles and 80 revolvers.

VIEWS OF THE FOREMOST ENGLISH NAVAL EXPERT

· The foremost authority on naval subjects in Europe is Vice-Admiral P. H. Colomb, of the British navy, and his views upon the lessons taught by our war with Spain are interesting and valuable. At a meeting of the United Service Institution, March 8, 1899, and presided over by Rear-Admiral A. K. Wilson, Admiral Colomb read an exhaustive paper upon the various features of the recent war upon the sea. Some of his references to the battle of Manila are given :

"On the American strategy in the East, there is nothing to be said. Dewey's objective was the Spanish fleet. He struck at it in the usual way, destroyed it, obtained command of the sea, and did what he liked afterward—all according to strategical routine.

"The American position in the matter of tactics began by being exceedingly anomalous. The United States were fully expecting, and spending a good deal of money and care in defending themselves from a particular kind of attack which they themselves never dreamed of making. The Americans expected all their coast towns to be blown about their ears, but they never took action about blowing Spanish towns about Spanish ears, except very specially and very half-heartedly, after their army was landed at Santiago. But the reporter, knowing what was expected of him by the ignorant, took care to leave no Cuban town unbombarded. So that I suppose—indeed, some remarkable utterances from the other side of the Atlantic make it certain—that popular belief in the bombardment of towns by ships has been confirmed by the war, though the war has only repeated the lesson of all former wars, namely, that this is not a thing to be expected and that it need not be guarded against.

"Five days after the declaration of war, Mr. Secretary Long telegraphed to Admiral Sampson words which briefly summed up and

ONE OF THE "MIANTONOMAH'S" FOUR TEN-INCH BREECH-LOADING RIFLES.

adopted the long-established practice of war in this respect: 'While the department does not wish a bombardment of forts protected by heavy cannon, it is within your discretion to destroy light batteries which may protect vessels you desire to attack, if you can do so without exposure to heavy guns.' Towns, we observe, are not in anybody's thoughts who is in authority. They only dwell in the imagination of the uninformed multitude. And then fortifications. Sampson had actually some idea that Havana could be carried by a close attack in the batteries, and afterward held by the navy alone. The wiser coun-

sels of authority prevailed against an attempt that all history pronounced a mistake. But it is a little remarkable that Mr. Long should
have mentioned the possibility of silencing batteries in order to get
at the ships they defended, because in all ages this has been a legitimate object, and because history has shown that batteries erected
with the object of supporting and defending ships very often fulfil
their object.

"A very significant commentary on the usefulness of batteries
in protecting towns was offered by Commodore Dewey at Manila.
There were found batteries protecting the town, and these batteries
began to exercise their protecting power by firing on Dewey's ships.
Dewey replied by message, not by gun. If the batteries did not
cease firing he would open fire upon the town ; and the batteries were
thenceforth silent. Really, the extreme of paradox was reached.

"The failure of the Cavite batteries and the general failure of
the Spanish batteries to contend against the American guns teaches
a very important lesson. There is no commoner belief—sometimes
expressed in so many words—than to say that once a fortification,
always a fortification ; that if you built and armed a ship, she would
become obsolete, but if you laid out the same money on a fort or
battery that had to be ready to contend with ships, that would remain,
and not become obsolete. But if there is one lesson more clear than
another to be drawn from this war, it is that if you intend to put
your strength into defensive batteries, those things grow obsolete
quite as fast as ships do. Batteries, such as those required at Cavite,
to do their appointed work, cannot be built and armed and left.
They are only ships on land."

Admiral Colomb expresses surprise that no legitimate use of
torpedo boats was made on either side in the war, and he concludes
that the status of the torpedo boat is just what it was before the war.
The Admiral adds :

"There were two sea fights in the war—the attack on the
Spanish ships at Manila by Commodore Dewey, and that resulting
from the attempt of Cervera to escape from Santiago with his squadron. In each of these cases all the Spanish ships were destroyed,
while the American ships hardly suffered at all. The sudden destruction and the character of the destruction would have been news

to us, if they had not been forshadowed by the results of the battle of Yalu. Admiral Sampson brought forward the outbreaks of fire in Cervera's ships as one of the lessons of the war. Without doubt this was so, but the battle of Yalu had already made the lesson confirmatory, and not new. This terrible destruction had no parallel in the days before steam and shells, though we were not unaccustomed to see ships that were mere wrecks and shambles surrender to conquerors that had not lost a mast or a man. *Sinope* had later taught what could be done in destruction with shell guns.

"But, speaking for myself, I am bound to say that the three battles of Yalu, Manila and Santiago have shaken my faith in the historical method more than any occurrences of modern times. I had certainly imagined that surrender would precede destruction, and I had

UNITED STATES 12-INCH BREECH-LOADING MORTAR, OR HOWITZER.

even gone so far as to suppose that it would be killed and wounded that would determine surrender, as it certainly did in old days ; and yet here are three battles where there has been no real surrender, and, otherwise, all destruction. One of the ablest of my naval friends comforts me by remarking that the nearness of the shore has in each of these cases had to do with the results, and that in a sea fight out of sight of land the old rule might remain intact. There may be something in the remark, though some of the Chinese' ships when beaten went down in deep water without making a sign.

And then I am afraid that we must allow that we have descended from the courtesies to the barbarities of war. The old rule certainly was that when the result became assured, when prolonging the dispute could be but a waste of life, the commander bowed to fate and surrendered the fruits of victory to the conqueror. We seem to say now that the fruits of victory must be denied to the conqueror at all hazards and that the spirit of the savage under the guise of gallantry is to dominate. If this is a lesson of the war, I fear it is a very sad one. Perhaps it is my feeling that turns me from this view and makes me think of other points.

"Regarding the pure tactical questions involved, it becomes plain that Dewey quietly took full advantage of the superiority of his guns and his gunnery, and placed himself in so distant a position that neither ships nor batteries could make an adequate reply to his fire. The thing was terribly businesslike on the American side, with a pathetic parade of quixotic gallantry on the other.

"In the case of Cervera, it seemed to me, and I think to most of those with whom I have discussed the matter, that his only chance was to have come out of port in close order in line ahead, and to have made at his utmost speed for the centre of the American ships. Sampson was prepared with two orders of battle, single column and double column, in line ahead. Cervera's chance was that the suddenness of his approach and the compactness of his formation might have found the American fleet not fully formed, so that the fear of hitting friends might disturb the aim of the American gunners and given Cervera a loophole. But the entire failure of Spanish speed must have made almost any plan, however well arranged, futile. In the result, as the Spanish ships came out one by one, and turned at once to starboard to run along shore, they showed no tactical aim, and left it to the Americans to follow them up as in a general chase and perfectly free to use their guns to the best possible effect.

"I am sure, however, that we must all feel that the discussion of material pros and cons is much complicated by a profound conviction of the dominating value of the man behind the gun. The overwhelming successes of the American Navy are only in part accounted for by superority of material. The entire failure of the Spanish guns, whether fired from ports or ships, to produce an adequate effect on the Americans could only have been due to bad shooting, and this was not wholly the fault of the weapons. The proof is conclusive that, if the gunnery is equal on each side, the greater number or the better quality will win, and that the policy we are pursuing is the only true one. But if the gunnery is equal, the inferior guns should do proportionate work, which the Spanish guns failed to do.

"A final word must be said on the utter change that has come over the organization and conduct of naval war. The change was marked in our conduct of the Egyptian difficulties. What was done, whether in principle or detail, was then done at and by the Admiralty. The Admirals abroad were pieces played by the Admiralty, and did not—as in old days—play themselves. However far we went in the Egyptian operations, the American Government in the Spanish war left us far behind. Everything was done from Washington, whether it was small, or whether it was great. It could not have been otherwise. All the intelligence went to Washington, and the men on the spot never had the information regarding what was round them that the Secretary of the Navy possessed. Hence, the ships were moved hither and thither from the office in Washington, and they had to gather what it all meant later on.

"It is a momentous change specially belonging to naval war; and to recognize the change is perhaps a chief lesson of the late contest."

FORCEFUL WORDS FROM ADMIRAL WILSON.

Among the declarations of Admiral Colomb was one that at the outbreak of the war, our Government should have sent a strong fleet across the Atlantic to blockade Spanish ships in Spanish ports. Referring to this plan of campaign, Admiral Wilson said:

"Think what the Americans would have had to do to send their ships across to Spain to blockade ships that were doing no harm to them. Where were they to get coal? Where was their base? Were they to take troops with them? If they took troops, what were they to do against the whole forces of the Spanish with the whole force of the peninsula at their backs? If the Americans had gone to St. Vincent, Admiral Cervera would not have been there. Fool as he was, he would not have stopped there if he knew the Americans were coming, and he would have gone somewhere else. Even if they had locked him up there, a properly organized squadron of ships of his speed, we know from all experience, cannot be blockaded in port without an enormously stronger force of ships, and when a squadron is once at sea how are you to know where that squadron goes?

"The great lesson we do learn from this war is, first of all, what everybody knew before, the immense value of the riches and resources of the country. We see the rich American country, and we see a miserably poor bankrupt country like Spain. But greater than that I think are the energy and perseverance and the directness of the race. I have not the slightest doubt that if the Americans had been turned over to Cervera's ships, bad as they were, they would have made a very good fight for it, and it is the energy and enterprise of the race, of which we as Englishmen claim a common share, that I think constituted the greatest factor in the success of the Americans in the recent war."

CHAPTER X

Tributes to the Genius of Admiral Dewey

Eloquent Tributes to the Genius That Won the Battle of Manila.—Dewey Made Admiral.—A Poetical Tribute by One of His Sailors.—The Trying Task That Followed the Great Naval Victory.—Dewey the Diplomat and Statesman.—His Personal Appearance and Character.

The great victory of Dewey in Manila Bay was fully acknowledged everywhere, and by none more freely than our cousins, whose proud boast of "being mistress of the seas," holds as good to-day as centuries ago. It was natural that we should be somewhat extravagant in our language and demonstrations, for we are a nation of hero-worshipers, and it is fortunate for Admiral Dewey's comfort that he postponed his return home for a year and a half. Many a victor in his situation would have eagerly seized the chance to hear the sweet music of his countrymen's plaudits and to receive the honors waiting to be showered upon him. One of his most admirable traits, however, is his modesty and dislike of adulation and display. It was by his own request that he was allowed to remain in the Philippines, where his services, fortunately indeed for our country, were still at the command of our Government. Moreover, the Admiral hoped that by thus deferring his visit he would be in a certain sense "forgotten," and not be overwhelmed with attentions even before he set foot on the shore of his native land; and, in nourishing that hope, the Admiral committed the greatest blunder of his life.

THE TRIBUTE OF ADMIRAL BRAND.

To return to the opinions of the greatest naval experts in the world, Admiral Thomas Brand, of the British navy, said of Dewey's victory:

"It will go down in history as one of the most brilliant victories in the naval history of the world. The American commander not only showed remarkable courage in entering the harbor and tackling the enemy's ships in the midst of a harassing fire from the land fortifications, but he demonstrated the fact that his plans had been most perfectly laid, and he had carefully obtained full particulars of the harbor navigation before entering. Hitherto I had believed the United States warships to be of inferior quality, and I fully expected them to fail in some particulars when the crucial test came ; but I am bound to say that I have changed my opinion, and from the showing of the American fleet so far, I am inclined to think it as good as any of its size in the world. That it is efficiently manned and commanded seems certain."

THE VIEWS OF H. W. WILSON.

Another equally famous naval expert, author of *Ironclads in Action*, said :

" Further details of the battle of Manila show that it was a great and glorious victory for the American fleet, under the brilliant lead of Commodore Dewey. The Americans deserve every credit for the exploit. It was a feat not far below the bombardment of Mobile by Admiral Farragut that carried Commodore Dewey's ships across the Spanish mine field, under the very muzzles of the ponderous guns which we know have been recently mounted at Corregidor Island."

DECLARATION OF CAPTAIN MAHAN.

Captain Alfred T. Mahan, who has no superior as a naval strategist, declared that the victory will rank as the greatest naval battle on record. It demonstrated the great value of our guns, and fully proved the excellent judgment displayed by our naval constructors in putting into service the armored vessels which had fully shown their utility in action. "The result of this engagement," said he, "plainly indicates that a cool-headed commander, who gets into the fight first and proceeds to business, has the best of the battle from the start. Commodore Dewey was backed up by a well-trained and brave crew."

OPINION OF EX-SECRETARY HERBERT.

Hon. Hilary A. Herbert, formerly Secretary of the Navy said :

" I know of no battle ever fought either on land or sea in which so much was accomplished with so little loss as in the battle of Manila. Jackson at New Orleans inflicted a loss upon the British of over 2,600 killed and wounded and prisoners, and his loss was only eight killed and fourteen wounded. Dewey destroyed eleven ships. the whole Spanish Navy in the Pacific, captured and blew up two fortifications, inflicted a loss of at least 150 killed and 250 wounded, took control of the Bay of Manila, and has a great city at his mercy, which he only fails to take possession of because his men are so few that he could not spare enough even to fill its policeman's walks on a moonlight night, and yet he lost not a single man killed, had only six wounded, and not a single one of his ships was injured. We may search naval annals for some parallel exploit, but it is not to be found. The nearest approach is the massacre at Minn River, where a French squadron in fifteen minutes destroyed the Chinese fleet. But the Chinese ships were mostly old junks, and the Chinese made little or no attempt to fight.

"The merit of Dewey's great deed is only equalled by the modesty with which he tells the story. There is not in his dispatches as published a single catch word, not a phrase seems to be written to hand himself down to posterity. He was only reporting what the squadron did. The results will be far-reaching. Spain must give up the Philippines as lost to her, at least during this war. She has no navy to spare from the defense of her own coast to send to the Philippines, and if she had she could not send ships over eight thousand miles without a coaling station on the way, and no base of operations at the end of the cruise except such as she could reconquer from Dewey."

COMMENTS OF REAR-ADMIRAL SCHLEY.

The comments of Rear-Admiral Winfield S. Schley were not only generous but discriminating, although uttered within a few days after news was received of the battle :

"Admiral Dewey's victory at Manila must deservedly take place side by side with the greatest naval victories of the world's history. It has been urged that the results show such decided inferiority in resistance as compared with vigor of attack that there is a diminution of the glory, but that is untrue, for it must first be remembered that the greatness of Dewey's success lies in the calm courage and daring displayed in his decision to enter a strange harbor at dark under the guns of many forts and braving the perhaps hidden torpedo or mine.

"It strikes me that with several advantageous fortified positions the preponderance of advantage was certainly with the enemy, and that with the great daring displayed by Dewey, there must fall upon his shoulders the mantle of Perry and Farragut.

"From the accounts that have been received of the battle it is evident that, despite the great risk every officer and every man knew was being taken, there was not a faint heart in all that squadron, but an enthusiasm and *esprit de corps* that could not but win with such a leader. I would note, too, that superior education which brings intelligence, coupled with perfection in marksmanship, aided greatly in winning the day and will, I believe, contribute to future victories. Admiral Dewey and every man in his squadron deserves every recognition that a grateful people and a nation can bestow."

WARM WORDS FROM THEODORE ROOSEVELT.

It was to be expected that Theodore Roosevelt, who, as has been stated, was the direct agent in sending Dewey to the Philippines, should express himself in eloquent language:

"Admiral Dewey has won a victory greater than any since Trafalgar, with the exception of Farragut's. It is one of the great sea fights of all times, and every American is his debtor. The chief thing that it shows is the absolute necessity, even with new engines of war themselves, to have the men in the conning towers and the men behind the guns trained to the highest possible point. Though the American fleet was superior to the Spanish, yet the Spanish batteries and the danger of navigating the bay made the material odds against the Americans. Yet so cool and daring was Dewey, so skillful his captains and so well-trained his gunners, that the Spaniards were smashed to atoms, while our people were practically unscratched. In fact, the American fire was so overwhelming that it practically paralyzed the Spaniards."

DEWEY MADE A FULL ADMIRAL.

The foregoing are only a few from the multitudes of tributes paid to one of the greatest naval heroes of history. On February 13, 1899, Mr. Hale, chairman of the Naval Affairs Committee reported a bill creating an Admiral of the Navy. This grade was established by Act of Congress on July 25, 1866, and the honor was conferred on Farragut in that year. Upon his death in 1870, Vice-Admiral David D. Porter succeeded to the rank, and at his death in 1891, it became extinct, to be revived and bestowed upon George Dewey. The bill, favorably reported by Chairman Hale, was unanimously passed and Dewey thus became the third full Admiral, to remain on the active list until retired by his own request.

It has been complained that the Spanish-American War has failed as yet to call forth a genuine poem worthy of the theme. The attempts have been innumerable, and some of them reveal considerable merit, but of all that have come under our eye the best was written by one of Dewey's own sailors and was published in the Manila *Times* under the caption of

"DEWEY WERE HIS NAME."

"He come an' raised his flag aboard the ship,
        An' mentioned how that Dewey were his name.
He didn't have no great amount o' lip,
        But wot he said he meant it, jist the same.
He put us thro' maneuvers short and long,
        An' kep' us at sub caliber, betweens,
Until we come to anchor at Hong Kong,
        An' got our orders for the Philippines.

"Then this 'ere Dewey struck a pow'ful gait,
        An' mentioned how that somethin' had ter drop;
He kep' the colliers workin' soon an' late,
        An' every blessed Jackie on the hop;
An' w'en 'e got 'is bunkers chock a-block,
        W'y, then he up an' filled his magazines,
An' tol' 'em w'en they asked him wot's o'clock,
        'A little game o' Spanish Philippines!'

"An' w'en all's done, he up an' goes to sea,
        The other ships a-trailing' in his rear;
An' w'en he sights them islands on his lee,
        He signals out fer every ship to clear.
We done it with a ringin', rousin' cheer,
        Fer why, we'd kind o' learned to like his style,
The which were sich, he made it to appear,
        He knowed wot he were doin' all the while.

"He kep' us on an' off till close o' day,
    An' then he kind o' squared around his chin
An' wig wagged out, 'Their ships is in the bay;
    They won't come out, so I'm a-goin in!'
He knowed the odds agin him in the game,
    He knowed the bay were mined for Uncle Sam;
He likewise knowed that Dewey were his name,
    An' bein' sich, he didn't care a damn.

"So on we went, a-creepin' thro' the night,
    Not knowin' whereabout that we was at;
With every barker stripped in trim fer fight,
    An' every blessed Jackie standin' pat;
An' w'en the mornin' broke, w'y, there we lay,
    Lined up, each crew a-standin' to its gun,
Right in the middle o' Manila Bay—
    Old Glory gleamin' pretty in the sun.

"There weren't no time ter talk about it then,
    Fer Spain cut loose her iron in a shower,
An' powder monkeys turned to fightin' men,
    An' fightin' men to devils, in an hour.
'Twere just one awful crashin', tearin' roar,
    That seemed like it were bustin' o' yer brain,
Along with shrieks of Yankee shells, thet bore
    A message labeled: 'Don't forget the *Maine!*'

"Lor' bless us, but it were a proper sight,
    Them ships an' forts a-spittin' shot an' shell,
An' Dewey, lookin' pleasant an' perlite,
    Requestin' from the bridge to 'give 'em hell!'
An' w'en we gits the order to retire,
    An' waits until the smudge has blowed away,
Their ships as wasn't sinkin' was afire,
    An' Uncle Sam were master of the bay.

"I hear there's some as says it weren't no fight,
    As does their fightin' home an' in a chair;
'If we'd been there,' they says, 'we'd done it right.'
    Well, mebbe so—God knows that they was there;
It weren't our fault the Spaniards couldn't aim,
    Our ships was there to hit, as well they knows,
But, bless their hearts! we'd licked 'em jist the same
    If they'd had gunners picked from all that grows.

"So, mates, these words is all I've got to say,
    I says 'em, an' I means 'em, every one;
They ain't no other man alive to-day
    Would tried to do wot Dewey tried an' done;
We knows it, us as sweat behind his guns;
    They knows it, them as writes the scroll of fame,
    An' w'en they tells o' heroes to our sons,
    W'y, mates, they'll head the list with Dewey's name."

THE MOST TRYING TASK OF ALL.

Great as was the victory of Manila, it was in one sense, the least difficult of the tasks performed by Admiral Dewey in the Philippines, for it was succeeded by days, weeks and months when all the resources of an unusually resourceful nature were taxed to the last degree. The force under his command was too small to occupy Manila, although he could have captured it on whatever day he chose. The insurgents were hovering around the city like a horde of wolves, eager to rush in to plunder, loot and to murder the defenceless inhabitants. The most unflinching sterness was necessary to keep these savages off, but the Admiral notified them that although he had come to help them secure their independence from Spain, he would turn his guns upon them the moment they attacked the Spaniards.

Aguinaldo, crafty and treacherous, soon gave cause for distrust, and the rebellion which he speedily set on foot against the authority of the United States has proven more stubborn and has cost more lives than our short and crushing campaign against Spain.

DEWEY THE DIPLOMAT AND STATESMAN.

More troublesome and trying than all this was the continual need of tact, firmness, moderation, self-restraint and real diplomacy and statesmanship in dealing with the foreign fleets in the Manila waters. England and Japan were specially friendly, but others were not. Germany particularly was a continual irritation. Not once but several times was the conduct of Admiral Von Diedrichs so exasperating that had almost any other man than Dewey been in command of the American fleet, an out and out conflict would have taken place, with ultimate consequences that one shudders to contemplate.

During the months preceding and following the fall of Manila, in August, 1898, Admiral Dewey demonstrated that he was not only a superb fighter, unsurpassed by any other naval commander, but a born diplomat and statesman. He spent hours in studying the manifold matters, often of the most diverse nature, that continually demanded his attention; he walked the deck all night, his whole thoughts, energies, brain and heart absorbed in deciding the momentous question: "How shall I best serve my country?"

'HE MADE NO MISTAKE!"

And what more eloquent tribute can be paid to the genius of Admiral George Dewey than the statement that from the first of May, 1898, when he sailed into Manila Bay, until May 1899, when his health compelled him to start for home, *he made no mistake?* Of what military or naval leader or statesman can such an assertion be made? And what a proof of the many-sided character of the true and unquestioned hero of the Spanish-American war!

PERSONAL APPEARANCE AND CHARACTER.

No commander appreciates his men more than Admiral Dewey. Oscar King Davis, who was on the *Olympia*, throughout her memorable battle, and who saw Dewey in all his moods, refers to this well-known characteristic. Looking at the white clad jackies lounging about, sleeping, reading, smoking, playing cards or checkers, he said:

"Just look at those men! Aren't they a fine lot? See the condition they are in, in spite of all the work of the summer. They haven't been off the ship for more than three months, and you know what hard work they have had. See that big fellow leaning against the rail. Isn't he a magnificent specimen? Suppose some sudden emergency should arise, do you know how long it would take to have this ship ready for action? Less than four minutes.

"Naturally I am proud of the work of the squadron. I should not be fit to command it, if I were not proud of its work; but I am proudest of my men. They are splendid fellows. They have done their work well. The people haven't realized how good their navy was. I would rather have command of this squadron than hold any office any people could give me."

In summing up some of the Admiral's characteristics, Mr. Davis says his mental process is lightning-like. He thinks like a flash, and goes all around his subject in less time than many a man would take to study one side. Yet he does not jump to conclusions and there are times when he is very deliberate. He reasons to his determinations, and, whatever his personal preferences, or beliefs or feelings, he can dissociate them entirely from his work. His logic machine is absolutely sound and in the finest order.

"It was my fortune," said Mr. Davis, "to be on more or less intimate and cordial terms with Admiral Dewey during six months of his operations in Manila Bay. I saw him many times, under constantly differing circumstances. I saw him well and ill, pleased and displeased, good natured and angry, in action and in repose, when everything was moving to his satisfaction, and when the gravest complications threatened him; but under whatever cloud of anxieties or difficulties he might be, he was always the same: self-reliant, confident, the George Dewey so dear to millions of Americans—the real George Dewey, cherished in the hearts of his fellows, whatever image of him his flamboyant frescoers set up for public worship; a plain man, simple, strong, great."

Regarding the personal appearance of Admiral Dewey, Edward W. Harden, United States Commissioner to the Philippines says: "There was, until recently, only one photograph of Admiral Dewey taken in late years; at least, there was only one which the public saw. All of the newspaper cuts and magazine drawings, and all of the paintings, busts and statues which have been made, are from this one photograph. He is the only officer in either the army or navy who took prominent part in the late war of whom many pictures are not obtainable. He was evidently too busy to have a lot of pictures taken before the war broke out to be used when he became famous. The photograph from which all of his pictures are made is a fair representation of him as he appears in naval uniform, though it is by no means flattering. It is far from representing him as he appeared in Manila Bay, however. This picture shows him in the double-breasted blue coat of a naval officer, while in Manila he was never seen except in a white, undress uniform, and unless it was to make some formal call, it is doubtful if he has had his sword on since

the war began.   In the battle of May 1st, and again at the bombardment on August 13th, he wore a white, undress uniform and a small
brown bicycle or traveling cap.   In most of the fancy pictures that
have been printed of him, he is shown in the full uniform of an
admiral, with cap and sword, leaning over the bridge and looking
anxiously through a pair of binoculars. On both occasions, in
reality, he walked around as he would do under ordinary circumstances, and there was no theatrical posing for the benefit of photo-
graphers.   He is about five feet, seven inches in height.   He stands
as straight as a ramrod, and is always dignified without being austere."

CHAPTER XI

The Philippines—Past and Present

A Rapid Review of History, Place and People.—The Story of Discovery.—The First World Girdlers.—Another Expedition.—Naming the Islands.—Struggles for Supremacy.—English take Manila.—Uprisings of the Natives.—The Last Struggle for Liberty.—A Warlike People.—Manila and other Towns.—Industries, Climate, Etc.—Admiral Dewey begins a New Era.

THE most important, and by far the most interesting, as well as the least known of America's new possessions, gained by her war with Spain, are the Philippine Islands. Comparatively few Americans have ever set foot upon that far-away and semi-civilized land, the possession of which enables America to say with England, "The sun never sets upon our flag."

The Philippines lie almost exactly on the other side of the globe from us. Approximately speaking, our noonday is their midnight; our sunset is their sunrise. There are some 1,800 of these islands, 400 of which are inhabited or capable of supporting a population; they cover about 125,000 square miles; they lie in the tropical seas, generally speaking, from five to eighteen degrees north latitude; and are bounded by the China Sea on the west and the Pacific Ocean or the east; they are about 7,000 miles southwest from San Francisco, a little over 600 miles southeast from Hong Kong, China, and about 1,000 miles almost due north from Australia; they contain between 8,000,000 and 10,000,000 inhabitants, about one-third of whom had prior to Dewey's victory, May 1, 18,8, acknowledged Spanish sovereignty to the extent of paying regular tribute to the Spanish crown; the remainder are bound together in tribes under independent native princes or Mohammedan rulers. Perhaps 2,500,000 all told have become nominal Catholics in religion. The rest are Mohammedans and idolaters. There are no Protestant churches in the islands.

THE STORY OF DISCOVERY.

It was twenty-nine years after Columbus discovered America that Magellan saw the Philippines, the largest archipelago in the world, in 1521. The voyage of Magellan was much longer and scarcely less heroic than that of the discoverer of America. Having been provided with a fleet by the Spanish king with which to search for spice islands, but secretly determined to sail round the world, he set out with five vessels on August 10, 1519, crossed the Atlantic to America, and skirted the eastern coast southward in the hope of finding some western passage into the Pacific, which, a few years previous had been discovered by Balboa. It was a year and two months to a day from the time he left Spain until he reached the southern point of the mainland of South America and passed through the straight which has since borne his name. On the way, one of his vessels deserted ; another was wrecked in a storm. When he passed through the Straight of Magellan he had remaining but three of his original five ships, and they were the first European vessels that ever breasted the waves of the mighty western ocean. Once upon the unknown but placid sea—which he named the Pacific—the bold navigator steered straight to the northwest. Five months later, about March 1st, he discovered the Ladrone Islands—which name Magellan gave to the group on account of the thieving propensities of the natives —the word *Ladrone* meaning robber.

After a short stay at the islands, he steered southwest, landing on the north coast of Mindanao, the second largest island of the Philippines. The natives were friendly and offered to pilot Magellan to the Island of Cebu, which lay to the north, and which they reported to be very rich. After taking possession of Mindanao in the name of his king, the discoverer proceeded to Cebu, where he gave such descriptions of the glory and power of Spain that he easily formed a treaty with the king of the island, who swore allegiance to his new-found master and had himself and chief advisers baptized in the Catholic faith. Magellan then joined the king in his war against some of the neighboring powers, and on April 26, 1521, was killed in a skirmish. The spot where he fell is now marked by a monument.

FIRST CIRCUMNAVIGATION OF THE GLOBE.

Trouble soon arose between Magellan's sailors and their new-found allies. The Spaniards were invited to a banquet, and twenty-seven of them were treacherously slain. The remainder, fearing for

their lives, escaped in their ships and sailed for home. It was soon
discovered that they had too few men to manage the three vessels,
and one of them was destroyed. The other two proceeded on their
voyage and discovered the spice island of Tidor, where they loaded
with spices ; but a few days later one of the vessels sprang a leak and
went down with her freight and crew. The other, after many hardships, reached Spain, thus completing the first circumnavigation of
the globe.

SECOND EXPEDITION TO THE PHILIPPINES.

In 1555, Philip II. came to the Spanish throne and determined
to send another expedition to the East Indies. His religious zeal
inspired him to conquer and christianize the islands. To shorten the
long and dangerous voyage, he decided to prepare and start with five
ships from the coast of Mexico. Miguel Lopez de Legaspi led the
expedition, consisting of four hundred soldiers and sailors and six
Augustine monks. In due time the expedition landed at Cebu. The
formidable appearance of the ships awed the natives, and on April
27, 1565—forty years after Magellan's remnant had fled from the
island—Legaspi landed and took possession. In honor of the Spanish
king the archipelago was given the name of the Philippine Islands.

In 1570 Legaspi sent his nephew, Salcedo, to subdue the island
of Luzon, the northernmost and the largest of the Philippine group.
He landed near the present site of Manila. The trustful natives
readily agreed to accept the Spanish king as their master, and to pay
tribute. Such slight tribal resistances as were offered were quickly
subdued. The next year Legaspi went to Manila to visit his relat-
ive ; and, seeing the importance of the situation and its fine harbor,
declared that city the capital of the whole archipelago, and the king
of Spain the sovereign of all the islands. Accordingly, he moved
his headquarters to that point, built houses and fortifications, and
within a year had the city well organized, when he died, leaving
Salcedo as his successor in command. It is remarkable how much
these two men accomplished with so small a force ; but they did not
so much by arms as by cajoling and deceiving the simple natives.
Furthermore, they allowed the conquered people to be governed by
their own chiefs in their own way, so long as they paid a liberal
tribute to the Spanish crown.

The history of the Philippines has been monotonous from their discovery until the present, a monotony broken at times by periods of adventures in which Manila has generally been the central scene.

STRUGGLES FOR SUPREMACY.

About 1580, Limahong a Chinese pirate, took the city with an armed fleet of sixty-two vessels, bearing 4,000 men and 1,500 women The met with stubborn resistance, but succeeded in scaling the wall; and entering the city. The Spanish forces were driven into a fort which the Chinese stormed. A bloody hand-to-hand conflict fol- lowed, and the Chinese were finally repulsed.

Early in the seventeenth century the Dutch attempted to obtain possession of the Philippines. They captured scores of Spanish merchantmen and treasure ships. Many naval engagements followed, the details of which read like the thrilling records of buccaneers and pirates, rather than the wars between two civil powers. Finally, after half a century of warfare, the Dutch were decisively beaten, and abandoned their efforts to capture the Spanish islands, much to the disadvantage of the Filipinos, for the islands of Java, Sumatra and other Dutch possessions to the south of the Philippines have been remarkably prosperous under the mild rule of the Netherlands.

MANILA TAKEN BY THE ENGLISH.

In 1662, the Chinese planned a revolution against the Spanish authorities. The governor heard of it, and a general massacre of the Mongolians followed. It was even planned to destroy every Chinaman on the islands, and they were in a fair way to do it, when, at length, the Spaniards bethought themselves that by so doing they would practically depopulate the islands of tradesmen and mechanics Accordingly, they offered pardon to those who would surrender and swear allegiance. In the year 1762, England sent a fleet under Admiral Cornish, with General Draper commanding the troops, against Manila. After a desperate battle the city fell, and the terms of surrender incorporated provisions for free trade, freedom of speech, and, best of all, freedom in religion to the inhabitants of the islands, and required Spain to pay England about $4,000,000 indemnity. By the Peace of Paris, in 1763, however, the war between England and

Spain was terminated, and one of the conditions was that Spain should retain the sovereignty of the Philippines. The English troops were withdrawn, and the unfortunate islands were again placed (as Cuba was by the same treaty) under the domination of their tyrannical mistress, and remained under Spanish rule from that time until the Americans freed them in 1898.

UPRISING OF THE NATIVES.

In nearly all the uprisings of the natives, the tyranny of the Church, as conducted by the friars and priests, was the cause. Such was the case in 1622, in 1649 and in 1660. The occasion of the revolt of 1744 is a fair example of the provocations leading to all. A Jesuit priest ordered all his parishioners arrested as criminals when they failed to attend mass. One of the unfortunates died, and the priests denied him rights of burial, ordering that his body be thrown upon the ground and left to rot in the sun before his dwelling. The brother of the man in his exasperation organized a mob, captured the priest, killed him, and exposed his body for four days. Thus was formed the nucleus of a rebel army. The insurgents in their mountain fastnesses gained their independence and maintained it for thirty-five years, until they secured from Spain a promise of the expulsion of the Jesuit priests from the colony.

Other revolutions followed in 1823, 1827 and 1844, but all were suppressed. In 1842, the most formidable outbreak up to that time occurred at Cavite. Hatred of the Spanish friars was the cause of this uprising also. Spain had promised in the Council of Trent to prohibit friars from holding parishes. The promises were never carried out, and the friars grew continually richer and more powerful and oppressive. Had the plan of the insurgents not been balked by a mistaken signal, no doubt they would have destroyed the Spanish garrison at Manila, but a misunderstanding caused their defeat. The friars insisted that the captured leaders should be executed, and it was done.

THE LATEST STRUGGLE FOR LIBERTY.

In 1896, the insurrection broke out again. Its causes were the old oppressions : unbearable taxes, and imprisonment or banishment, with the complete confiscation of property of those who could not pay ; no justice except for those who could buy it ; extortion by the friars ; marriage ceremony so costly that a poor man could not pay the fee ; homes and families broken up and ruined ; burial refused to the dead, unless a large sum was paid in advance ; no provision and no chance for education. Such were some of the causes that again goaded the natives to revolution and nerved them with courage to achieve victory after victory over their enemies until they were promised most of the reforms which they demanded. Then they laid down their arms, and, as usual, the Governor-General failed to carry out a single pledge.

Such was the condition, and another revolt, more formidable than any of the past, was forming, when Commodore Dewey with his American fleet entered Manila Bay, May 1, 1898, and by a victory unparalleled in naval warfare, sunk the Spanish ships, silenced the forts, and dethroned the power of Spain forever in a land which her tyranny had blighted for more than three hundred years.

THE PEOPLE—THEIR MANNERS AND CUSTOMS.

It is impossible within the scope of this article to give details concerning all the inhabitants of this far-away archipelago. Professor Worcester, of the University of Michigan, tells us that the population comprises more than eighty distinct tribes, with individual peculiarities. They are scattered over hundreds of islands, and one who really wants to know these peoples must leave cities and towns far behind, and, at the risk of his life, through pathless forests, amid volcanic mountains, at the mercy of savages, penetrate to the innermost wilds. Notwithstanding the fact that for hundreds of years bold men, led by the love of science or by the spirit of adventure, have continued to penetrate these dark regions, there are many sections where the foot of civilized man has never trod ; or, if so, he came not back to tell of the lands and peoples which his eyes beheld.

DIFFICULTIES OF EXPLORING THE COUNTRY.

There have been great obstacles in the way of a thorough exploration of these islands. Spain persistently opposed the representatives of any other nation entering the country. She suspected every man, with a gun, of designing to raise an insurrection or make mischief among the natives. The account of red tape necessary to secure guns and ammunition for a little party of four or five explorers admitted through the customs at Manila is one of the most significant, as well as one of the most humorous, passages in Professor Worcester's story of his several years' sojourn while exploring the archipelago.

In the second place, the savage tribes in the interior had no respect for Spain's authority, and will have none for ours for years to come. Two-thirds of them paid no tribute, and many of them never heard of Spain, or, if so, only remembered that a long time ago white men came and cruelly persecuted the natives along the shore. These wild tribes think themselves still the owners of the land. Some of them go naked and practice cannibalism and other horrible savage customs. Any explorer's life is in danger among them; consequently most tourists to the Philippines see Manila and make short excursions around that city. The more ambitious run down to the cities of Iloilo and Cebu, making short excursions into the country from those points, and then return, thinking they have seen the Philippines. Nothing could be further from the truth. Such travelers no more see the Philippine Islands than Columbus explored America.

Even near the coast there are savages who are almost as ignorant as their brethren in the interior. Mr. Stevens tells us that only "thirty miles from Manila is a race of dwarfs that go without clothes, wear knee-bracelets of horsehair, and respect nothing but the jungle in which they live." The principal native peoples are of Malayan origin. Of these, to the north of Manila are the Igorrotes, to the south of Manila are the semi-civilized Visayas, and below them in Mindanao and the Sulu Archipelago are the fierce Moros, who originally came from the island of Borneo, settling in the Philippines a short time before the Spanish discovery. They are Mohammedans in religion, and as fanatical and as fearless fighters as the Turks themselves. For three hundred years the Spaniards have been fighting these savages, and while they have overcome them in nearly all the coast towns, they have expended, it is said, upward of $100,-000,000 and sacrificed more than one hundred thousand lives in doing so.

The fierce Moro warriors keep the Spanish settlers along their coasts in a constant state of alarm, and the visitor to the towns feels as if he were at an Indian outpost in early American history, because of the constant state of apprehension that prevails. Fortunately, however, the Moros along the coast have learned to distinguish between the Spaniard and the Englishman or American, and through them the generosity of the *Englese*, as they call all Anglo-Saxons, ha· spread to their brethren in the interior. Therefore, American and English explorers have been enabled to go into sections where the Spanish friars and monks, who have been practically the only Spanish explorers, would meet with certain death. The Mohammedan fanaticism of the Moros, and that of the Catholic friars and Jesuits, absolutely refuse compromise.

The Negritos (little Negroes) and the Mangyans are the principal representatives of the aboriginal inhabitants before the Malayan tribes came. There are supposed to be, collectively, almost 1,000,000 of them, and they are almost as destitute of clothing and as uncivilized as the savages whom Columbus found in America, and far more degenerate and loathsome in habits.

THE CITY OF MANILA.

The Island of Luzon, on which the city of Manila stands, is about as large as the State of New York, its area being variously estimated at from 43,000 to 47,000 square miles. It is the largest island in the Philippine group, comprising perhaps one-third of the area of the entire archipelago. Its inhabitants are the most civilized, and its territory the most thoroughly explored. The city of Manila is the metropolis of the Philippines. The population of the city proper and its environs is considered to be some 300,000 souls, of whom 200,000 are natives, 40,000 full-blooded Chinese, 50,000 Chinese half-castes, 5,000 Spanish, mostly soldiers, 4,000 Spanish half-castes and 300 white foreigners other than Spaniards. Mr. Joseph Earle Stevens, already referred to, who represented the only American firm in the city of Manila, under Spanish rule (which finally had to turn its business over to the English and leave the island a few years since), informs us that he and three others were the only representatives of the United States in Manila as late as 1893.

The city is built on a beautiful bay from twenty-five to thirty miles across, and on both shores of the Pasig River. On the right bank of the river, going up from the bay, is the old walled town, and around the walls are the weedy moats or ditches. The heavy guns and frowning cannon from the walls suggest a troubled past. Th.. old city is built in triangular form, about a mile on each side, and is regarded as very unhealthful, for the walls both keep out the breeze and keep in the foul air and odors. The principal buildings in the old part of the city are the cathedral, many parish churches, a few schoolhouses and the official buildings. The population in the walled city is given at 20,000. Up to a few years ago, no foreigner was permitted to sleep within its walls on account of the Spaniards' fear of a conspiracy. A bridge across the Pasig connects old Manila with the new or unwalled city, where nearly all of the business is done and the native and foreign residents live. This section of the city is known as Binondo and its chief street is the Escolta.

EARTHQUAKES AND TYPHOONS.

It does not take one long to exhaust the sights of Manila, if the people, who are always interesting, are excepted. Aside from the cathedral and a few of the churches, the buildings of the city are anything but imposing. In fact, there is little encouragement to construct fine edifices because of the danger from earthquakes and typhoons. It is said that not a year passes without a number of slight earthquake shocks, and very serious ones have occurred. In 1645 nearly all of the public buildings were wrecked and 600 persons killed. A very destructive earthquake was that of 1863, when 400 people were killed, 2,000 wounded and 46 public buildings and 1,100 private houses were badly injured or completely destroyed. In 1874 earthquakes were again very numerous throughout the islands, shocks being felt at intervals in certain sections for several weeks. But the most violent convulsion of modern times occurred in 1880, when even greater destruction than in 1863 visited Manila and other towns of Luzon. Consequently there are very few buildings to be found more than two stories high ; and the heavy tile roofs formerly in use have, for the most part, been replaced by lighter coverings of galvanized iron.

9 D.D.

These light roofs, however, are in constant danger of being stripped off by the typhoons, terrible storms which come with a twisting motion as if rising from the earth or the sea, fairly pulling everything detachable with them. Masts of ships and roofs of houses are frequently carried by these hurricanes miles distant. The better to resist the typhoons, most of the light native houses are built on bamboo poles, which allow the wind to pass freely under them, and sway and bend in the storm like a tree ; whereas, if they were set solidly on the earth, they would be lifted up bodily and carried away. Glass windows being too frail to resist the shaking of the earthquakes and the typhoons, small, translucent oyster shells are used instead. The light thus admitted resembles that passing through ground glass, or, rather, stained glass, for the coloring in the shells imparts a mellow tinted radiance like the windows of a cathedral.

MANILA AS A BUSINESS CENTER.

The streets of Manila are wretchedly paved or not paved at all, and, as late as 1893, were lighted by kerosene lamps or by wicks suspended in dishes of cocoanut oil. Lately an electric plant has been introduced, and parts of the city are lighted in this manner. There are two lines of street cars in Manila. The motive power for a car is a single small pony, and foreigners marvel to see one of those little animals drawing thirty-odd people.

The retail trade and petty banking of Manila is almost entirely in the hands of the half-castes and Chinese, and many of them have grown immensely wealthy. There are only about three hundred Europeans in business in the whole Philippine group, and they conduct the bulk of the importing and exporting trade. Manila contains a number of large cigarette factories, two of which employ 4,000 and one 10,000 hands. There is also a sugar refinery, a steam rice mill, and a rope factory worked partly by men and partly by oxen, a Spanish brewery and a German cement factory, a Swiss umbrella factory and a Swiss hat factory. The single cotton mill, in which $200,000 of English capital is invested, runs 6,000 spindles.

The statistics of 1897 show that the whole trade of Manila comprised only forty-five Spanish, nineteen German, and seventeen English firms, with six Swiss brokers and two French storekeepers having large establishments. One of the most profitable businesses is said to be that of selling cheap jewelry to the natives. Breastpins which dealers buy in Europe for twelve cents each are readily sold for from $1.50 to $2.00 each to the simple Filipinos. Almost everything that is manufactured abroad has a fine prospective market in the Philippines, when the condition of the people permits them to buy.

A certain charm attaches to many specimens of native handiwork. The women weave exquisitely beautiful fabrics from the fiber of plants. The floors of Manila houses are admired by all foreigners. They are made of hard wood and polished with banana leaves and greasy cloths until they shine brightly and give a cool airiness to the room.

Any kind of amusement is popular with the Filipinos—with so much leisure on their hands—provided it does not require too great exertion on their part. They are fond of the theatre, and, up to a few years ago, bullfighting was a favorite pastime; but the most prominent of modern amusements for the natives and half castes is cockfighting. It is said that every native has his fighting cock, which is reared and trained with the greatest care until he shows sufficient skill to entitle him to an entrance into the public cockpit where he will fight for a prize. The chickens occupy the family residence, roosting overhead; and, in case of fire, it is said that the game "rooster" is saved before the babies. Professor Worcester tells an amusing story of the annoyance of the crowing cocks above his head in the morning and the devices and tricks he and his companions employed to quiet them. The Manila lottery is another institution which intensely excites the sluggish native, and takes from him the money which he does not lose on the cockfights. Under the United States Government this lottery will, no doubt, be abolished in time. It formerly belonged to the Spanish Government, and Spain derived an annual profit of half a million dollars from it.

GENERAL COMMERCE OF THE PHILIPPINES.

It is hardly necessary, so far as the commercial world is concerned, to mention any other locality outside of the city of Manila. To commerce, this city (whose total imports in 1897, were only $10,000,-000, and its exports $20,000,000) is the Philippine Islands. Its present meagre foreign trade represents only an average purchase of about one dollar per inhabitant, and an average sale of two dollars per inhabitant for the largest archipelago in the world, and one of the richest in soil and natural resources. The bulk of these exports was hemp, sugar, and tobacco; and, strange as it may seem, the United States received 41 per cent. of her hemp and 55 per cent. of her sugar for the year 1897, notwithstanding the fact that we had not one commercial firm doing business in that whole vast domain.

The city of Iloilo is on the southern coast of the fertile island of Panay, and, next to Manila, the chief port of the Philippines. It has an excellent harbor, and the surrounding country is very productive, having extensive plantations of sugar, rice and tobacco. The population of Iloilo is only 12,000, but there are a few larger towns in the district, of which it is the seaport. Though the city at springtides is covered with water, it is said to be a very healthful place, and much cooler than Manila.

The other open port, Cebu, on the eastern coast of the island of the same name, is a well-built town, and has a population of about 13,000. From this point the bulk of the hemp for export comes.

GENERAL CHARACTER OF THE ISLANDS.

It is impossible to speak of the other islands in detail. Seven of the group average larger than the State of New Jersey; Luzon is as extensive as Ohio, Mindanao equals Indiana; and, as we have stated before, about four hundred of the islands are inhabitable, and, like Java, Borneo, and the Spice Islands, all are rich in natural resources. They are of a volcanic origin, and may be described in general as rugged and mountainous. The coasts of most of the islands are deeply indented by the sea, and the larger ones are well watered by streams, the mouths of which afford good harbors. Many of the mountainous parts abound in minerals. Mr. Karuph, President of the Philippine Mineral Syndicate, in May, 1898, addressed a letter to Hon. John Hay, at that time our ambassador to England, in which he declares that the Philippines will soon come prominently forward as a new center of the world's gold production. "There is not a brook," said Mr. Karuph, "that finds its way into the Pacific Ocean whose sands and gravel do not pan the color of gold. Many valuable deposits are close to deep water. I know of no other part of the world, the Alaskan Treadwell mines alone excepted, where pay ore is found within a few hundred yards of the anchorage of sea-going vessels." In addition to gold, iron, copper, lead, sulphur, and other minerals are found, and are believed to exist in paying quantities. The numerous mineral springs attest their presence in almost every part of the principal islands.

FORESTS AND TIMBER.

The forest products of the islands are perhaps of greater value than their mineral resources. Timber not only exists in almost exhaustless quantity, but—considering the whole group, which extends nearly a thousand miles from north to south—in unprecedented diversity, embracing sixty varieties of the most valuable woods, several of which are so hard that they cannot be cut with ordinary saws, some so heavy that they sink in water, and two or three so durable as to afford ground for the claim that they outlast iron and steel when placed in the ground or under water. Several of these woods are unknown elsewhere, and, altogether, they are admirably suited for various decorative purposes and for the manufacture of fine implements and furniture.

Here also are pepper, cinnamon, wax, and gums of various sorts, cloves, tea, and vanilla, while all tropical fruits, such as cocoanuts, bananas, lemons, limes, oranges of several varieties, pineapples, citrons, bread-fruits, custard apples, pawpaws, and mangroves flourish and most of them grow wild, though, of course, they are not equal to the cultivated fruit. There are fifty odd varieties of the banana in the archipelago, from the midget, which makes but a single mouthful, to the huge fruit eighteen inches long. There seems to be no limit to which tropical fruits and farm products can be cultivated.

The animal and bird life of the Philippines offer a field of interesting research to naturalists. There are no important carnivorous animals. A small wild cat and two species of civet cats constitute about all that belong to that class. The house cats of the Philippines have curious fishhook crooks in the ends of their tails. There are several species of deer in the archipelago. Hogs run wild in large numbers. The large water buffalo (*carabao*) has been domesticated and is the chief beast of burden with the natives. The *timarau* is another small species of buffalo, very wild and entirely untamable ; and, though numerous in certain places, is hard to find, and when brought to bay dies fighting.

Birds abound in all of the islands ; nearly six hundred species have been found, over fifty of which exist nowhere else in the world. One of these species builds a nest which is highly prized by Chinese epicures as an article of diet. Prof. Worcester tells us "the best quality of them sometimes bring more than their weight in gold." Crocodiles are numerous in fresh-water lakes and streams, attaining enormous size, and in certain places causing much loss of life among stock and men as well. Snakes also abound, and some of them are very venomous. Cobras are found in the southern islands. Pythons are numerous, some of the smaller sizes being sold in the towns and kept in houses to catch rats, at which they are said to be more expert than house cats.

All the domestic animals, aside from the *carabao*, have been introduced from abroad. Cattle are extensively raised, and in some of the islands run wild. The horses are a small Spanish breed, but are very strong and have great endurance. Large European horses do not stand the climate well.

CLIMATE, VOLCANOES, ETC.

The mean annual temperature of Manila is 80 degrees F. The thermometer seldom rises above 100 degrees or falls below 60 degrees anywhere in the archipelago. There is no month in the year during which it does not rise as high as 91 degrees. January and December are the coldest months, the average temperature being 70 to 73 degrees. May is the warmest, the average being 84 degrees. April is the next warmest, with an average of 83 degrees ; but the weather is generally very moist and humid, which makes the heat more trying. The three winter months have cool nights. Malaria is prevalent, but contagious diseases are comparatively few. Yellow fever and cholera are seldom heard of.

The Philippines are the home of many volcanoes, a number of them still active. Mayon, in the island of Luzon, is one of the most remarkable volcanic mountains on the globe. It is a perfect cone, rising to the height of 8,900 feet, and is in constant activity; its latest destructive eruption took place in 1888. Apo, in the island of Mindanao, 10,312 feet high, is the largest of the Philippine volcanoes. Next is Canloon in Negros, which rises 8,192 feet above the sea. Taal is in a lake, with a height of 900 feet, and is noteworthy as being the lowest volcano in the world. To those not accustomed to volcanoes, these great fire-spouting mountains, which are but prominent representatives of many lesser ones in the islands, seem to be an ever-present danger to the inhabitants; but the natives and those who live there manifest little or no fear of them. In fact, they rather pride themselves in their possession of such terrifying neighbors.

Such is an outline view of the Philippine Archipelago of the present day. A new era has opened up in the history of that wonderful land with its liberation from the Spanish yoke. The dense ignorance and semi-savage barbarities which exist there must not be expected to yield too rapidly to the touch of human kindness and brotherly love with which the Christian world will now visit those semi-civilized and untamed children of nature. Nevertheless, western civilization and western progress will undoubtedly work mighty changes in the lives of those people, in the development of that country, during the first quarter of the twentieth century, which ushers in the dawn of its freedom.

THE BATTLE OF MANILA.

In all the annals of naval warfare there is no engagement, terminating in so signal a victory with so little damage to the victors, as that which made the name of George Dewey immortal on the memorable Sunday morning of May 1, 1898, in Manila Bay. The world knows the story of that battle, for it has been told hundreds of times in the thousands of newspapers and magazines and scores of books throughout the civilized world. But few, perhaps, who peruse these pages have read the simple details of the fight as narrated by that most modest of men, Admiral Dewey himself. We cannot better close this chapter on the Philippines than by inserting Admiral Dewey's official report of the battle which wrested the Filipinos from Spanish tyranny and placed nearly ten millions of oppressed people under the protecting care of the United States.

ADMIRAL DEWEY'S STORY OF MANILA.

"UNITED STATES FLAGSHIP OLYMPIA, CAVITE, May 4, 1898.

"The squadron left Mirs Bay on April 27th, arrived off Bolinao on the morning of April 30th, and, finding no vessels there, proceeded down the coast and arrived off the entrance to Manila Bay on the same afternoon. The Boston and the Concord were sent to reconnoitre Port Subic. A thorough search was made of the port by the Boston and the Concord, but the Spanish fleet was not found. Entered the south channel at 11.30 P.M., steaming in column at eight knots. After half the squadron had passed, a battery on the south side of the channel opened fire, none of the shots taking effect. The Boston and McCulloch returned the fire. The squadron proceeded across the bay at slow speed and arrived off Manila at daybreak, and was fired upon at 5.15 A.M. by three batteries at Manila and two near Cavite, and by the Spanish fleet anchored in an approximately east and west line across the mouth of Bakor Bay, with their left in shoal water in Canacao Bay.

"The squadron then proceeded to the attack, the flagship Olympia, under my personal direction, leading, followed at a distance by the Baltimore, Raleigh, Petrel, Concord and Boston in the order named, which formation was maintained throughout the action. The squadron opened fire at 5.41 A.M. While advancing to the attack, two mines were exploded ahead of the flagship, too far to be effective. The squadron maintained a continuous and precise fire at ranges varying from 5,000 to 2,000 yards, countermarching in a line approximately parallel to that of the Spanish fleet. The enemy's fire was vigorous, but generally ineffective. Early in the engagement two launches put out toward the Olympia with the apparent intention of using torpedoes. One was sunk and the other disabled by our fire and beached before they were able to fire their torpedoes.

"At 7 A.M. the Spanish flagship Reina Christina made a desperate attempt to leave the line and come out to engage at short range, but was received with such a galling fire, the entire battery of the Olympia being concentrated upon her, that she was barely able to return to the shelter of the point. The fires started in her by our shells at the time were not extinguished until she sank. The three batteries at Manila had kept up a continuous fire from the beginning of the engagement,

which fire was not returned by my squadron. The first of these batteries was situated on the south mole-head at the entrance of the Pasig
River, the second on the south position of the walled city of Manila,
and the third at Malate, about one-half mile further south. At this
point I sent a message to the Governor-General to the effect that if
the batteries did not cease firing the city would be shelled. This had
the effect of silencing them.

"At 7.35 A.M. I ceased firing and withdrew the squadron for
breakfast. At 11.16 I returned to the attack. By this time the
Spanish flagship and almost all the Spanish fleet were in flames. At
12.30 the squadron ceased firing, the batteries being silenced and the
ships sunk, burned and deserted.

"At 12.40 the squadron returned and anchored off Manila, the
Petrel being left behind to complete the destruction of the smaller
gunboats, which were behind the point of Cavite. This duty was
performed by Commander E. P. Wood in the most expeditious and
complete manner possible. The Spanish lost the following vessels:
Sunk, Reina Christina, Bastilla, Don Antonio de Ulloa; burned, Don
Juan de Austria, Isla de Luzon, Isla de Cuba, General Lezo, Marquis
del Duero, El Correo, Velasco, and Isla de Mindanao (transport);
captured, Rapido and Hercules (tugs), and several small launches.

"I am unable to obtain complete accounts of the enemy's killed and
wounded, but believe their losses to be very heavy. The Reina Christina alone had 150 killed, including the captain, and ninety wounded.
I am happy to report that the damage done to the squadron under
my command was inconsiderable. There were none killed, and only
seven in the squadron were slightly wounded. Several of the vessels
were struck and even penetrated, but the damage was of the slightest,
and the squadron is in as good condition now as before the battle.

"I beg to state to the department that I doubt if any commander-in-chief was ever served by more loyal, efficient and gallant
captains than those of the squadron now under my command. Captain Frank Wildes, commanding the Boston, volunteered to remain
in command of his vessel, although his relief arrived before leaving
Hong Kong. Assistant Surgeon Kindelberger, of the Olympia, and
Gunner J. C. Evans, of the Boston, also volunteered to remain, after
orders detaching them had arrived. The conduct of my personal

3

staff was excellent. Commander B. P. Lamberton, chief of staff, was a volunteer for that position, and gave me most efficient aid. Lieutenant Brumby, Flag Lieutenant, and Ensign E. P. Scott, aidè, performed their duties as signal officers in a highly creditable manner; Caldwell, Flag Secretary, volunteered for and was assigned to a subdivision of the five-inch battery. Mr. J. L. Stickney, formerly an officer in the United States Navy, and now correspondent for the New York *Herald*, volunteered for duty as my aide, and rendered valuable service. I desire especially to mention the coolness of Lieutenant C. G. Calkins, the navigator of the Olympia, who came under my personal observation, being on the bridge with me throughout the entire action, and giving the ranges to the guns with an accuracy that was proven by the excellence of the firing.

"On May 2d, the day following the engagement, the squadron again went to Cavite, where it remains. On the 3d the military forces evacuated the Cavite arsenal, which was taken possession of by a landing party. On the same day the Raleigh and the Baltimore secured the surrender of the batteries on Corregidor Island, paroling the garrison and destroying the guns. On the morning of May 4th, the transport Manila, which had been aground in Bakor Bay, was towed off and made a prize."

CHAPTER XII

Behind Admiral Dewey's Guns

The Magnificent Naval Battle of May 1st Described by an Officer who stood by Dewey during the Fight.—The Personal Side of the Nation's Greatest Hero. —A Brush with German Officers.—The Surrender of Cavite.

MAY 1, 1898, will go down in history as the date of the greatest naval battle the world has ever seen. Farragut made himself immortal by his famous order, "Damn the torpedoes; go ahead." Commodore George Dewey, taught in the school of Farragut, went ahead in Manila Bay, regardless of torpedoes or glowering forts.

On the night of April 30th the United States squadron was off Manila Bay. Darkness came on, and all aboard the vessels were in a state of keen expectancy. At 10 o'clock all hands were piped to fighting quarters, and all lights were "doused." No one knew what the next few hours would bring.

Commodore Dewey had been warned that Spanish mines and torpedoes had been sunk at the mouth of the bay. Balloon-shaped, with the island of Corregidor across the neck, the bay lent itself naturally to defence. The path to Manila was a narrow and dangerous one, but Dewey, fearless and confident, decided to make the dash, and either win or lose all in one stroke.

What a picture the scene conjures up to one's mind! The inky blackness of the night, the ships themselves lightless, the men keyed to a state of excitement, anxious as to what their fate would be, their Commodore calm as though there was no enemy ahead or danger beneath. All is silence except the swish of the waters as the fighters ploughed through. Then a spark or two blown from the funnel of the *McCulloch* against the black sky betrays to the sentinels on the forts at the harbor the presence of the fleet. The sharp boom of a gun, another, and still another, echo across the bay. They give to the Spanish forces the first inkling of the approaching battle.

The story of that battle, so modestly and simply told in the report of Commodore Dewey, has already been given. At his side on the flagship *Olympia* all through the engagement stood a young naval officer, Ensign W. Pitt Scott. His name was mentioned by Commodore Dewey in the report to the War Department, and he was specially commended for bravery in the battle.

ENSIGN SCOTT'S STORY OF THE BATTLE.

It is stated by Colonel George A. Loud, who witnessed the battle from the Revenue Cutter *McCulloch*, that a six-pound shell cut the rigging four feet over Commodore Dewey's head just as Ensign Scott was raising a signal flag and the halyards were shot away. Ensigh Scott has told the story of the battle, which is given herewith. He writes:

"The Spaniards had ten ships fighting to our six, and, in addition, had five or six shore batteries, some of which bothered us a great deal. We steamed by their line and fired some deadly shot at them. We had anticipated that once across their line would be sufficient to silence them, but they did not yield, and so, when we got to the end of the line, we turned and went back at them again. It was getting really interesting now, for many of their shots were coming close to us, and the screech of the missiles as they whistled over our heads was anything but pleasant. Now and then we would see a shot strike in the water ahead of us and explode and the pieces of it come at us. I will never forget it.

"I was surprised to find how little it disturbed us. I never believed I would ever feel so unconcerned while the shots were falling around us. No one seemed to care an iota whether the shells dropped on us, or fell a distance away, and in the intervals, between which we were making signals, the most commonplace remarks were made.

"We passed across the enemy's line the second time; but that did not seem to silence them any more than the first, and we had to try it a third time, with no better result, although perhaps their fire was not so heavy as at first. A small torpedo boat came out and attempted to get within striking distance of the *Olympia*, but our secondary battery drove her in; a second time she came out and at us, but again our fire was too much for her, and some of our shots striking her, she had barely time to get back to the beach, or she would have sunk.

THE FLAGSHIP BORE THE BRUNT OF THE FIRE.

"It soon became apparent that the Spaniards were concentrating their fire on the *Olympia* (as flagship), and we then received the brunt of the fight. At one time the *Reina Christina*, the Spanish flagship, attempted to come out from her position and engage us at closer distance, but we turned our fire on her and drove her back.

"A fourth time we steamed across their line, and a fifth, and it began to look as if they were not going to give in until after all our ammunition would be exhausted, which would leave us in a very serious predicament, in the midst of the enemy and in one of their ports, 7,000 miles from supplies; so after the fifth time across their line we withdrew to count up our ammunition, to see how we stood, and get breakfast.

"It was only 7.30 A.M., but it seemed to us as if it were the middle of the day. Then we began to count our casualities, and found that no one had been killed and no one injured, with a few slight exceptions.

"But it was the dirtiest-looking crowd I have ever seen, and by far the oddest. It was so hot that nearly all of the men had stripped off all their clothes,—in fact, in the turrets they did strip off about everything but their shoes, which they kept on to protect their feet from the hot floor. Commodore Dewey himself, the most dressed man in the battle, was in white duck; the rest of us appeared without collars and some without shirts, an undershirt and white blouse being more than sufficient for our needs, and, if our blouses were not off, they certainly were not buttoned.

STANDING UNDER SHARP FIRE.

"We were a mighty dirty crowd. Our faces and clothes were full of smoke and powder and saltpetre, and the perspiration rolling around in that made us picturesquely handsome. I would have given a good deal for a picture of the ship's company, men and officers.

"Then we looked around to see where the ship had been

injured, and found that she had been struck several times, none of which materially hurt her. On the bridge where we stood was, perhaps, the hottest place of all, for at least four shots struck within thirty or forty feet of it. One of the ugly shots flew over our heads with a screech, but its cry was a little different from most of the others, and several of us said, 'That hit something', and we looked aloft to see if it had, and found the halyards on which we had a signal flying cut in two, and the signal out to the leeward. Another shot cut the wire-rigging ten feet over our heads, while any number flew close over us without striking anything.

"About halfpast ten we returned to the attack, and gave the *Baltimore* the post of honor in leading, as we were very short of 5-inch ammunition, and the way that the *Baltimore* did fire into the Spanish batteries was a caution. It was not long before the enemy was completely silenced and the white flag run up. Two of their ships were on fire and burning fiercely, and one was sinking. The *Don Antonio de Ulloa* was the last to give in, and after she was abandoned by her crew, she still kept her flag flying, which necessitated our firing at her until it was lowered ; but as no one was left on board to lower it, we kept firing at her until she slowly began to sink. It was a grand sight to see her settle aft, with the flag of Spain upon her.

"Then we sent one of the smaller ships in to destroy those that were still afloat, and the *Petrel* burned and sunk four or five of them, while the *Concord* fired a large transport, which, we afterward learned, was quite full of coal and stuff for the Spaniards. Altogether our six ships, the *Olympia, Baltimore, Raleigh, Boston, Concord,* and *Petrel,* burned and sunk almost the entire Spanish fleet that is in the East, as follows, viz.: Sunk, the *Reina Christina* (flagship), *Castilla* and *Antonio de Austria,* the *Isla de Cuba,* the *Isla de Luzon,* the *Marques del Duero,* the *Velasco,* the *General Lezo,* the *El Correo,* and the transport *Isla de Mindanao.* There is still one small vessel, the *Argus,* on the ways, but she is so badly damaged by shot that I doubt if she would float if we tried to put her into the water. Besides, we captured the *Manila,* a splendid 1900-ton vessel, which they used as transport, and on which we expect to send home our trophies in the way of captured guns, etc. We also captured any number of tugs and steam launches, some of which we are now using. Some of them were very fine tugboats.

ALL WERE PROUD OF THE SHIPS' WOUNDS.

"Everyone seemed proud of the wounds to the ships. The evening of the fight I had to go around to the different ships on an errand for Commodore Dewey, and on each one all hands made it a point to take me around and show me where each shot hit them.

"The harbor presents quite an unusual appearance with eight or nine ships showing just above water, the masts charred, and their upper works (those that can be seen) nothing but a twisted mass of iron. It looks as if we had done something to pay for the *Maine*.

"I got ashore several days after the engagement and walked through the navy yard. It presents a woeful sight. The barracks had any number of holes in the sides, and things were strewn all over. In one room of the the commandant's house we saw where a large 8-inch shell had gone through the roof, and after carrying away the thick planking had exploded, knocking down the side of the room and wrecking everything in it. In another building I saw where a shell had gone through the side of it, and had scattered the bricks all over the room."

In this remarkable battle, Admiral Montojo, the Spanish Commander, fought with the bravery that won from Admiral Dewey compliments and congratulations. His flagship, the *Reina Maria Christina*, the best of his fleet, dashed bravely towards the long line of belching vessels of Dewey's squadron, hoping to cripple at least one of the warships, that was pouring such an awful fire into his fleet. It was the madness of despair.

Dewey signalled for a concentration of fire upon the on-coming vessel, and as she neared the *Olympia*, the latter discharged her 8-inch guns both fore and aft, killing sixty of the Spaniard's crew, including her captain, chaplain and a lieutenant, and causing her boilers to explode. The flagship was a burning wreck, and was forced to retire. Admiral Montojo transferred his flag to the *Isla de Cuba*, which maintained a vigorous fire until she too sank at her moorings.

Admiral Montojo's own account of the fight is interesting as giving a Spanish view of the greatest of naval encounters. The

Admiral is a spare man, of small stature, about 65 years old, with an air of an old Spanish Grandee. He speaks English fluently, but with a slight accent, and the following are his own words in describing the battle :

THE SPANISH ADMIRAL'S ACCOUNT OF HIS DEFEAT.

"About 5 o'clock on Sunday morning I observed the American squadron coming in line straight across the bay towards Cavite. We prepared to receive them. A few minutes after 5 o'clock the engagement opened, the battery on Pont Sangley (Cavite) firing on each ship as she came within range. The American ships did not reply. All the Spanish ships were in Cavite Bay at anchor—the *Reina Christina* (my flagship), *Castilla*, *Don Juan de Austria*, *Ulloa*, *Isla de Cuba*, *Isla de Luzon*, *Marques del Duero*, and some small gunboats. The *Reina Christina* and the *Don Juan*, as you know, were old cruisers ; the *Castilla* was a wooden cruiser, but was unable to steam owing to the breakdown of her engines ; the *Ulloa* and *Velasco* were helpless, and were undergoing repairs off the arsenal.

"The *Olympia*, *Baltimore*, *Raleigh*, and *Boston* engaged my flagship in turn about 5.30, attracted by my flag. I recognized the necessity of getting under way, and accordingly slipped both anchors, ordering the other ships to follow my example. Although we recognized the hopelessness of fighting the American ships, we were busy returning their fire. The *Reina Christina* was hit repeatedly. Shortly after 6.30 I observed fire forward. Our steering gear was damaged. rendering the vessel unmanageable, and we were being subjected to a terrific hail of shell and shot. The engines were struck, and we estimated that we had 70 hits about our hull and superstructure. The boilers were not hit, but the pipe to the condenser was destroyed. A few moments later I observed the afterpart on fire. A shell from the Americans had penetrated and burst with deadly effect, killing many of our men.

"My flag lieutenant said to me, 'The ship is in flames. It is impossible to stay on the *Christina* any longer.' He signalled to the gunboat *Isla de Cuba*, and I and my staff transferred to her, and my flag was hoisted on her. Before leaving the *Christina* my flag was hauled down. My flagship was now one mass of flame. I ordered away all the boats I could to save the crew. Many of the men jumped overboard without clothing and succeeded in reaching the shore, several hundreds of yards away. Only a few men were drowned, the majority being picked up by the boats.

" Before jumping overboard, Captain Cadarso's son, a lieutenant on board the *Christina*, saw his father alive on deck, but others state that as the Captain was about to leave a shell burst overhead and killed him. We estimate that 52 men were killed on board the *Christina* and about 150 wounded. The chaplain was killed. The assistant physician, the chief engineer, and three officers were wounded. The boatswain and chief gunner were both killed. In the *Castilla* only about 15 men were killed, but there were many wounded, both on the *Castilla* and the *Don Juan*, on which 13 men were killed. Altogether, so far as we know at present, 400 men were killed and wounded in our ships.

" As soon as I translated myself from the *Reina Christina* to the *Isla de Cuba* all the shots were directed upon the *Cuba*, following my flag. We sought shelter behind the pier at Cavite, and, recognizing the futility of fighting more, I prepared to disembark, and gave orders for the evacuation of the remainder of our ships. The *Castilla* had been on fire from end to end for some time, and was, of course, already abandoned. The *Ulloa* was also burning.

THE LAST SPANISH SIGNAL.

" My last signal to the Captains of all vessels was—' Scuttle and abandon your ships.'

" This was about 7.30. The *Reina Christina, Castilla, Don Juan de Austria, Velasco,* and *Ulloa* were all destroyed in this engagement. To prevent the guns being of use to the Americans, the Captains, on abandoning, brought away portions of the mechanism, and also succeeded in saving all the ships' papers and treasure. At this point there was a cessation of firing. The *Boston* sent ashore a boat with an officer carrying a white flag, and parleyed with the Chief of the Arsenal. He asked permission to destroy the vessels completely without interference from the shore. After consultation with me, the Chief of the Arsenal replied that it was not competent on my part to give any pledge ; the ships were at his mercy and he could do with

them as he liked.   While the parleying was proceeding, the *Petrel* and
Concord went across the bay, and fired a large number of shots into
the *Isla de Mindanao*, which was lying ashore near Bacoor, and she
soon caught fire.   Her captain had run her ashore when the American
squadron was observed making for Cavite Bay.   She never fired a
shot.

"I was wounded in the left leg by an iron splinter, and my son,
a lieutenant, was wounded in the hand by a shell splinter.   We were
both wounded on the *Reina Christina*.   I directed the movements of
my squadron from the bridge.   There was no conning tower.   The
Captain of the *Boston* said to my chief of staff, Captain Boado, 'You
have combated with us with four very bad ships, not warships.   There
was never seen before braver fighting under such unequal conditions.
It is a great pity that you exposed your lives in vessels not fit for
fighting'.   Commodore Dewey also sent me a message by the British
Consul, saying that, peace or war, he would have great pleasure in
clasping me by the hand, and congratulating me on the gallant manner in which we fought."

A WILD EXULTANT CHEER OF VICTORY.

And so the great fight ended.   When the little *Petrel* announced
that the Spanish fleet had scuttled their vessels and fled, a great
cheer went up from all the men who had braved the perils of the
Spanish fire, and that cheer was doubled and redoubled when, later
on, it was announced that not one man of the American fleet had
lost his life.   The only death was due to apoplexy brought on by the
intense heat.   The Chief Engineer of the *McCulloch* was the victim;
he suddenly expired, not in the battle, but just as the fleet was
entering the mouth of the bay.

Fighting ceased about 12.15 P. M., by which time all the Spanish
ships were sunk or burned.   The arsenal was ablaze, and throughout
the night explosions were occurring in Cavite Bay—an alluring
spectacle of destruction.

It was in the smaller incidents of this great battle that Commodore (thereafter to be known as Admiral) Dewey showed to his men,
and to the whole world, what manner of man he was.   The withdrawal of his fleet so that his men, exhausted by the severe work of

battle, might have breakfast has thrilled every heart. His kindness and courtesy in complimenting a defeated foe for personal bravery, proved him a gentleman even in war. His cablegrams to the Navy Department show him a man of rare modesty. One sentence in the second of his dispatches, harmonizing as it does with the keynote of the whole war—"humanity"—will live in history with the sayings of the greatest men the world has had. Let us repeat his own words: "I am assisting in protecting the Spanish sick and wounded. Two hundred and fifty sick and wounded in hospital within our line." That was humanity's own voice. When in naval history had such a spectacle ever been witnessed. Before the smoke of battle had even cleared away, the victorious commander was plying the hand of brotherly charity to stay the sufferings of the men with whom he had been engaged in deadly combat.

GEORGE DEWEY, ADMIRAL, HERO, STATESMAN, GENTLEMAN.

The United States Navy has never had, perhaps, as remarkable a figure as George Dewey. From Maine to Mexico, from the Atlantic to the Pacific, his name is as familiar, and he is as beloved, as any of the great figures of the nation's history.

Admiral Dewey is not only a great fighter, but has proved himself a great statesman. The situation after the downfall of Cavite was a perplexing one; immediately after the battle, Dewey had cut the cable that connected Manila with the rest of the world and he was, therefore, thrown upon his own resources as to what to do in an emergency. He could not be directed by the government at Washington. He had gone to the islands seeking only the Spanish fleet, and determined to carry out the cabled instructions he had received at Hong-Kong, ordering him to "find the Spanish fleet and capture or utterly destroy it." How well he did this has already been told. But now the question of holding an arsenal, captured by him, without having at his disposal any considerable force of armed soldiers confronted him.

The insurgent forces under General Aguinaldo had moved upon Manila, when the attack had been made upon the fleet in the bay. After the withdrawal of the Spanish forces from Cavite the insurgents were eager to plunder the houses left by the terror-stricken people.

They did not hesitate to rob even the dead. But Admiral Dewey determined not to allow such things, and immediately he had his hands full.

DEWEY HAS NEED FOR FIRMNESS.

To add to his troubles the German Emperor sent to Manila Bay several of his mighty battleships in command of Admiral von Diedrich. The sympathies of Germany were apparently with Spain, and the German Admiral let no opportunity go by without showing his feelings in the matter. An incident occurred when the insurgents were making an attack upon the Spanish outposts which is worth recording. The fighting between the Spaniards and insurgents was always done under cover of darkness, partly because of the extreme heat, and partly because of the guerrilla style of warfare which was carried on. When the battle was begun the German vessels in the harbor turned their powerful search-lights upon the places where the insurgent army was concealed, thus putting them in the glare of the light and rendering them an easy mark for the Spaniards who were hidden effectually by the darkness. But the light rested there only for a moment. Admiral Dewey sent peremptory orders to the German Admiral that if the lights were not extinguished immediately, or if the action were repeated, he would consider it an act of war against the United States, and take steps accordingly. The lights were never again flashed upon the struggling insurgents.

When Admiral Dewey was ready to shell the Spanish forces, he ordered all of the vessels of the foreign powers then in the harbor to remove to a distance of three miles from his fleet. The attitude of the German fleet, though not openly hostile, had been significantly unfriendly. When the German Admiral received Dewey's order he removed to the required distance, but lined up his vessels in such a way that they bore directly upon the American fleet so that in case there was a display of open partisanship on the part of Germany, Dewey's fleet would be between two fires,—the fires of the forts on the one hand, and the fires of the German warships on the other.

A FRIENDLY ACT BY THE BRITISH ADMIRAL.

It was then that the British friendliness, which had been such a prominent feature at home, displayed itself as a reality. The British

Admiral moved his warships and came at anchor in a position immediately between the vessels of Germany and those of the United States. If Germany, therefore, had fired a shot, it would have fired through the warships of England. The trouble ended then and there, although the German Admiral kept up petty annoyances for some time. Finally, Admiral Dewey turned to one of the German Admiral's Lieutenants and said to him, " If Germany wants war with my country, it can have it in five minutes." The invitation, it is needless to say, was not accepted.

It was thus that Admiral Dewey met emergencies—ever polite, ever the cultured man of the world, but ever the firm, fearless officer, ready to fight if need be to uphold the dignity and honor of his nation and himself. It is fitting that the nation has especially singled out such a man for the highest office that can be given to men of the navy. The President personally tendered him the thanks of the people; Congress made him Rear Admiral, and revived for him the grade of Admiral, which went out of existence many years ago with Admiral Porter. Although his personal history has already been given, it may be well to recall the leading facts in his career:

Admiral Dewey is a man to admire at close range. Many heroes lose their gloss on close acquaintance. With Dewey this is not so. Through a long line of sturdy stock he has inherited a culture, an integrity, and a force of character that make him a man to honor. He was born in a fine old Colonial mansion in Montpelier, Vt., sixty years ago. He was a young man when he first fell in love with his life work. He wanted to go to sea, but his father did not take kindly to the idea. A compromise was effected. The boy at 14 left the Montpelier public school to enter the Norwich University at Northfield, Vt., a military school, where his useful enthusiasm was temporarily appeased by musket practice and drills. But the craving for the sea life was still strong with Dewey.

THE EARLY CAREER OF DEWEY.

So his father secured for him an appointment to the Naval Academy at Annapolis in 1854; he graduated in 1858. When Fort Sumter was fired on in 1861, Dewey received his commission as a Lieutenant on the seventeen-gun steam sloop *Mississippi.* His

Yankee blood was hot for fight, and he and his vessel participated in the terrific actions of the West Gulf squadron. History tells how young Dewey received the baptism of battle, and how owing to the terrible fire of the shore batteries on the Mississippi River the crew were forced to abandon their vessel. The last to leave the ship were the Captain and his First Lieutenant, George Dewey. Again and again through the war he showed his metal. He served on the famous *Kearsarge* and afterward on the flagship *Colorado*. He received his first command in 1870, the *Narragansett.* Passing through various years of service, Dewey became, in 1884, a Captain and Commander of the *Dolphin*, one of the first craft of the new navy. His promotion continued rapidly. From 1885 to 1888 he commanded the *Pensacola*, flagship of the European squadron.

On account of his devotion to method, his close application to detail and his wide knowledge of naval science he was elevated, in 1888, to the head of the Bureau of Equipment and Recruiting, with the rank of Commodore. In 1893 he served as a member of the Light-house Board, and three years later, having reached the actual rank of Commodore, he became President of the Board of Inspection and Survey. He left that important post to take command of the Asiatic squadron.

His son, George Dewey, speaking of his father a few days after the great victory, said : "When I said good-bye to him at the station I told him, 'I hope you will have a most pleasant and successful cruise.' He said with a laugh, 'Well, I guess I will, I am the first Commodore to go out there since Perry, and that ought to mean something?' All the others have been Admirals since Perry, and that rather seemed at the moment to have attached some significance to the fact that he was the first Commodore on the Asiatic squadron since then."

THE MAN IN WHITE IN A PERSONAL WAY.

Admiral Dewey is known as the Man in White in the Philippines. He is a stickler for dress, is himself always immaculate, and insists that those around him shall be careful about their personal appearance. Those who think, from his photograph, that he is a small man, are mistaken. He weighs fully 185 pounds, and is so near 6 feet in height, that he gives one the impression of being fully that. He carries himself well, is graceful, though somewhat quick and nervous in his movements, and his face reflects keenness, cleverness, and an appreciation of good humor. He has a quick temper which sometimes leads him to say stinging things, but his self-control is so excellent, that one cannot but admire how well he holds himself in check. He is the idol of every man in his command, and what is more to his credit, he was their idol before he became the victor at Manila Bay.

When ashore, he is a great club man, a fine horseman, and an expert gunner. His wife died many years ago, shortly after the birth of their only son, George. Dewey is an early riser when on shore, temperate to the degree of abstemiousness. He enjoys a good table, but eats sparingly ; he is fond of a good cigar after dinner, and occasionally smokes between times. He is methodical, business-like, cool and very deliberate ; he does his own work well, and expects everybody else to do the same. He is very fond of children, and in his younger days, when he visited his native town, it was very often a familiar spectacle to see him on the piazza of the old Dewey home surrounded by a group of wide-eyed youngsters, telling them stories about daring men-of-warsmen and sea battles.

Eugene Field's verse is not a bad description, in many respects of George Dewey :

> " A single man, perhaps, but good ez gold and true ez steel,
> He could whip his weight in wild cats and you never heard him squeal,
> Good to the helpless and the weak ; a brave an' manly heart,
> A cyclone couldn't phase, but any child could rend apart ;
> So like the mountain pine that dares the storm which sweeps along,
> But rocks the wind in summertime, an' sings a soothin' song."

CHAPTER XIII

The Second Battle of Manila

How 8,000 American Soldiers Swept into a Heavily Entrenched City, Garrisoned by Nearly Twice that Number of Spaniards.—Insurgent Army Kept from Plunder. —Rare Bravery and Sacrifice.—What Major-General Wesley Merritt, Commanding the Expedition, General Frank V. Greene, General Arthur McArthur and General Thomas Anderson Said Officially of the Battle.—The Peace Protocol.

AFTER the occupation of the arsenal at Cavite by Admiral Dewey that officer waited without further fighting until he could receive reinforcements from the United States sufficient to enable him to take and hold Manila. The insurgents, however, kept up a continuous fighting in the region around Manila until they practically held all of the territory except that city in their grasp. They fought with great bravery, and, although checked by Admiral Dewey at the outskirts of the city, they managed to drive the Spanish behind their fortifications and force them to the wall. They held Malabon, Tarlac, and Bakkoor, Aguinaldo establishing a provisional government at the latter place and announcing himself dictator of the islands. The insurgents were eager to rush upon the city, but Dewey refused to allow "Hordes of passionate semi-savages to storm a civilized metropolis." He forbade them to cross the Malate River, seven miles south of Manila, threatening to bombard them with the *Petrel*.

In a campaign of two weeks the insurgents took 3,000 prisoners, including 2,000 soldiers of the regular Spanish army. On July 13th Dewey sent the following cablegram to the Naval Department: "Aguinaldo informs me his troops have taken all of Subic Bay except Isla Grande, which he was prevented from taking by the German man-of-war *Irene*. On July 7th the *Raleigh* and *Concord* went there; they took the island and about 1,300 men with arms and ammunition. No resistance. The *Irene* retired from the bay on their arrival."

This last sentence contains in a nutshell one of the most exciting incidents in the history of the war, an incident which almost involved our nation in a war with Germany. This was the first open action of the German Admiral against the United States. When the insurgents were about to take the island, the German warship *Irene* appeared on the scene and protected the Spaniards there from attack. Dewey, when informed of the matter, sent the *Boston* and *Raleigh* to the island, and the *Irene* slunk away. One shot from the *Raleigh* caused the Spaniards to raise the white flag. The captain of the *Irene* explained that he interfered "in the cause of humanity," and for a time it seemed as though the German meddling would prove a serious matter. The German government, however, repudiated the incident, and that, together with Dewey's splendid handling of the situation, prevented the affair from assuming the proportion it threatened.

In the meantime three expeditions were on their way across the ocean to take charge of matters, and reinforce Admiral Dewey. General Wesley Merritt was appointed Commander-in-Chief of all the forces in the Philippines, and arrived at Cavite July 25th. Some days before, on June 30th, the first expedition under General Thomas Anderson had landed. Another expedition under General Frank V. Greene arrived on July 17th, and the third, under General McArthur, arrived July 30th, five days later than General Merritt.

Immediately upon the arrival of General Merritt it was decided, after a conference with Admiral Dewey, to attack and take Manila. No time was lost. General Merritt stated in his dispatch that "to gain approach to the city Greene's outposts were advanced to continue a line from Camino Real to the beach. On the night of July 31st, Spanish attacked sharply. Artillery outposts behaved well. Held position. Necessary to call out brigade. Spanish loss rumored heavy." Our loss was 9 killed, 9 seriously wounded and 38 slightly wounded.

This plain statement of facts gives no idea, however, of the real battle which initiated our soldiers into the warfare of the Philippine Islands. The fighting took place amid a terrible rainstorm, a rainstorm such as we are not familiar with in the United States; 3,000 Spanish troops made a concerted sortie from Manila on the outposts and trenches of Camp Dewey, near Malate. The attack was directed

4

at the American right flank held by the Tenth Pennsylvania troops. The trenches of the Americans extended from the beach to the left flank of the insurgents. Sunday was the insurgent feast day, and their left flank withdrew, leaving the American right flank exposed. Companies A and E of the Tenth Pennsylvania and Utah Battery were ordered to reinforce the right flank ; it was there that the attack was made. The brave Pennsylvania men never flinched, but stood their ground under a withering fire. The alarm spread and the First California Regiment with two companies of the Third Artillery who fight with rifles were sent as reinforcements.

The Utah battery covered itself with glory, and all the men showed the greatest pluck under the trying deluge of nature and of the Spaniards. The enemy was repulsed and retreated in disorder. The Spanish loss was about 350 killed and 900 wounded. On the night of August 1st the fighting was renewed, but the enemy had been taught a lesson and made the attack at long range with heavy artillery. The Utah Battery replied, and the artillery duel lasted about an hour.

General Greene, in his report of the battle, says : " Major Cuthbertson, Tenth Pennsylvania, reports that the Spaniards left their trenches in force and attempted to turn our right flank, coming within 200 yards of his position. But as the night was intensely dark, with incessant and heavy rain, and as no dead or wounded were found in front of his position at daylight, it is possible that he was mistaken, and that the heavy fire to which he was subjected came from the trenches near Block House 14, beyond his right flank, at a distance of about 700 yards. The Spaniards used smokeless powder, the thickets obscured the flash of their guns, and the Mauser bullet penetrating a bamboo pole makes a noise very similar to the crack of the rifle itself ; hence, the difficulty of locating the enemy.

" This attack demonstrated the immediate necessity of extending our intrenchments to the right, and, although not covered by my instructions (which were to occupy the trenches from the bay to Calle Real, and to avoid precipitating an engagement), I ordered the First Colorado and one battalion of the First California, which occupied trenches at 9 A.M., August 1st, to extend the line of trenches to the Pasay Road. The work was begun by these troops, and continued every day by the troops occupying the trenches in turn, until a strong line was completed by August 12th, about 1,200 yards in length, extending from the bay to the east side of the Pasay Road. Its left rested on the bay, and its right on an extensive rice swamp, practically impassable."

The right flank was refused, because the only way to cross a smaller rice swamp, crossing the line about 700 yards from the beach, was along a crossroad in rear of the general line. As finally completed the works were very strong in profile, being five or six feet in height and eight to ten feet in thickness at the base, strengthened by bags filled with earth.

" The only material available was black soil saturated with water, and without the bags this was washed down and ruined in a day by the heavy and almost incessant rains. The construction of these trenches was constantly interrupted by the enemy's fire. They were occupied by the troops in succession, four battalions being usually sent out for a service of twenty-four hours, and posted with three battalions in the trenches and one battalion in reserve along the crossroad to Pasay ; Cossack posts being sent out from the latter to guard the camp against any possible surprise from the northeast and east.

TERRIBLE SERVICE IN THE TRENCHES.

" The service in the trenches was of the most arduous character, the rain being almost incessant, and the men having no protection against it ; they were wet during the entire twenty-four hours, and the mud was so deep that the shoes were ruined and a considerable number of men rendered barefooted. Until the notice of bombardment was given on August 7th, any exposure above or behind the trenches promptly brought the enemy's fire, so that the men had to sit in the mud under cover and keep awake, prepared to resist an attack, during the entire tour of twenty-four hours.

" After one particularly heavy rain a portion of the trench contained two feet of water, in which the men had to remain. It could not be drained, as it was lower than an adjoining rice swamp, in which the water had risen nearly two feet, the rainfall being more than four inches in twenty-four hours. These hardships were all endured by the men of the different regiments in turn, with the finest possible spirit and without a murmur of complaint.

"August 7th the notice of bombardment, after forty-eight hours, or sooner if the Spanish fire continued, was served, and after that date not a shot was fired on either side until the assault was made on August 13th. It was with great difficulty, and in some cases not without force, that the insurgents were restrained from opening fire and thus drawing the fire of the Spaniards during this period.

"Owing to the heavy storm and high surf it was impossible to communicate promptly with the division commander at Cavite, and I received my instructions direct from the Major-General commanding, or his staff officers, one of whom visited my camp every day, and I reported direct to him in the same manner. My instructions were to occupy the insurgent trenches near the beach, so as to be in good position to advance on Manila when ordered, but meanwhile to avoid precipitating an engagement, not to waste ammunition, and (after August 1st) not to return the enemy's fire unless convinced that he had left his trenches and was making an attack in force. These instructions were given daily in the most positive terms to the officer commanding in the trenches, and in the main they were faithfully carried out.

AMMUNITION WAS WASTED.

"More ammunition than necessary was expended on the nights of August 2d and 5th, but in both cases the trenches were occupied by troops under fire for the first time, and in the darkness and rain there was ground to believe that the heavy fire indicated a real attack from outside the enemy's trenches. The total expenditure of ammunition on our side in the four engagements was about 150,000 rounds, and by the enemy very much more.

"After the attack of July 31st, August 1st I communicated by signal with the captain of the United States steamship *Raleigh*, anchored about 3,000 yards southwest of my camp, asking if he had received orders in regard to the action of his ship in case of another attack on my troops. He replied:

"'Both Admiral Dewey and General Merritt desire to avoid general action at present. If attack too strong for you, we will assist you, and another vessel will come and offer help.'

" In repeating this message, Lieutenant Tappan, commanding United States steamship *Callao*, anchored nearer the beach, sent me a box of blue lights, and it was agreed that if I burned one of these on the beach the *Raleigh* would at once open fire on the Spanish fort."

General Greene issued this address to the troops : " Camp Dewey, near Manila. The Brigadier-General commanding desires to thank the troops engaged last night for gallantry and skill displayed by them in repelling such a vigorous attack by largely superior forces of Spaniards. Not an inch of ground was yielded by the Tenth Pennsylvania Infantry and Utah Artillery stationed in the trenches. A battalion of the Third Artillery and First Regiment California Infantry moved forward to their support through a galling fire with the utmost intrepidity. The courage and steadiness shown by all in their first engagement is worthy of the highest commendation."

THE DOWNFALL OF MANILA.

Manila fell before American arms on August 13th. The combined land and naval forces took the city with little or no opposition. The official story of its downfall is told in the following dispatch sent by General Merritt to the War Department:

" Manila, August 13th.—On the 7th instant Admiral Dewey joined me in forty-eight-hour notification to Spanish commander to remove non-combatants from city. Same date reply received, expressing thanks for humane sentiments, and stating Spanish without places for refuge for non-combatants now within walled towns.

" On 9th instant sent joint note, inviting attention to suffering in store for sick and non-combatants in case it became our duty to reduce the defences, also setting forth hopeless condition of Spanish forces, surrounded on all sides, fleet in front, no prospect of reinforcements, and demanded surrender as due to every consideration of humanity. Same date received reply, admitting their situation, but stating Council of Defence declares request for surrender cannot be granted, but offered to consult government, if time was granted necessary for communication via Hong Kong. Joint note in reply declining.

" On the 13th joined with navy in attack with following results : After about half hour's accurate shelling of Spanish lines. McArthur's

Brigade on right and Greene's on left center under Anderson made vigorous attack and carried Spanish works. Loss not accurately known—about 50 in all. Behavior of troops excellent ; co-operation of the navy most valuable. Troops advanced rapidly on walled city, upon which white flag shown and town capitulated. Troops occupy Malate, Bynondo, walled city San Miguel. All important centers protected. Insurgents kept out. No disorder or pillage."   •

The fleet under Admiral Dewey opened the engagement at ⸴.30 o'clock in the morning. A sudden cloud of smoke, green and white, against the stormy sky completely hid the *Olympia*, and a shell screamed across two miles of turbulent water, and burst near the Spanish fort at Malate. Then the *Petrel* and *Raleigh* and the active little *Callao* opened a rapid fire directed toward the shore end of the intrenchments. The Spaniards replied feebly.

Less than half an hour after the bombardment began, General Greene reported that it was possible to advance. Thereupon six companies of the Colorado regiment leaped over their breastwork, dashed into the swamp and opened volleys within 300 yards of the Spanish lines. The land forces under General Anderson advanced from the South, General Greene in command of the First Brigade held the left wing, General McArthur of the Second Brigade was on the right of the line and covered two miles.

The Spanish made a hard fight against the right and left wings, but after a while were forced to retreat inside the Malate fort, from which they were driven by the fire from the ships. The American troops speedily captured the fort. Our land forces followed closely upon the retreating Spaniards. The Second Battalion of the First California headed the advance on the city. A company of the First Nebraska did effective work with Gatling guns.

TOOK A BLOCKHOUSE AT PISTOL'S POINT.

The Astor Battery gave a splendid example of daring in this assault. At the call of General McArthur, Captain Peyton C. March volunteered to dislodge some Spanish soldiers occupying a blockhouse which controlled the roads at Passay. Fifteen or more of his men accompanied him, armed only with pistols, in the rush up the hill in the face of deadly Spanish fire. Of these fifteen but three.

including Captain March, remained when the Spaniards fled from the blockhouse. All the others had been either killed or wounded in the charge. It was a costly and magnificent show of bravery, but it served the purpose, and practically ended the fighting for the day.

General Greene, in his report of the battle, says :

"Captain Grove and Lieutenant Means, of the First Colorado, had been particularly active in this work and fearless in penetrating beyond our lines and close to those of the enemy. As the time for attack approached, these officers made a careful examination of the ground between our trenches and Fort San Antonio de Abad, and, finally, on August 11th, Major J. F. Bell, United States Volunteer Engineers, tested the creek in front of this fort and ascertained not only that it was fordable, but the exact width of the ford at the beach, and actually swam in the bay to a point from which he could examine the Spanish line from the rear. With the information thus obtained it was possible to plan the attack intelligently. The position assigned to my brigade extended from the beach to the small rice swamp, a front of about 700 yards.

"After the sharp skirmish on the second line of defence of the Spaniards, and after Greene's brigade moved through Malate, meeting a shuffling foe, the open space at the Luneta, just south of the walled city, was reached about 1 P.M. A white flag was flying at the southwest bastion, and I rode forward to meet it under a heavy fire from out right and rear on the Paco Road.

KEPT THE INSURGENTS OUT.

"At the bastion I was informed that officers representing General Merritt and Admiral Dewey were on their way ashore to receive the surrender, and I therefore turned back to the Paco Road. The firing ceased at this time, and on reaching this road I found nearly 1,000 Spanish troops who had retreated from Santa Ana through Paco, and coming up the Paco Road had been firing on our flank. I held the commanding officers, but ordered these troops to march into the walled city. At this point the California regiment a short time before had met some insurgents who had fired at the Spaniards on the walls, and the latter in returning the fire had caused a loss in the California regiment of 1 killed and 2 wounded.

"My instructions were to march past the walled city on its sur-render, cross the bridge, occupy the city on the north side of the Pasig, and protect lives and property there. While the white flag was flying on the walls yet, very sharp firing had just taken place out-side, and there were from 5,000 to 6,000 men on the walls, with arms in their hands, only a few yards from us. I did not feel justified in leaving this force in my rear until the surrender was clearly estab-lished. and I therefore halted and assembled my force, prepared to force the gates if there was any more firing. The Eighteenth Infan-try and First California were sent forward to hold the bridges, a few yards ahead, but the Second Battalion, Third Artillery, First Ne-braska, Tenth Pennsylvania and First Colorado were all assembled at this point. While this was being done, I received a note from Lieu-tenant-Colonel Whittier, of General Merritt's staff, written from the Captain-General's office within the walls, asking me to stop the firing outside, as negotiations for surrender were in progress.

"I then returned to the troops outside the walls and sent Cap-tain Birkhimer's battalion of the Third Artillery down the Paco road to prevent any insurgents from entering. Feeling satisfied that there would be no attack from the Spanish troops lining the walls, I put the regiments in motion toward the bridges, brushing aside a consid-erable force of insurgents who had penetrated the city from the direc-tion of Paco, and were in the main street with their flag, expecting to march into the walled city and plant it on the walls. After crossing the bridges the Eighteenth United States Infantry was posted to patrol the principal streets near the bridge, the First California was sent up the Pasig to occupy Quiapo, San Miguel and Malacanan, and with the First Nebraska I marched down the river to the captain of the Port's office, where I ordered the Spanish flag hauled down and the American flag raised in its place.

"The resistance encountered on the 13th was much less than anticipated and planned for, but had the resistance been greater, the result would have been the same, only the loss would have been greater. Fortunately, the great result of capturing this city, the seat of Spanish power in the East for more than three hundred years, was accomplished with a loss of life comparatively insignificant."

General McArthur is strong in his expression of approval of heroic work. In his report he says:

"The combat of Singalong can hardly be classified as a great military event, but the involved terrene and the prolonged resistance created a very trying situation, and afforded an unusual scope for the display of military qualities by a large number of individuals.

"The invincible composure of Colonel Ovenshine, during an exposure in dangerous space for more than an hour, was conspicuous and very inspiring to the troops; and the efficient manner in which he took advantage of opportunities as they arose during the varying aspects of the fight was of great practical value in determining the result.

"The cool, determined and sustained efforts of Colonel Reeve, of the Thirteenth Minnesota, contributed very materially to the maintenance of the discipline and marked efficiency of his regiment.

"The brilliant manner in which Lieutenant March accepted and discharged the responsible and dangerous duties of the day, and the pertinacity with which, assisted by his officers and men, he carried his guns over all obstacles to the very front of the firing line, was an exceptional display of warlike skill and judgment, indicating the existence of many of the best qualifications for high command in battle.

"The gallant manner in which Captain Sawtelle, brigade quartermaster, volunteered to join the advance party in the rush, volunteered to command a firing line, for a time without an officer, and again volunteered to lead a scout to ascertain the presence or absence of the enemy in the blockhouse, was a fine display of personal intrepidity.

"The efficient, fearless, and intelligent manner in which Lieutenant Kernan, Twenty-first United States Infantry, Acting Assistant Adjutant-General of the brigade and Second Lieutenant Whitworth, Eighteenth United States Infantry, aid, executed a series of dangerous and difficult orders, was a fine exemplification of stall work under fire.

"The splendid bravery of Captains Bjornstad and Seebach, and Lieutenant Lackore, of the Thirteenth Minnesota, all wounded, and, finally, the work of the soldiers of the first firing line, too, all went to make up a rapid succession of individual actions of unusual merit."

THE SPANIARDS HOIST THE WHITE FLAG.

At 11.30 A.M. the Spaniards hoisted the white flag. A conference to arrange the terms of surrender was held at the palace of the Governor-General at 4 P.M. General Jandenes agreed to surrender and the American flag was raised at 5.30 P.M. by Lieutenant Brumby, of the *Olympia*. The total number of Spanish soldiers who surrendered exceeded 8,000, and there was an unlimited supply of arms and ammunition. In the attack 5 were killed and 43 injured.

The terms of capitulation, as given in General Merritt's report, were as follows :

"The undersigned having been appointed a commission to deter-mine the details of the capitulation of the city and defences of Manila and its suburbs and the Spanish forces stationed therein, in accordance with the agreement entered into the previous day by General Wesley Merritt, United States Army, American Commander-in-Chief in the Philippines, and His Excellency Don Fermin Jandenes, acting General-in-Chief of the Spanish Army in the Philippines, have agreed upon the following :

"1. The Spanish troops, European and native, capitulate with the city and its defences, with all the honors of war, depositing their arms in the places designed by the authorities of the United States, and remaining in the quarters designated and under the orders of their officers, and subject to the control of the aforesaid United States authorities, until the conclusion of a treaty of peace between the two belligerent nations. All persons included in the capitulation remain at liberty, the officers remaining in their respective homes, which shall be respected as long as they observe the regulations prescribed for their government and the laws in force.

"2. Officers shall retain their side arms, horses and private property. All public horses and public property of all kinds shall be turned over to staff officers designated by the United States.

"3. Complete returns in duplicate of men by organization, and full lists of public property and stores shall be rendered to the United States within ten days from this date.

"4. All questions relating to the repatriation of officers and men of the Spanish forces and of their families, and of the expenses which said repatriation may occasion, shall be referred to the Government of the United States at Washington.

"Spanish families may leave Manila at any time convenient to them.

"The return of the arms surrendered by the Spanish forces shall take place when they evacuate the city, or when the American army evacuates.

"5. Officers and men included in the capitulation shall be supplied by the United States, according to their rank, with rations and necessary aid as though they were prisoners of war, until the conclusion of a treaty of peace between the United States and Spain. All the funds in the Spanish treasury and all other public funds shall be turned over to the authorities of the United States.

"6. This city, its inhabitants, its churches and religious worship, its educational establishments, and its private property of all descriptions are placed under the special safeguard of the faith and honor of the American Army.

<table>
<tr><td>F. V. GREENE,
Brigadier-General of Volunteers, U. S. A.</td><td>NICHOLAS DE LA PETRA,
Auditor-General Excmo.</td></tr>
<tr><td>B. P. LAMBERTON,
Captain, United States Navy.</td><td>CARLOS,
Coronel de Ingenieros.</td></tr>
<tr><td>CHARLES A. WHITTIER,
Lieut.-Colonel and Inspector-General.</td><td>JOSE,
Coronel de Estado Major."</td></tr>
<tr><td>E. H. CROWDER,
Lieut.-Colonel and Judge-Advocate.</td><td></td></tr>
</table>

PEACE.

While the battle was planned, overtures had been made through the mediation of the French Ambassador at Washington, on behalf of the Spanish Government for a cessation of hostilities, to culminate in a treaty of peace. The peace protocol was signed at 4.23 P.M. on Friday, August 12th. The sixth article of the protocol was as follows: "On the signing of the protocol hostilities will be suspended, and notice to that effect will be given as soon as possible by each government to the commander of its military and naval forces."

As the Manila cable had been cut and was not in use, it was impossible to communicate the news of peace to Admiral Dewey or General Merritt. Consequently they were ignorant of the fact that peace had been declared when they assailed and took Manila. Allowing for difference in time, the surrender of Manila took place a few hours after the signing of the peace protocol. This proved the turning point of most of the arguments which took place later, when the Peace Commissioners met together at Paris to discuss the conditions of the treaty.

In the meantime, however, General Merritt ruled supreme in the captured city, keeping out insurgents and protecting people and property.

CHAPTER XIV

The Trouble With Aguinaldo

Face-to-Face View of the Insurgent Leader.—A Man of Craft and Cunning.—Sold out His Own People.—Fought against Uncle Sam.—Insurgents Swept into the Sea.—Immense Sacrifice of Life and Property.—The Flight of Agoncillo to Canada.—The Oregon Sent for by Dewey "for Political Reasons."—Germany Takes a Friendly Step.—Emperor William Removes All His Warships from Manila Bay, and Places German Interests in American Hands.

THE fighting in the Philippines did not end with the downfall of Manila or the signing of the Peace treaty. The insurgents had to be reckoned with. From the beginning they proved even harder to handle than the Spanish. Inflated with victory, General Aguinaldo, the insurgent leader, proclaimed himself Dictator of the islands, and it was with difficulty that his followers were held in check by the American forces without open hostility. It became evident that we should have trouble with the insurgents. That it would be as serious as after-events proved, was not imagined.

On June 13th Aguinaldo issued a "declaration of independence," of which the following is a rough translation:

"To the district headmen and village headmen of the province of Bulacan. from the Political Military Governor of this province, whose headquarters are now transferred to the town of San Francisco de Malabon, and combined with the section under his orders at Bacoor, Binacayan, Imus, Novaleta, Salinas and Cavite Viejo. They only require to be combined with the other forces in Indiang and Silang, near by, and then our troops will be sent forward, and within a few days will be found in possession of almost the whole province, which, being maritime, will be found in a position to proclaim effectively our independence. This proclamation will not be long deferred, because the ultimate object of this government will thus be best attained notwithstanding the suggestions of some of our principal associates. It is better and more convenient to select as the place on account of its being near the sea, the township of Cavite Viejo, which is an old port, originally the town of Cavite.

"Wherefore I decree as follows :

"The 12th day of this month is fixed for the declaration of the independence of this our beloved country, in this township of Cavite Viejo, for the due and proper solemnization of which auspicious event there should be on the day named an assemblage of all district headmen and commanders of our forces, and through the proper representatives there should be a notification issued for the purpose of inviting the attendance of all who have in any way assisted in the good work, such, for example, as the distinguished Admiral of the American squadron and his commanders and officers, to all of whom, as having lent invaluable aid in the glorious work, a courteous invitation will be sent. After the formal reading of the declaration, the same will be signed by all who wish to give support thereto.

"Given under our hand and seal at Cavite this 9th day of June, 1898.   EMILIO AGUINALDO,
                                   Dictator of the Philippines."

Various congresses were convened within the succeeding months, and Aguinaldo thought it wiser to change his title from that of Dictator to President of the Revolutionary Government of the Filipinos. He experienced some trouble in securing a suitable cabinet, and the list was changed several times. The following is the latest make-up of the Cabinet : President of the Cabinet and Minister of Foreign Affairs, Mabini ; Minister of the Interior, Teodoro Sandica, civil engineer, educated in England and Belgium, and taken to Manila from Hong Kong by Admiral Dewey ; Minister of War, General Baldomero Aguinaldo, a cousin of Aguinaldo, the President of the so-called Filipino Government, and a leader of the insurrection from the beginning, said to be a large landowner of Cavite ; Minister of Finance, General Trias, a close ally of Aguinaldo ; Minister of Public Works, Gregorio Gonzaga, a lawyer, formerly the Filipino Agent at Hong Kong, and formerly Spanish Attorney-General in Visayas.

The following description of Aguinaldo by Joseph L. Stickney. who was with Admiral Dewey during the battle of May 1st and

landed later, gives a good view of the insurgent leader and his character.   He says:

"Having been on terms of friendly association with General
Aguinaldo and his staff during the last half of May and the whole
of June, I had an opportunity to get some idea of the man who is
to-day one of the most important individual factors in our dealings
with the Filipinos.

"Emilio Aguinaldo, now about 29 years old, is a man of an
intelligence far beyond that of most of his people.   He comes of a
good family in the province of Cavite, near Manila, where he was
educated and where he entered the bar.   He joined the insurgents
immediately after the outbreak of the rebellion in the latter part of
1896, but it was not until after the execution of Dr. Rizal that he
became one of the leaders of the revolt.

"The blockade maintained by the Spanish squadron in Philippine waters against the importation of arms for the insurgents gradually drove the Filipinos to the wall, and in December, 1897, the
celebrated 'pacification' of the islands was negotiated, the go-between
being Senor Pedro Paterno, director of the Manila museum, a Filipino, who had remained at least passively loyal to the Spaniards.
The Filipino junta at this time was composed of Emilio Aguinaldo,
who exercised such executive powers as were possible to so feeble an
organization; Senor Artacho, Home Secretary; Senor Montenogro,
Foreign Secretary; Vito Bilarmino, War Secretary; and Baldomero
Aguinaldo, Secretary of the Treasury.

"The so-called 'pacification' consisted in a purchase of the
insurgent leaders for the sum of $800,000 (Mexican), equal to about
$400,000 in gold.   Aguinaldo and his associates agreed to surrender
all the arms in the possession of the natives and to quit the archipelago, remaining away at the pleasure of the Spanish government,
and to use their utmost influence to disband and disarm all the insurgent forces.

"Aguinaldo was to go to Hong Kong to receive the first install-
ment of the Spanish money, amounting to $400,000 (Mexican), and
he was then to cable to Artacho, who surrendered himself to the
Captain-General as a hostage.   On receiving Aguinaldo's cable message that the money had been paid, Artacho was to dissolve the

insurgent organization, disband the troops and give up their arms. This part of the programme was carried out in December, 1897, or the early part of January, 1898.

"The cash payment was divided among the junta and Aguinaldo started for Paris. He had gone no farther than Singapore, however, when the destruction of the *Maine* in Havana harbor brought on an acute tension of the relations between the United States and Spain and he remained in Singapore to see whether the Filipinos might not profit by Spain's difficulties.

"General Aguinaldo sailed from Hong Kong for Manila Bay in the dispatch boat *McCulloch*, May 17, 1898. He landed in Cavite on the 19th. As I accompanied him from Hong Kong, and was able to be of some service to him, I was received at his headquarters with great cordiality until after the arrival of the first detachment of troops. About that time Aguinaldo began to think he was a great man, and as he was tiresome and often ridiculous when trying to live up to his own estimate of himself, I saw less and less of him.

"He took possession of one of the numerous abandoned houses in Cavite, and at first he acted with good judgment and simplicity. In a day or two the natives flocked into Cavite in droves, and as a small steamer arrived from Hong Kong, laden with arms and ammunition, in a week there were more than 1,000 men ready to take the field against the Spaniards in Cavite Province.

"On the night of May 26th Aguinaldo sent 600 men across the Bay of Bacoor in canoes. This force was attacked by 300 Spaniards on the morning of the 28th, and all the latter were captured. Sharp and continuous fighting occurred for a week, during which—after having succeeded in witnessing the fighting for two days without Aguinaldo's consent or assistance—I obtained from him a guide and a passport which enabled me to go into battle with more comfort and less risk.

"When Manila was fairly invested by the insurgents, Aguinaldo's ideas of his own importance and power underwent a very apparent expansion. He had been obliged to quit Cavite, as our troops needed the town; but he moved his headquarters to Bacoor, and there he was as inaccessible to ordinary mortals as if he had been the Emperor of China.

"Anyone who expects Aguinaldo to make gross blunders in dealing with our people will probably be disappointed. He is an exceptionally shrewd man. He is of the distinctly Japanese type in appearance, having the broad, square forehead, which betokens intellect, re-enforced by the bumps in the back of his head, which indicate the endurance and persistence of a strong animalism.

"He has rather large eyes, set wide apart, and a straight but sensual nose. His lips are full, and his chin round and not determined. His height is about 5 feet 4 inches, and he carries himself very erect. His color is a light chocolate. He speaks and writes Spanish and Tagalog, the native language of the island of Luzon. He understands English fairly well, though he always made a pretense of not being able to speak or comprehend it. I had reason for believing that he could have held all his conversation with us in English without an interpreter if he had wished to do so."

BELIEVED TO BEAR A CHARMED LIFE.

One of Aguinaldo's great holds over the insurgents was through their superstition. They believed that he bore a charmed life. The Spaniards had often placed large sums on his head, at one time $25,000 having been offered for him dead or alive. He managed, however, to escape both capture from the Spanish and treachery from his own men. At one time some of the insurgents, who were envious of his power, poisoned the food which was to have been given him at dinner. In some lucky way, however, Aguinaldo happened not to taste the meal, and he escaped what would have otherwise been certain death.

The following interesting account of a visit to Aguinaldo's headquarters at Cavite, once the home of a rich native, is given: "The house is broad, low, roomy, and typically Spanish. There is a paved court at the street entrance, and, while Aguinaldo occupied it, a guard of insurgents lined it on either side. They would come to present arms as you passed by, and good form called for a salute in return. A stairway leads from the court, and the landing at the top is large, and makes a good ante-chamber.

Here stand guards in uniforms of blue. There is little delay, and the summons to enter the reception-room comes quickly. Aguinaldo comes in, extends his hand, and then motions the visitor to a seat. He wears a spotless suit of white linen, a white shirt with well-polished front, a high collar and a black cravat tied in a bow, and red velvet slippers embroidered in gold. At first sight you would take him for a Japanese student. It takes a long stretch of the imagination to believe that this youthful-looking man in white is a leader of a large force of warlike people.

In his office he has a modern desk, backed with a beveled edge mirror that came from Europe, a couple of large, strong iron boxes, an abundance of easy chairs, an old grand piano, and a large hat-rack of fanciful design. The only signs of war were the ends of sword chains that peeped through holes in the coats of the officers who were with him.

Such was the man with whom the American commanders had to deal,—a man who sold out his own countrymen, and, because the full price of their slavery had not been paid to him, he returned from his voluntary exile and again placed himself at the head of the people he had betrayed. There is little wonder that the American commanders viewed him with suspicion and checked his onward march.

While the peace conference was being held at Paris to discuss the terms of a treaty, General Merritt was present to consult with the American members of the commission on the subject of the situation in the Philippines. General Otis was ordered to replace him in control of the island. The situation which confronted General Otis was not a pleasant one, but no serious outbreak occurred for some time.

Toward the end of December, however, Aguinaldo assumed an attitude of open defiance against American arms. He ensconsced himself at Malloas, about twenty miles from Manila, and made that the seat of the so-called Revolutionary Government. He began to run things in a high-handed manner, and became even more despotic and overbearing toward his own people than the Spaniards ever were. In the interior cities, controlled by the insurgents, he levied taxes upon the natives much more excessive than any exacted by the old rulers of the islands.

It became evident to General Otis that something had to be done. The insurgents were inflamed by reports sent to them from the United States by Agoncillo, who had been sent to this country by the Junta of the Filipinos to keep an eye on the legislation here. The behavior of this envoy of the Philippine insurgents was such that it was deemed wise to place secret service agents on his track. It was found that he and other Filipinos in this country were plotting against our Government, consequently the watch kept upon him was made so keen that Agoncillo fled for Canada, fearing arrest.

THE ATTACK OF THE INSURGENTS.

About the same time that he fled, the news was cabled across the sea that the Filipinos had attacked Manila, and that on the 5th of February a desperate battle had been waged, in which the insurgents were utterly routed and lost nearly 2,000 men.

The story of the battle, as briefly told in the official cablegram of General Otis, is as follows :—" Adjutant-General : Insurgents in large force opened attack on our outer lines at 8.45 last evening ; renewed attack several times during night ; at 4 o'clock this morning entire line engaged ; all attacks repulsed ; at daybreak advanced against insurgents, and have driven them beyond the lines they formerly occupied, capturing several villages and their defence works ; insurgents' loss in dead and wounded large ; our own casualties thus far estimated at 175 ; very few fatal. Troops enthusiastic and acting fearlessly. Very splendid execution on flanks of enemy ; city held in check, and absolute quiet prevails ; insurgents have secured a good many Mauser rifles, a few field pieces, and quick-firing guns, with ammunition, during last month."

In another dispatch General Otis states that our casualities aggregate 250. He buried 500 of insurgent dead and held 500 prisoners. Their total loss was 4,000.

The fighting was not the result of the aggression on the part of the Americans, but was precipitated by the action of two native soldiers who refused to obey the order of a sentry who challenged them as they attempted to pass his post. These two natives advanced to the outpost of the First Nebraska Regiment, stationed to the northeast of Manila. The sentry ordered them to halt, but they insolently refused to do so. He called upon them again, and as they paid no attention to his order, he leveled his rifle and fired upon them.

No sooner had the shot been fired than the Filipinos, who were occupying block-house No. 7, fired a signal for a general attack upon the Americans. Immediately the insurgents moved against the American troops, the Nebraska Regiment being the first to meet the attack. It was evident that the insurgents expected to take our troops by surprise, consequently they were not prepared for the vigorous reception which they received. The Nebraska, Montana, and North Dakota outposts replied briskly until reinforcements arrived. The Filipinos concentrated at three points, Caloocan, Gagalangin, and Santa Mesa. At about 1 o'clock the insurgents opened fire simultaneously from all three places, supplementing the attack by the fire of two seige guns at Balik-Balik, and advancing their skirmishes at Paco. The Utah Light Artillery and the Third Artillery did splendid work. The engagement lasted over an hour. The United States cruiser *Charleston* and the gunboat *Concord*, stationed off Malabon, opened fire, and did great damage to the insurgents.

At 2.45 A.M. there was a fusilade along the entire line, and the monitor *Monadnock* opened fire from off Malate. With daylight the Americans advanced. The California and Washington regiments made a splendid charge and drove the Filipinos from the villages of Paco and Santa Mesa. The Nebraska regiment also distinguished itself, capturing a very strong position at the reservoir, which is connected with the waterworks. The Kansas and Dakota regiments compelled the enemy's right flank to retire to Caloocan.

FILIPINOS DROWNED LIKE RATS.

The brigade under General King charged upon a strong force of the enemy, and, yelling wildly, drove them helter-skelter into the Pasig River, where, in a frenzy of terror, they were drowned like rats.

The utter fearlessness of the American soldiers was never better demonstrated than in this onward charge. The Ygorates, armed with bows and arrows, made a very determined stand, in the face of the fire of artillery, and left many dead upon the field. Evidently they did not know what guns were, for they stood in the face of the fire without realizing that they were at a disadvantage, and were mowed down like wheat. One of the chiefs, who was captured, said he had never seen a modern field piece before.

The next day General Hale's brigade advanced and took the waterworks outside of the city. They had a sharp skirmish with the enemy, which made no determined stand. The pumps were damaged, but the missing parts were found later, and the works were soon placed in good order.

The terrible loss of the rebels may be gained from the fact that one hundred and sixty of them were buried in one field on one day, and eighty-seven in another. The Americans worked hard to bring hundreds of the suffering insurgents to the hospital for treatment. The character of the insurgents may be judged from the fact that they used the flag of truce as a defence for their own fire. All through Manila white flags were shown from the houses of the natives, and, as the soldiers passed by, they were shot at from these very windows.

A Filipino Colonel went out from his line under a flag of truce. Several American officers promptly went to meet him, but when the parties met the concealed insurgents opened fire, whereupon the Colonel apologized for the barbarous conduct of his troops and returned to his lines.

On February 10th an advance was made upon Caloocan, the stronghold of the insurgents. It was taken after some brisk fighting, and with slight loss on our part; but General Otis was not satisfied. He pushed on to Malabon, to which the insurgents had retreated, and soon was in possession of the town. Before leaving, however, Aguinaldo's savage hordes set fire to the town, and much damage was done to property.

The trouble was not confined to the Island of Luzon. Brigadier General M. D. Miller sent an ultimatum on February 10th to the commander of the rebels at Iloilo, notifying him that it was his intention to take the town by force, if necessary.

WARNING NON-COMBATANTS TO LEAVE.

The warships began to shell the town at eight o'clock the next morning, and soon cleared the trenches of the insurgent force. A detachment from the cruiser *Boston* and the *Petrel* were landed and marched into the town, hoisting the Stars and Stripes over the fort. Not a single man on the American side was injured.

After the taking of Caloocan, General Otis pressed the advantage, and Haytay and Canita were taken by the American advance guard without a shot having been fired. While this was going on, the insurgents inside of Manila made determined efforts to burn down the city. Buildings were fired in three different sections at the same time, and the flames were controlled by the troops only after severe labor. A considerable number of the incendiaries were shot, and a few of our soldiers were wounded. The fire was most successful at Tongo, the northernmost suburb of the city, which lies on the shore of the bay. The rebels in hiding were very active while the Americans were fighting the fire and caused a great deal of annoyance. For a time business was suspended in this district, and many suspects were placed under arrest. The *Monadnock*, of Dewey's fleet, joined in the work of dispersing the Filipinos, effectively shelling the rebel lines under the direction of the signal corps on shore. In the skirmish a surprising discovery was made, that many of the insurgents were armed with dummy rifles, there being about three of these to one of the Mausers, which explained in part the secret of the apparently good equipment of the Filipinos.

While the skirmishing was going on, Admiral Dewey telegraphed the Naval Department as follows :

" MANILA, February 24th.

For political reasons, the *Oregon* should be sent here at once.

DEWEY."

This dispatch was made public by an accident. Secretary Long inadvertently handed it with a number of others to some newspaper men, and for a time the department was kept busy, trying to explain exactly what Dewey meant. The general opinion was that the Admiral wanted the famous vessel, not for any effect on the insurgents, but as a notice to foreigners to keep hands off. The *Oregon* was promptly dispatched to Manila. Not long after this the German war vessels at Manila were withdrawn, and the interests of German residents were placed in the hands of the American officials there. Admiral von Diederichs, who had proved so offensive to Dewey, was withdrawn by his Government, and in his place Prince Henry of Germany was sent to take charge of the German squadron which had been sent to Hong Kong. It was stated at the time of the change

that Admiral von Diederichs had shown a lack of tact in the management of affairs at Manila Bay, and consequently the trouble which
had hampered Dewey at first disappeared, and the Germans apparently assumed a friendly attitude toward our Government.

CEBU IS TAKEN.

The United States gunboat *Petrel*, commanded by C. Cornwell,
visited Cebu, the most important of the Visayas group, on February
22d. The Commander sent an ultimatum ashore declaring the intention of the Americans to take possession peaceably, if possible, by
force if necessary. The rebels immediately vacated, taking their
guns to the hills. A party of marines was landed, and the American
flag soon floated over the Government building there.

For some time the fighting was confined to the region around
Caloocan, and this was not aggressive, but defensive. The insurgents,
kept up a guerilla warfare at night, which proved rather troublesome,
but, as usual, not serious. On March 3d General Otis stated that he
had captured 1,500 insurgents since February 4th.

March 3d was a red-letter day among both the army and navy
people in the island. President McKinley sent to the Senate the
name of George Dewey to be an Admiral of the Navy under the act
approved the day before, and Brigadier-General Elwell S. Otis,
United States Army, to be Major-General by brevet to rank from
February 4th, and the Senate confirmed both nominations. Secretary Long and Secretary Alger cabled congratulations for themselves
and for the President, and the news was received with great enthusiasm everywhere in the Philippines where American soldiers or sailors were stationed. Admiral Dewey raised his four-starred flag on
the *Olympia*, and was saluted by the guns of the forts, the foreign
warships, the British cruiser *Narcissus* and the German cruiser *Kai-
serin Augusta*, and all the American ships in port.

On March 4th the United States cruiser *Baltimore* arrived at
Manila from Hong Kong, having on board Professor J. G. Shurman
and Professor Dean C. Worcester, the two of the civil members of
the United States Philippine Commission. The transport *Senator*
arrived on the same day with six companies of the Twenty-second
Infantry as reinforcements to Otis' command. Reinforcements, aggre-

gating 4,800 men, were hurried forward as fast as possible, bringing
the total number of officers and men up to 41,800. The force then
there consisted of twenty regiments of infantry, one engineer battalion, seven troops of cavalry and eleven batteries of artillery. Nineteen vessels with an aggregate of 297 officers, 2,990 men and 253
marines made up the naval contingent, which did not include the
transport *Solace* with 162 officers and men which was constantly passing back and forth from Manila.

On March 10th the United States transport *Grant* arrived, having
on board Major-General Henry W. Lawton, who had so distinguished
himself in Cuba and was an old Indian fighter, together with the
Fourth United States Infantry and a battalion of the Seventeenth
United States Infantry.

WHEATON'S FLYING COLUMN.

General Wheaton was put in charge of a new divisional brigade
and advanced on March 13th from San Pedro Macati for the purpose
of corralling the enemy. He moved on Pasig, meeting with slight
resistance, as the enemy was in full retreat. His Flying Column sought
to cut off communication between the south and north insurgents'
armies. Guadalupe and the city of Pasig were quickly captured.
The enemy fought furiously under a heavy fire and were caught in a
trap with the Flying Column on one side and the Pasig River on the
other. They made a stand for an hour and were finally forced into
the jungle in full retreat.

The American advance began at daybreak, the cavalry leading at
a sharp trot. A dash across the open brought the column to a clump
of timber commanding the rear of Guadalupe. The advance, supported by the Oregon troops, opened a heavy fire on the insurgents,
and then the column divided, the right swinging towards the town of
Pasig, and the left advancing with a telling fire into the brush where
the insurgents were concealed.

At Guadalupe church a handful of the rebels made a sullen
stand, but finally broke and ran. The rebels who had taken refuge
in the jungle were discovered by river gunboats, which poured a disastrous fire into them. Everywhere the followers of Aguinaldo fled
for safety, and for a time the troops were ordered to cease firing to

get some rest before attacking Pasig itself. When the attack was finally begun, a heavy rain was falling. After a vigorous fight, the Filipinos finding themselves outwitted and defeated fled to the northward, and by 5 o'clock the whole American line bivouaced around the city. The next day the column advanced beyond Pasig to the shore of Laguna Bay, sweeping everything before it. The enemy made a running fight and suffered severe loss. Their avenues of communication north and south were effectively closed.

A BRUSH WITH THE ENEMY.

Between Pateros and Taguig General Wheaton with the Twentieth and Twenty-second Infantry, the Oregon and Washington troops, section six of the Sixth Artillery, and a squad of the Fourth Cavalry came upon the enemy massed in such a force as to cause an unusually heavy fight. The enemy was driven back with great loss.

On March 16th the First Battalion of the Twentieth United States Infantry advanced from Pasig, clearing the country to Caintia, a well-defended village of seven hundred inhabitants. The enemy was dislodged after a half-hour's fighting, during which the American troops advanced in splendid order under heavy fire, charging across the rice fields against overwhelming odds.

General Otis sent the following cablegram on March 15th : "Three thousand insurgents moved down last night to the towns of Pasig and Pateros, on shore of Laguna Bay, fronting Wheaton's troops on Pasig River line ; by heavy fighting Wheaton has dislodged and driven them back, taking 400 prisoners and inflicting heavy loss in killed and wounded ; he reports his loss as very moderate ; he now occupies these towns with sufficient force to hold them."

Our troops found 106 dead Filipinos and 100 new graves near Pasig. The prisoners were unarmed, and, it is presumed, they executed their threat of throwing their arms into the river.

In the meantime a number of the Filipinos had grown tired of the continuous victories of our troops, and some of the prominent leaders among the insurgents advised surrender to the United States and an acceptance of our terms of government. Twelve adherents of the plan of independence were sentenced to death by Aguinaldo, because they wrote, advising surrender, and General Legarda, who

visited Malolos for the purpose of advising Aguinaldo to give up the
unequal struggle, was executed on the spot by orders of the rebel
leader.

ON TOWARD MALOLOS.

It was decided to make a concentrated effort to capture Malolos,
the capital of the insurgent temporary government and the headquarters of the insurgent leader. Here the Filipinos had massed
their forces, and here, too, they had thrown out protection and
trenches, and had prepared themselves for a fierce fight. It was
hoped that, by taking this place, the backbone of the insurgent struggles would be broken. In order to meet the American advance,
Aguinaldo's forces concentrated in large number about Malabon,
which lies to the north of Manila, on the railway and on the shore of
the bay. They had constructed several lines of trenches around
Malabon, and there they awaited the onward movement of our army.

The fighting began when, on March 25th, General MacArthurs'
division, consisting of the brigades of General Harrison Gray Otis,
General Hale and General Hall, supplemented by General Wheaton's
brigade, advanced and captured the towns of Novaliches on the left,
and San Francisco del Monte and Mariquina on the right, clearing
the rebel trenches in front of the line north from the river to Caloocan. They also secured possession of the railroad, practically corner-
ing the flower of Aguinaldo's army at Malabon and in the foothills
of Singalon, twenty miles apart. The plan was to strike north of Polo.

The attack was begun at 6 o'clock in the morning. The Nebraska
and Colorado Volunteer Regiments encountered the first strong resistance. This was at San Francisco del Monte, and in the surrounding trenches. The Cavalry outflanked the enemy, who broke and
ran, but later made a stubborn stand in the woods north of the Laloma
church.

The rebels adopted the American tactics of holding their fire
until the enemy were about 1,000 yards away, and they fired lower
than usual ; but the boys from the United States fired volleys with
terrible effect, and then rushed forward, cheering and sweeping everything before them. The Twentieth Kansas and Tenth Pennsylvania,
with the Montana Volunteers on the left, protected by the Utah Battery, advanced over the open rice fields on the double-quick, yelling

fiercely and occasionally dropping in the grass and firing by volley.
The enemy, strongly entrenched in the woods, kept up a steady fire
until the Americans were in close quarters, and then they broke and
fled. The bodies of 125 of their dead were found in the trenches
and many more in the woods.

Within ninety minutes after the advance was made, the whole
front, for a distance of three miles to the north, had been cleared.
General Hale's brigade had simultaneously swept in a northwesterly
direction, routing the enemy. Our advance was over open ground
for a mile and a half. The Third Artillery, under command of Major
William A. Kobbe, at the apex upon which the line was to turn, got
the hardest fighting and lost nine per cent. of its men.

BRAVERY OF THE KANSAS TROOPS.

As the line swung northwest, and came to the Tuliahan River,
General Wheaton's brigade moved out from Caloocan, where it had
been held in the trenches, and swept the insurgents directly in front,
making the American line stretch along six miles of the south bank
of the river. The bridge at Caloocan had been destroyed, and there
were solid lines of insurgents in trenches across the river. Bullets
were flying all around, but the Third Kansas Artillery boldly waded
across the stream, and fiercely stormed the blockhouse which commanded the approach. They were forced almost to swim owing to
the depth of the water, but, soaking wet, they charged the trenches
and the blockhouse with the wildest cheers, and the Filipinos, who
had never heard of such fighting, fled at their approach. It was a
most inspiring spectacle of heroism to all who saw it,—a spectacle
that shall ever live in history.

In this fight General MacArthur and General Hale, with their
staffs, were frequently under heavy fire. The heat was terrific, and
at times all of the officers, except the two Generals, were forced to
dismount, overcome by the heat. The next day MacArthur dashed
beyond Pôlo and to the northeast, and captured Meycauavan, two
miles from Polo. It is at the base of the rough hills and the jungles,
and the whole way is lined with trenches. The fight here was a brisk
one, and among those who fell was Captain Krayenbuhl, who had
been promoted for individual bravery at the battle of Manila, as

described in another chapter. He was one of the most popular and efficient young men of the campaign, and his death was deplored by everybody who knew him.

General MacArthurs' plan was to cut off the 5,000 insurgents in Malolos from the rest of the insurgents, but he was unable to carry it out, owing to the roughness of the ground and the thickness of the jungle, which prevented him from getting far enough around to the north of Polo to shut the enemy in.

THE TRAGIC DEATH OF COLONEL EGBERT.

In this engagement Wheaton's brigade figured almost exclusively. There were engaged the Fourth, Twenty-second, and Twenty-third Infantry, the Utah Troop, the Third Artillery, and the Oregon troops. These were stretched out along the railroad from Caloocan to the Tuliahan River. The rebels had destroyed the bridge over the river, and on the further side made their stand, while the engineers were trying to replace the floor of the bridge on the iron girders. The Second Oregon Regiment dashed across the river, wading and swimming. The Twenty-second and four companies of the Twenty-third gained the west bank of the river about the same time. From the river the land rose steadily for half a mile to Malinta, which stands at the summit of the hill. The crest was torn up with intrenchments, but the Americans moved steadily forward, yet no reply came from the hidden foe. They waited until our troops were within 300 yards of them, and then the seemingly deserted trenches belched forth a deadly fire.

The Twenty-second, which was in the advance, with gallant Colonel Harry C. Egbert at their head, dashed at the entrenchments. The Oregon and Kansas troops at the right and left were fighting with great gallantry, but they were in the woods, while the men of the Twenty-second were in the open, and as these heroes of Santiago made that magnificent charge up the hill in the face of the deadly fire of the insurgents, Colonel Egbert fell forward in his saddle mortally wounded.

Close behind him struggling through the grass came General Wheaton and his staff. The soldiers bore the litter with the dying Colonel back, and, as they passed the General, he bared his head and

gave a soldier's greeting to the dying officer. " It was done nobly,"
said the General. " I am done for, I am too old," gasped Egbert ;
and his words proved only too true, for the gallant hero of two wars
was dead before they got him to the rear. Thus ended a record of
continuous service as a line officer for nearly forty years.

Colonel Egbert was appointed a first lieutenant in the army from
civil life in 1861. He was taken prisoner at the Battle of Gettysburg,
but escaped and rejoined his command. He was severely wounded
in 1864 in the Battle of Bethesda Church, Va. In the Santiago
campaign he commanded the Sixth Infantry until shot through the
body on July 1, 1898, when he was disabled. For his distinguished
service in this battle he was appointed a Brigadier-General of volunteers, which grade he held until December 1, 1898, when, in the
reduction of volunteers, he was honorably discharged. He had been
promoted Colonel in the regular army on July 1, 1898, and was
assigned to the Twenty-second Infantry, whose Colonel, Charles A.
Wikoff, was killed at San Juan. The Twenty-second sailed for
Manila February 1st, and in this great charge, so similar to that up
the hill at Santiago, it again sacrificed its commanding officer to the
bullets of the foe.

The advance to Malinta was made over the Nivalichaes Rial.
The Filipinos fled along the railroad, burning rice mills, tearing up
the tracks and obstructing everywhere. They took refuge in the
church of Malinta and made a stand there, but the American troops
came on a run and took the place by assault.

MALABON IS TAKEN.

General MacArthur's division pressed on along the torn up railroads toward Malabon, and at his near approach the insurgents set
fire to that place and fled back to Malolos as fast as they could. The
condition of the country was such that rapid progress was not possible, but with every step of the advance the Americans carried
victory with them. Try as they would, the American forces were
unable to carry out their plan of catching Aguinaldo and his whole
army between the two advancing lines. The Filipinos were able to
make more rapid progress than the American troops, owing to their
familiarity with the country.

On March 27th, the American forces advanced from Meycauavan, General Harrison Gray Otis leading his brigade on the left of the railroad track and General Hale's brigade taking the right of the track. The resistance was small until the Americans approached the Marilao River within sight of Marilao itself. Again the Filipinos made a stand on the river bank, and when the Americans came near they delivered an effective fire. The river was too deep to ford, and the infranty consequently could not accomplish much. The fire of the Filipinos was such as to lead to the opinion that they were well trained soldiers, probably members of the Milita which the Spaniards organized. The entrenchments of the Filipinos were a revelation to our troops, and were found to have been designed by capable engineers and constructed with care and thoroughness.

A BOLD CHARGE BY COLONEL FUNSTON.

Behind them the Filipinos did effective work, but when the American field artillery came into action it put a dramatic end to the battle. Approaching under cover of the bushes to a clear space not more than sixty yards from the trenches, the artillerymen dashed into plain view, shouting as though in full charge and prepared to fire. Knowing the effect of our artillery the Filipinos were eager to quit before they received a rain of shell. A hundred or more fled from their trenches, while others remaining displayed a white flag and shouted, "Amigos," (meaning friends). The infantry had been chafing at not getting into action, and Colonel Funston with twenty of his Kansas followers again jumped into the river and swam across to the opposite side. They forthwith made a charge and captured 80 prisoners with all their arms. It was a foolhardy act according to the books, but it made the name of Colonel Funston and his Kansas Regiment famous all over the world. A lot of men from the Tenth Pennsylvania also crossed the river and captured 40 prisoners. Finally the town fell before the Americans. They were now but eight miles away from Malolos, the insurgent capital, and everybody was eager to press on to what they thought would be the final contest of the war. But General MacArthur thought it best to give the men a rest for a little while. Early on the 29th, he advanced rapidly to Bocave, and at 11.45 he advanced toward Bigaa, and at 3.15 in the afternoon he turned toward Guiguinto, 3½ miles from Malolos. There was some fierce fighting in the afternoon. Troops crossed the river at Guiguinto by working artillery over the railroad bridge by hand and swimming mules against fierce resistance.

AGUINALDO IN COMMAND.

During the fight Aguinaldo commanded his troops in person for the first time since the war against our troops began. Prisoners who were captured, say that officers stood behind the Filipino soldiers with whips instead of swords and lashed the men to keep their position. As the enemy fled they tore up the tracks of the railroad, making the progress of our troops very slow.

During the approach to Malolos, General MacArthur and his staff, while walking abreast of the line, came near losing their lives. Everything was quiet when suddenly a shower of bullets came on all sides from sharp shooters in trees and on house tops. These were speedily dislodged. The march towards Malolos was rapidly accomplished.

ENTERING THE INSURGENT CAPITAL.

As the troops neared the outskirts of the city, General Hale's and H. G. Otis' brigades were stretched between the sea and the mountains. The scene was a magnificent one; the splendid line with its waiving colors looked like a rainbow, and as it neared the outskirts of the city a number of Filipinos bearing a flag of truce came out to meet it. At the sight of the white signal of surrender, our troops broke into cheers and song, but when our messengers approached, the bearers of the flag of truce turned and ran back to their capital. An instant pursuit was begun and our troops were received with heavy volleys from the outskirts of the town. On the right the jungle swarmed with little blue figures. It was the rear guard, protecting the retreat of the rebel army and destroying the railroad track as they swept on.

The Americans camped all night outside the city. The Generals held a council of war, for they believed that, on the morrow, they might have to fight 20,000 men. The battle opened at daybreak with the bombardment of the trenches in front, and for half an hour the shells fell in a shower. From the huts natives threw knives at Kansas men, while showers of arrows flew on all sides. The right wing unbroken advanced over fields and through streams, taking the main trenches south of the city. They found them deserted. A few men came out to meet the advancing line and informed the soldiers that the army had gone by railway toward the interior.

The Kansas men led the left, and at the end of the main street of the city they were met by a barricade of stones from which a hot fire was poured by a few insurgents, but Colonel Funston leaping from his horse and swinging his hat led the Kansas men over the barricade and down the street with terrific yells, firing volleys as they ran. But the town was deserted and there the victorious American army rested and feasted, while the American flag flew over the Government building of Aguinaldo's capital. The shattered army had fled for its life into the interior, and Aguinaldo and his cabinet had left two days before, and could not be found.

And for a time, at least, the backbone of the rebellion was broken.

A FEW PROCLAMATIONS BY AGUINALDO.

It was evident, from later information, that Aguinaldo had determined to stake all in an attack upon the American forces. He issued several proclamations defining his position, on February 2d, 3rd and 5th.

The first declares the Americans opened the fight, and calls upon the Filipino Congress to sustain the Constitution. The second says:

"We have fought our ancient oppressors without arms, and we now trust to God to defend us against the foreign invaders."

His proclamation of February 3rd says:

"I order and command:

"First—That peace and friendly relations with the Americans be broken and that the latter be treated as enemies, within the limits prescribed by the laws of the war.

"Second—That the Americans captured be held as prisoners of war.

"Third—That this proclamation be communicated to the Consul, and that Congress order and accord a suspension of the constitutional guarantee, resulting from the declaration of war."

Aguinaldo's proclamation of February 5th says the outbreak of nostilities was "unjustly and unexpectedly provoked by the Americans," and refers to his manifesto of January 8th, publishing the alleged grievances of the Filipinos at the hands of the army of occupation, and the "constant outrages and taunts which have been causing misery to the Manilians," and refers to the "useless conference" and "contempt shown for the Filipino Government" as proving a "premeditated transgression of justice and liberty."

The rebel leader also refers to the former losses of the Filipinos, but says "slavery is bitter," and calls upon them to "sacrifice all upon the altar of honor and national integrity."

He insists that he tried to avoid, as far as possible, an armed conflict, but claims that all his efforts were "useless before the unmeasured pride of the American representatives" whom he charges with having treated him as a rebel "because I defended the interests of my country, and would not become the instrument of their dastardly intentions."

Aguinaldo concludes with saying:

"Be not discouraged. Our independence was watered freely by the blood of martyrs, and more will be shed in the future to strengthen it. Remember, that efforts are not to be wasted that ends may be gained. It is indispensable to adjust our actions to the rules of law and right, and to learn to triumph over our enemies."

The attack upon Manila by the insurgents was made at a time when the country was watching expectantly to see what the Senate would do in the ratification of the Peace Treaty, which had been framed in Paris. The day preceding the rebel uprising it looked as though the treaty would not be ratified. The news of the slaughter of our troops reached this country the day before the vote was to be taken in the Senate. Immediately the whole nation was swept with feeling. Everybody deplored the sacrifice of life, and everybody looked to the Senate to see what the effect of the news would be. When a vote was taken the Paris Peace Treaty was ratified by a vote of 57 to 27, amid the greatest excitement.

The Peace Treaty was ratified by Spain, and, on April 11th, the last act in the Spanish-American drama was played. This formal and final scene took place at the White House, and, curiously enough, it

6

happened on the anniversary of the day on which President McKinley, in a Message to Congress, asked for authority to intervene in the Cuban situation.

The final scene was the exchange of the ratifications of the Peace Treaty. The French Ambassador, M. Cambon, handed President McKinley the Spanish copy of the treaty, handsomely engrossed and bound in morocco. The President took from his desk and handed to the Ambassador, who represented the Government of Spain, the American copy of the treaty, also engrossed and bound in dark blue morocco. Each bowed as the exchange took place, and the ceremony so simple, yet so full of meaning, was over.

After the exchange of the ratifications, President McKinley issued his proclamation, which reads :—

"Whereas, A Treaty of Peace between the United States of America and Her Majesty, the Queen Regent of Spain, in the name of her august son, Don Alfonso XIII., was concluded and signed by their respective plenipotentiaries at Paris on the 10th day of December, 1898, the original of which convention being in the English and Spanish languages, is word for word as follows :

(Here the full text of the treaty is given.)

And whereas, The said convention has been duly ratified on both parts, and the ratifications of the two Governments were exchanged in the city of Washington, on the eleventh day of April, one thousand eight hundred and ninety-nine.

"Now, therefore, Be it known that I, William McKinley, President of the United States of America, have caused the said convention to be made public to the end that the same and every article and clause thereof may be observed and fulfilled with good faith by the United States and the citizens thereof.

"In witness whereof, I have hereunto set my hand and caused the seal of the United States to be affixed.

"Done at the city of Washington this eleventh day of April, in the year of our Lord, one thousand eight hundred and ninety-nine, and of the Independence of the United States, the one hundred and twenty-third.   "William McKinley.

[SEAL]   " By the President.

"John Hay, Secretary of State."

The Home Coming of Admiral Dewey

IF any man ever earned a vacation, it was Admiral George Dewey. It has been shown that the winning of the battle of Manila, brilliant and overwhelming as it was, bore no comparison to the tension throughout the weeks and months that succeeded, when patience, fortitude and all the extraordinary resources of the masterful diplomat were keyed to the highest point. Refusing the rest that an appreciative government offered him, the naval hero remained at his post of duty until it may be said his great work was finished, and the continuous strain made it absolutely necessary that he should seek repose for the wearied body and mind.

And so it came about that at four o'clock, on the afternoon of May 20, 1899, the *Olympia* steamed out of Manila Bay, on her long voyage homeward to the other side of the world. The day was an ideal one, with a clear sky, a moderate sun, and enough breeze to give a cool freshness to the wind which sent the little whitecaps chasing one another in a race that never ended. The *Olympia* was still in her blue-gray fighting suit, and before starting lay near the breakwater, with the *Oregon*, in spotless white and buff, but a short distance away. Just in advance lay the *Baltimore* and smaller *Concord*, their color matching the flagship, while over to the westward were the huge army transports *Warren* and *Hancock*, still showing the smoke and grime of their long voyage across the Pacific. The monitor *Monadnock* lay off the Paranaque, alert and watchful, for the Filipinos were still troublesome, and every now and then it was necessary to hurl " hot shot " among their ranks. The *Monterey* was at Cavite, but the *Manila*, one of Dewey's first prizes, steamed up from the lower bay to bid goodbye to the Admiral.

All the formalities of such an important occasion were carried out to the letter. In the morning General Otis visited the *Olympia* and called upon the Admiral, who, a few hours later returned the call, after which a reception was held aboard the ship, which lasted almost until she was ready to sail. Among the callers were many citizens of Manila, officers of the army and every officer who could leave his ship.

As the engines of the *Olympia* began moving, the immense four-starred blue flag, the insignia of Dewey's rank, floated from the main truck. Since flag officers do not fly pennants, a huge new flag flew from the main gaff, forming a picture of beauty as it streamed outward in the breeze. Turning to port, the *Olympia* steamed ahead of the *Oregon* and astern of the *Baltimore* and *Concord*. The first gun of the salute to the departing Admiral came from a 6-pounder on the *Oregon*, speedily followed by the guns of the other ships. The booming was still traveling over the sea when the *Olympia* neared the huge British cruiser *Powerful*, the American band led off with "El Capitan," the march played by our English cousins, when our ships sailed from Mirs Bay on their Philippine campaign, and which was played again by the band of the *Immortalite*, as the *Olympia* went into action on August 13, 1898. Music came from the *Olympia* and her sister ships, but amid the thunderous salutes, it was hard to distinguish all the tunes, though from the quarter deck of the *Baltimore* (which now took her place as flagship) rose the sweet strains of "Home, Sweet Home," and nothing could have been more appropriate or touching.

In passing the *Powerful*, the *Olympia* saluted her with "God Save the Queen," to which the British sailors, lined along the rail two deep, responded with a cheer so tremendous that the Americans almost split their throats in making proper answer. The signal flags continued to wave their goodbyes, untill at last the *Olympia* faded from view in the horizon, on her voyage home, where a nation was waiting to welcome her gallant commander, officers and crew.

The voyage was timed precisely as the Admiral desired. There was no cause for haste and the government desired him to consult no one's wishes and convenience but his own. He, his officers and men

nad been exposed to the fierce heat of the tropics so long that the
cooler breezes and more invigorating climate soon produced the
most beneficial effects. Passing through the Suez Canal and making
a brief halt at Colombo, Ceylon, the *Olympia* arrived at Trieste on
the morning of July 20th. She entered the port with her flags flying,
and exchanged a twenty-one-gun salute with the fort, and, as soon as
her anchor was down, Consul Hossfield boarded the cruiser. Admiral
Dewey was on deck, and advancing cordially shook hands with him.
Later the Port Captain, the Captain of the warship *Amphitrite* and
the Admiralty Captain, in absence of the Austrian Admiral, boarded
the *Olympia* and welcomed the American Admiral.

Amiral Dewey expressed delight with the cool air and beautiful
Bay of Trieste. He said his health was excellent and his strengh
had steadily increased from the time he left Colombo. He explained
the delay in the arrival of the *Olympia* as being due to an accident
to the propeller while she was in the Suez Canal.

The next arrival on the warship to welcome the Admiral was
Minister Harris followed by the local authorities. Among other
visitors were the German, French and British Consuls and the
Captain of the King of Greece's yacht. The affability and modesty
of Admiral Dewey charmed every one. In referring to the naval
engagement off Cavite, he said : "I ordered coffee, but they brought
a tepid beverage, which I drank quickly. Consequently, I was terribly
seasick just before the battle. I was sick during the whole battle."

Minister Harris gave a banquet to the Admiral in the Town
Hall on the evening of July 21st. The hall was brilliantly decorated with
the Stars and Stripes and was fragrant with rare and beautiful flowers.
Among those present, besides Minister Harris and the staff of the
legation, were the American and other Consuls, Mr. Foss, President
of the Maritime Commission at Washington, and the Admiral and
officers of the *Olympia*. Although it was intimated that there would
be no speeches at the banquet which was over at 10 o'clock, several
were made, that of the Admiral being in reply to Mr. Harris. In the
course of his remarks he said that he did not find a more loyal flag
before Manila than that of Austria.

The following morning, Admiral Dewey accompanied by Minster
Harris, visited the Emperor's magnificent castle at Miramar, built by

the unfortunate Ferdinand Maximilian, Emperor Francis Joseph's brother, who, duped and deserted by Emperor Louis Napoleon, was captured and shot in Mexico, after vainly striving to establish a monarchy there.

Everything possible was done to make the stay of the Admiral at Trieste enjoyable. On July 23d, accompanied by the United States Consul Hossfield, he went to Optchina, a favorite excursion place, three miles from the city and 1,150 feet above the sea. On the way thither, they stopped to witness the national game of bowls, called bocce. The Admiral was particularly interested in the local costumes and delighted with the views. He declared the afternoon's enjoyment perfect.

At the banquet given on Saturday evening by the Admiral on board the *Olympia*, there were twenty-two covers. The naval hero drank to the prosperity of his old home and the land of his birth and to the health and prosperity of Minister Harris. He gracefully expressed his appreciation of the generous hospitality extended to him and his officers and men by the city of Trieste.

A letter received from Mayor Van Wyck, of New York City, on the next day, said : "The people of this city, profoundly impressed with your services to their country, and desirous of expressing their appreciation of your victory, have, through the Municipal Assembly, taken action providing for an official reception to you on your return to this country.

"As Mayor, and acting on behalf of the people and their official representatives, I have, therefore, the honor to tender to you, on behalf of the city of New York, a public reception on your arrival, and to extend to you, as the guest of the city, its hospitalities and courtesies."

To which the Admiral replied :

"TRIESTE, July 24, 1899.

"To Mayor Van Wyck, New York :

"Letters received and invitation accepted. Expect to arrive about October 1st. Will cable definitely from Gibraltar. Have written.

"DEWEY."

An interesting account by an eyewitness of the battle of Cavite, in Manila Bay, was published in the *Piccolo*, in which the narrator said the Admiral stood on the bridge of the *Olympia* fearlessly, distributing orders amid a hailstorm of shells and bullets, or stirring his men by word or deed. The Admiral, says the writer, is the same in peace as in war. He sees everything and attends personally to the smallest matters. He is a severe disciplinarian, but his subordinates love him like a father. During the battle two sailors played, "There'll be a Hot Time in the Old Town To-night" on a banjo and fiddle.

Admiral Dewey complimented the Austrian warships at Manila on their strict observance of the laws of neutrality, in which no nation surpassed them, but he said the conduct of the German officers was most displeasing to him. In one instance he was obliged to fire at their flagship because, that vessel disregarded the rules of the blockade. This firing, of course, meant the discharge of a signal gun, but the Admiral added that he had no antipathy to the German nation whatever.

On the afternoon of August 1st Admiral Dewey received farewell visits from a number of officials at a hotel, after which he boarded the *Olympia*, and at four o'clock in the afternoon sailed for Naples.

In a letter written on board the *Olympia*, August 1st, and addressed to the Acting Secretary of the Navy, Allen, the Admiral refers in the following terms to his visit at Trieste :

"Leaving Trieste to-day, I desire to bring to the attention of the Department the uniform courtesy and kindly feeling shown not only to me, but to the ship and its whole personnel as representing our country, by the officials of Trieste and Austria. The Austrian Minister of Marine arrived from Vienna to velcome us officially, and remained several days awaiting us, but was obliged by his duties to return before our arrival. The naval, military and civil officials stationed here have been most cordial.

"The people also have exhibited a most friendly feeling toward our nation, and have visited the ship in large numbers. It is estimated that 40,000 people attended the funeral of Rask, an electrician, who died in the hospital, and they showed many marks of sympathy. Naval Constructor Capps, who visited the dock yards at Pela, was shown every courtesy there and also at the naval and private ship yards of Trieste."

The *Olympia* arrived at Naples on the morning of August 5th, and exchanged salutes with the shore batteries and Italian warships. An immense crowd had assembled and enthusiastically cheered the Admiral as he landed. Many buildings displayed the American colors and no welcome could have been more cordial than that of the Prefect and municipal authorities. The Mayor of the city called on the Admiral the following day, and he returned the visit on the 7th. On the same evening, Vice-Admiral Gonzales gave a banquet in honor of Admiral Dewey. Among those present were Mr. Lewis, M. Iddings, Secretary of the United States Embassy at Rome; M. R. C. Parsons, Second Secretary of the Embassy; Mr. H. de Castro, United States Consul-General at Rome; the officers of the *Olympia* and the Italian authorities. There had been considerable uneasiness in this country lest some slight or indignity should be shown the Admiral when he called at the Italian ports, because of the lynching some time before of a number of Italian miscreants in Louisiana. It was gratifying, therefore, that nothing of the kind occurred, the treatment accorded the naval hero being as courteous and cordial in Italy as it was everywhere else. He declared himself enchanted with Naples, and in the course of an excursion through the city, invited a troupe of wandering musicians on board the *Olympia*, where they gave a performance. When they took their departure, the dusky faces were wreathed in smiles, for the fee received by them was a big one indeed.

Much the same story is to be told of Leghorn, where the *Olympia* arrived at noon on the 13th. Thousands welcomed the Admiral with shouts, and did him every honor in their power. Unfortunately, however, he was feeling far from well, and was so weak from fever that he was obliged to spend the next day on the *Olympia* where the visits of officials and others were received by the captain. The newspapers *Gazetta Livornese* and *Il Telegrafo* made a hit by publishing appreciative biographical sketches of the "Victor of Cavite."

In the course of a few days the Admiral recovered from his illness and on the 18th he received visits from Mr. James A. Smith, the United States Consul and members of the American colony.

Some discussion was caused in this country by a statement in the N. Y. *Herald* to the effect that Admiral Dewey had expressed an opinion that our next war would be with Germány. This statément was authoritatively denied, his assertion being that if such a war ever occurred it vould be begun by the Germans, and not by us. Moreover, he did not believe any such war would ever occur.

On August 22d, the *Olympia* arrived at the French port of Villefranche with the intention of remaining a week. As usual the newspapers tried to draw an expression of views from the Admiral, but he firmly declined saying he had come to rest, not to talk. The next day the Prefect of Nice went aboard the warship and saluted the Admiral in the name of the French government. The band frequently landed and drilled for the purpose of getting into form for the grand parade awaiting them in the metropolis of the new world.

The *Olympia* left Villefranche on the afternoon of August 31st, for Gibraltar. Deputy Mayor Achiardi, accompanied by Attilio, American Vice-Consul at Nice visited Admiral Dewey and explained that the Mayor would have paid his respects, but for his unavoidable detention in Switzerland. Through his deputy he sent salutations from himself and the municipality. The Admiral thanked M. Achiardi for the courtesies shown him, and left his best wishes for the prosperity of Nice. It was remarked by all who saw Admiral Dewey that he looked bronzed, rugged, and in the best of health.

A STRIKINGLY BEAUTIFUL SCENE

The start for Gibraltar was picturesque. About the middle of the afternoon large crowds assembled on the shore to witness the departure of the famous Admiral and his warship. The crew, dressed in spotless white, were busy in hauling the boats and launches and making all the preparations necessary for leaving the port. Soon afterward, Attilio, the American Vice-Consul at Nice, arrived with the latest mails and despatches for the Admiral and boarded his vessel. He stayed only a short time, and a few minutes before four o'clock the *Olympia* weighed anchor and steamed out of the harbor.

The scene was strikingly beautiful. The sun was shining brightly and a brisk breeze was blowing. As the cruiser passed out, the multitude on shore cheered again and again. Very rarely has the warship of any natiop roused the enthusiasm there that was created by the *Olympia*. Admiral Dewey gained much benefit at

13 D.D.

Villefranche from his restful sojourn on shore. The care necessary regarding his health prevented him from accepting any invitations except those of the Vice-Consul to drive and to take dinner with him, but he often expressed his pleasure at again visiting Villefranche and Nice. His frank, open courtesy won the admiration of every one with whom he came in contact.

DEWEY AT GIBRALTAR

The flagship arrived at Gibraltar a few minutes before eight o'clock on the morning of September 4th. When she had come to anchor, Admiral Dewey visited the Governor, and was received by a guard of honor on landing. The Governor returned the visit shortly afterward. As the flagship entered the harbor, she fired a national salute in honor of the British flag, which was responded to by a land battery and the British warship *Devastation*, whose crew manned the rails, while the band played "Hail Columbia." The band of the *Olympia* acknowledged the courtesy by playing "God Save the Queen," and by dipping the American ensign three times as the cruiser anchored.

While the health of the crew was excellent, Admiral Dewey was somewhat indisposed. Upon landing he made his quarters at the Bristol Hotel, and in the afternoon took lunch at the American con-sulate. All the generals and field officers visited him on the same day at the hotel, and were received with the fullest courtesy. Prudence compelled the Admiral to decline a large number of dinner invitations, his preference being to attend few social functions. He declined Admiral Drury's invitation to become a guest at the Admiralty House, but accepted an invitation to dine there on Friday, September 8th. He also attended an afternoon tea at the Governor's cottage, which that official was occupying, while his regular residence was undergoing repairs.

On the 8th of September the Admiral visited the school-ship *Saratoga* and the training-ship *Alliance*. Well aware of the over-whelming ovation awaiting him in America, he wisely husbanded his strength for that event. While the *Olympia* was coaling he remained on shore, and, as a result of his prudence, his health and strength were greatly benefited.

On the morning of the 10th, after a stay of six days at the famous port, the flagship headed westward. She was now on the homestretch of her long voyage from the other side of the world, having started from Manila May 20th, almost four months before. Honors had awaited the gallant hero at every point at which the famous flagship stopped, and she sped homeward amid the best wishes of those she left behind, and the prayers of the millions awaiting the arrival of the great Admiral in his beloved native land.

The expectation was that Admiral Dewey would reach New York, on Thursday the 28th of September. Indeed, he himself did not expect to arrive before that date. The metropolis of the country and indeed the whole Union were busy making their preparations to give him suitable welcome on the day named, when to the astonishment of every one, the *Olympia* steamed up the bay in the gray misty light of the morning of Tuesday the 26th, two days ahead of time.

When the news reached the city, it was turned topsy turvy with excitement. From the moment the *Olympia* came round Sandy Hook, until the sun went down, on the close, rainy "muggy" day, she was not left alone for a single minute. Visitors swarmed over her decks, and little boats circled about her, while the passengers intently studied every point of the wonderful craft that had made such a glorious record on the other side of the world.

It was half-past seven when the *Olympia* dropped anchor. While a portion of the crew was hard at work making the ship as white as wax from stem to stern, the others were kept busy returning the salutes of passing steamboats and sailing vessels. The hundreds of visitors who swarmed aboard were made welcome, for from the Admiral down, all were in jolly spirits, and so glad to get home that they were ready to grasp the hand and hug every one who came within reach.

The first callers, of course, were the reporters, and directly after them came Sir Thomas Lipton owner of the *Shamrock*, which had crossed the Atlantic to race the *Columbia* for the world's championship. Admiral Dewey greeted Sir Thomas and his companions and lugged them off to his cabin.

Shortly after their departure, the *Dolphin* ran alongside with Rear Admiral Sampson and Captain Chadwick. Standing at the

24

head of the gangway, Admiral Dewey grasped the hands of Admiral Sampson as he came up the steps. The visitors, of course, were in full dress uniform, and being taken below remained for an hour chatting together.

Hardly had they left, when George G. Dewey, only son of the Admiral, came aboard. The young man, who had not seen his father for two years, was nervous and anxious, his wish being to surprise his parent, who did not see him until he came up with the salutation :

" How are you, father ?"

It was a joyous meeting indeed, and young Dewey remained close by his father throughout the remainder of the day at the receptions and all. The next important arrival was Rear Admiral Philip, who as soon as he came within sight roared : " *Hello-o-o-o ! Dew-ey !*" And the Admiral roared back again just as lustily : " *Hello-o-o-o ! Philip !*" Then followed the meeting, the laughter and handshaking. Thence forward, there was a steady stream of visitors until nightfall. The Admiral was in high spirits, jovial and charmed all by his brightness and vivacity. A committee explained to him the arrangements that had been made for the reception, and he expressed himself pleased with everything that had been done.

Wednesday was like a clear crisp day in October, and the multitudes who steadily poured into the city from all directions were delighted over the promise of fine weather for the magnificent demonstration. Of course, the Admiral passed the night on board the *Olympia*, since his official landing could not take place before the day set, September 30th.

At about ten o'clock in the morning, the Admiral and the *Olympia* ran the forts in the lower bay and sailed on along the Staten Island coast to the head of the fleet of warships, which had been waiting for a week to take part in the great demonstration. The first gun firing was when the flagship came within sight of Fort Wadsworth. The *Olympia* thundered her reply, and then Fort Hamilton struck in and was responded to as before. After this it was cannon war, the shrieking of whistles and the cheering of thousands. Amid it all, Dewey stood on deck, smiling and as happy as a schoolboy.

When the forts had finished, the fleet of warships took up the tremendous work. The *New York*, the *Chicago*, the *Massachusetts*, the *Indiana*, the *Texas*, the *Lancaster* and the *Dolphin* never made more noise, and it is safe to say never will surpass what they did in honor of the hero of Manila. Admiral Howison of the *Chicago*, ranked Admiral Sampson by a few months, and was therefore commander of the fleet. As the *Olympia* came up, Howison's blue flag was pulled down and up went the red field with the two stars, showing merely the flagship of a Rear Admiral. Through the turmoil and bedlam of steam whistles, waring guns and yelling human beings steamed the *Olympia*, with her four-starred blue flag, indicating the rank of a full admiral, to the head of the column of warships, where she dropped her anchor and returned the salute of Admiral Howison.

The anchorage was just below the Staten Island Ferry, and there the *Olympia* was beset hour after hour by every species of boat that floats, crammed full of jubilant, shouting, frenzied multitudes, who seemed completely to lose their senses, whenever the Admiral showed himself for a few minutes on his ship.

The first visit of the day was by the government tug *Markeeta*, on which were the relatives of the Admiral. They numbered fifteen, not counting George, the son, who remained all night on the *Olympia*. The reunion lasted about an hour, and it need not be said was a delightful one to all and to none more than the bronzed hero himself.

After this, Admiral Howison who was in Dewey's class at the Naval Academy, and has always been a warm personal friend, came on board and was followed by Admiral Sampson. These calls of course had to be returned in full uniform which is gorgeous enough to dazzle the eyes of those even who are accustomed to military display. One of the most pleasant calls was upon his old friend Admiral Jack Philip in command of the Brooklyn Navy Yard. As an announcement of his intention to leave the ship for a time, the Admiral's flag was first lowered on the *Olympia*.

The day was as busy as the preceding one. Visitors swarmed over the ship ; a floral horseshoe six feet high was presented to the Admiral ; schoolboys took his picture ; a lion cub born in Philadelphia was presented to him by the Director General of the Hagenbach's Aggregation of Trained Animals, and received with delight by the Admiral. After the departure of the visitors, a concert was held on board the *Olympia*, and at a late hour the tired ones were allowed to rest and sleep.

Thursday, the 28th, was absolutely perfect,—the skies blue, the sunshine clear and the temperature neither too warm nor too cold, but such as to make exercise pleasant, and to cause the blood to bound through the veins to tingle the cheeks and to make one glow with health and high spirits.

The *Olympia* was anchored down the bay off Tompkinsville, where she was literally taken possession of by the swarms whose enthusiasm was irrestrainable. Frequent salutes were exchanged with the other warships, and the whole day was another bedlam of hurrahs, cheers, steam whistle and booming cannon.

The most interesting visitor of the day was Commodore George W. Baird. Commander Baird had with him the flag of Admiral Farragut. When Farragut was made a Rear-Admiral in the Civil War a quartermaster named Knowles, the same man who passed lashings around Farragut in the rigging of his ship, improvised a Rear-Admiral's flag, which was used on the *Hartford*. When Farragut was promoted to full Admiral, Knowles added two stars, making it four, and this was the original Admiral's flag of the United States Navy. The flag was deposited later in the Naval Academy at Annapolis, Md., where it remained until 1881, when the bronze statue of Admiral Farragut was unveiled in Washington. The flag was used in the celebration attending the unveiling of the statue. Later it came into the possession of Commander Baird, who was an old shipmate of Admiral Dewey.

Admiral Dewey was taken by surprise when Commander Baird came aboard the *Olympia*, and when he learned that this flag was to be given to him the tears came into his eyes and he was unable to speak. As the Commander handed the flag to him he said:

"Admiral, I wish to present to you the first Admiral's flag ever broken out in the Navy of this country. That grand old Admiral, whose name and memory we all so revere, first hoisted this ensign upon the good ship *Hartford* before New Orleans and afterward upon the *Franklin*, and since it came down from that masthead it has never been whipped by the wind nor worn by the elements.

And you, the worthy successor of that great Admiral, whose tactics you so successfully followed a short while ago, I deem the proper person for Farragut's mantle to fall upon."

Admiral Dewey did not speak for a moment. Then he said, his voice trembling :

" This is the last flag I'll fly. It was the first Admiral's flag, and I feel the honor that it brings to me."

The tears were still in his eyes as he turned to the committee with Commander Baird and said :

"You do me too great an honor by bringing me this beautiful flag."

Among the numerous official visits was that of the committee which had in charge the reception of Admiral Dewey when he should reach Washington. It was headed by Major-General Nelson A. Miles and Rear-Admiral Higginson. As the General of the Army came aboard, the *Olympia* fired the fifteen guns due to his rank. He and the Admiral chatted together, the other members of the committee were introduced, and the full Washington programme was explained.

After the departure of General Miles and his party, General Merritt, officially representing the army and in full dress uniform came alongside and was received with fitting honors. It will be remembered that Dewey and Merritt were closely associated in the capture of Manila, and they met with all the warmth of two old comrades in arms.

The most striking call, however, was that of Governor Roosevelt, to whom the Admiral impulsively declared " I owe everything to you," alluding to the work of Roosevelt when Assistant Secretary of the Navy, through which the victory of Manila was rendered possible. The meeting between two such brave, patriotic men could not have been more cordial and demonstrative. After there had been innumerable exchanges of compliments, Governor Roosevelt turned to Captain Lamberton, who stood beside the Admiral and said : " You don't realize what you are. I have read of the achievements of Nelson and I have read Mahan about Trafalgar. You fellows are greater than either of them. You will go down in history. Every schoolboy will read it, and I tell you that's a great thing and' a great responsibility, too."

The Admiral turned to the Governor and said again : " You are the man who sent us to the Philippines. I owe everything to you, and I want to tell you, Governor, that you are the only visitor I've had for whom I've turned out the men."

When the Governor and his party left, seventeen guns were fired, an Admiral's salute, and Roosevelt was the only visitor accorded that honor. The Lieutenant-Governor of Vermont and the Governor's staff in gorgeous uniforms called and attempted to inflict a set speech upon the Admiral, but he cleverly dodged it, being neither an orator himself nor fond of listening to orations by others.

Friday was another crisp, sunshiny day, the ideal one for what may be termed the official welcome to Admiral Dewey and the heroes of Manila, Not counting the thousands who crowded the innumerable crafts of all descriptions, a moderate estimate of the number of spectators in the city and on land was a million.

The show opened in the upper bay off Tompkinsville and off St. George, where the warships of Admiral Sampson's squadron were anchored below the *Olympia* and the vast swarming multitude began surging in the morning toward Staten Island. Self-defence compelled the exclusion of visitors, but when between nine and ten o'clock the Admiral appeared on the quarter-deck he was cheered with the wildest enthusiasm.

The steamboat *Sandy Hook* arrived a few minutes before eleven o'clock, bearing Mayor Van Wyck, President Guggenheimer, of the Council, and President Woods, of the Aldermen, the Governors of fifteen States, and most of the officers of the city administration. As they came abord, the Admiral warmly shook the hand of the Mayor and invited him and his friends to go below. All entered the cabin, where the Admiral stood on one side of a long table, with the Mayor directly opposite. The Mayor said :

" Admiral Dewey, with pleasure and by the direction of the city of New York, I meet you at her magnificent gateway to extend to you in her name and of her million visitors, leading citizens of forty-five States, representing almost every hamlet in the nation, a most cordial welcome, congratulating you upon being restored to family and home.

" A loving and grateful nation is gladdened by your safe return from the most remarkable voyage of history, so far-reaching in its results that the clearest mind cannot yet penetrate the distance. It has already softened the voices of other nations in speaking of ours; changed permanently the map of the world; enlarged the field of American pride and completed the circle of empire in its western course. Your courage, skill and wisdom, exhibited in a single naval engagement of a few hours, brought victory to our country's arms, and then you dealt with your country's new relations to the world with the judgment of a trained diplomat. By common consent, you have been declared warrior and statesman—one who wears the military uniform until the enemy surrenders, and then dons the habit of the diplomat.

"The greatest reception awaits you that was ever tendered military or civil hero. Such an outpouring of the people was never dreamed of before. Never has the heart of America turned with such perfect accord and trusting confidence to one of her sons as it does to you.

" I place at your disposal the freedom and unlimited hospitality of the city of New York."

The Admiral replied that he was deeply touched by the many evidences of good-will that had been shown him, and fully appreciated the honor which the city and the American people had done him. Then the Mayor drew from his pocket the gold badge, decorated with diamonds, which the city had struck for Admiral Dewey.

" How beautiful !" said the Admiral, who called his steward, and, indicating the place where he wished to have the medal pinned, had him pin it.

Then the Mayor said that he trusted the Admiral would call on him on his ship. The Admiral said he would be very glad to do so, and the whole party left the cabin, entered the barge and went directly to the *Patrol*, on which the police crew was lined up along the starboard rail. The policemen all saluted by raising their right hands to the visors of their caps as the Admiral stepped over the rail. Led by the Mayor he entered the cabin of the *Patrol*, where a light breakfast was served. The Mayor remarked that a great victory was won at Manila and the *Olympia* was a great fighting ship.

"Yes," replied the Admiral, "she is certainly a great fighter. She is a great ship ;. but we won at Manila for another reason. That reason was that the Government at Washington has always been ready to spend a lot of money to let. the crews of our vessels have plenty of target practice. The crews on the ships in the Asiatic squadron had lots of target practice and they could shoot well and hit well. The reason that we beat the Spaniards so easily, in fact, was because of the forethought of Roosevelt in letting the Navy have all the money that it wanted for gunnery practice. The Spaniards, on the other hand, had never had any practice at all, to speak of. Some of them had never shot at a target in their lives."

After breakfast, Admiral Dewey and the rest of the party entered the barge and returned to the *Sandy Hook*, where the crush was terrific. On board the *Sandy Hook* were the following members of the Admiral's family : Mr. and Mrs. Charles Dewey, Mr. and Mrs. C. Robert Dewey, Miss Kate Dewey Squire, Mr. and Mrs. McCuen, Mr. and Mrs. F. J. Howland, Lieutenant and Mrs. Thomas G. Dewey, George P. Dewey, William T. Dewey, James S. Dewey, Mr. and Mrs. Martin and Miss Martin. None of them except Mr. Charles Dewey tried to take any part in the welcome to the Admiral. They remained together on an upper deck throughout the day.

The Governors who were on the *Sandy Hook* were Stone of Pennsylvania, McSweeny of South Carolina, Tunnell of Delaware, Voorhees of New Jersey, Dyer of Rhode Island, McMillin of Tennessee, Atkinson of West Virginia, Wells of Utah, Russell of North Carolina, Bushnell of Ohio and Richards of Wyoming.

The time set for the parade was one o'clock, and a few minutes before that time the Admiral's own flag was hauled down, and that of Admiral Farragut, the first Admiral of the Navy, was run up to the main truck. The cheering whistle blowing and shouts were overpowering and indescribable. Then the *Olympia* gracefully headed up the river at quarter speed, followed by the other warships, the start being made at exactly one o'clock.

The fireboats *New Yorker* and *Zophar Mills* took positions as outsiders of the *Olympia* and kept the route clear, by each starting its tremendous hose and keeping a huge stream of water going. Any

raft that got in the way of this miniature Niagara was sure of a ducking and all scooted frantically from under the deluge.

At either quarter of the *Olympia*, there was a protecting torpedo boat, and behind them came the other ships of the fleet of war
vessels. First there was the *New York*, flying three big American
ensigns and the red flag with two stars of Admiral Sampson. Next
came the *Indiana* with the flags that she flew in the battle at Santiago.
After her were the *Massachusetts*, the *Texas*, the *Brooklyn*, the *Ma-
rietta* the *Lancaster*, the *Scorpion*, and then Rear-Admiral Howison's
flagship the *Chicago*. She flew three ensigns too, and the red flag
of two stars, and that denoted the rank of Admiral Howison. The
torpedo boats that were spread along the line included the *Ericsson*,
the *Winslow* and the *Cushing*. The *Porter* and the *Dupont* were the
afterguard of the *Olympia*. After the warships came the revenue
cutters *Manning, Algonquin, Gresham, Windham,* and *Onondaga*.
The transports *Sedgwick, McPherson* and *McClellan* were up the bay
waiting until the more pretentious ships passed them in order to fall
in line.

The fleet had just about straightened out when Admiral Dewey
and Colonel Bartlett went up to the after-bridge. Admiral Dewey
spent three or four minutes looking around, first with the naked eye
and then with his glasses. He saw the bay closely dotted with ships
of all sizes and all styles. In the distance the Staten Island shore
was black with people ; in the other direction he saw Liberty Island
and Liberty herself with flags flying from every corner of her
pedestal, and the greensward running from the foot of the pedestal
down to the water's edge, full as it would hold of men and women
waving hats and flags in his honor. He saw the Brooklyn Bridge,
the tall poles on which the lights had been fixed, spelling the words
" Welcome Dewey," decorated from top to bottom with the flags of all
nations ; he saw every pier on the Brooklyn side decked with human
beings as thick as mustard on a plaster. Up the river, as far as he
could see with the aid of his glasses were crowds of boats, seemingly
without end. Looking upon the magnificent welcome, the like of
which no living hero ever received, the Admiral was deeply affected,
and for a long time paced back and forth, silent, thoughtful, grateful
and profoundly happy.

As Governor's Island was reached the guns of Old Castle Williams began to boom out their salute for the Admiral. The side of Governor's Island that was nearest to the line of the parade was filled with people who were waving flags and cheering. Castle Williams fired seventeen guns.

The moment the last sounded, the *Olympia* began returning the salute, and her firing started up the bedlam of whistles again.

Castle Williams passed, the Battery was in sight and then was seen for the first time the real magnitude of the reception that was awaiting the victorious Admiral and his ship. From the deck of the *Olympia* the Battery appeared to be one mass of humanity. The Barge Office roof was covered to the cupola; the Aquarium seemed planted in the centre of the crowd in Battery Park, and its circular roofs were crowded until they appeared to be roofs made wholly of human beings. Every pier on the New York side beginning with the first one above the Battery had a load of humanity that threatened to sink it. The boats that lay alongside the piers were likewise crowded and they were all dressed in holiday attire. Without the aid of glasses it could be seen that the roof of every house along the river front held its load, the windows of every house that showed above the pier houses were filled with people and the roofs of the great buildings of lower Broadway made a tremendous showing. The Bowling Green building, towering high as it does above the Washington building, was made still higher by an immense stand erected there, and from the *Olympia* the people seemed to go right up and form a peak. The Produce Exchange tower was crowded and the roof of the Produce Exchange building. And so every building that could be seen appeared to be as full as it could stick, and the people leaning out of the windows made it look as if the buildings themselves were stocked with humanity and the contents were running over.

As the *Olympia* began to pass the piers the craft that were lying alongside blew their whistles and the crowd around sent up cheers. The ferryboats that were running back and forth across the river were as badly crowded as were the excursion boats that were taking part in the holiday. They too were decked out in all the flags that could be plastered over them, and the sight of the on-

coming parade set their captains adding to the bedlam that the holi-
day-makers were sending up. The big double-deck ferryboats of the
Pennsylvania Railroad towering above the pier-houses themselves,
were a mass of women, and when they began blowing their whistles
it seemed to be a signal for an uproar of noise from the Jersey coast.
The ships on that side of the river, the engines in the railroad yards
and the factory whistles joined in. On the end of the Starin Line
pier was an immense banner reading "Welcome Dewey," and then a
stand that reached from the water line clear up to the end of the
pier. The American Line pier, next to it, is about twice as big and
the stand on the end of that also reached to the roof and was filled
with women who wore gay colors and who made a sight that attracted the attention of the Admiral.

"Look at them," he said; and stepping to the port rail of the
bridge he took off his hat and waved it at the crowd, bowing again
and again as he did so.

On up the river, as the *Olympia* proceeded, the noisy welcome
grew louder. The first open space on the New York shore after the
Battery was passed was at Canal Street, and, as in the case of the
Battery, this seemed to be a solid mass of people. But it could not
have been solid, for there was room for them to move enough to
wave flags, and they waved hundreds of them. The Admiral
returned the salute by waving his hat. The houses along the river
at Canal Street are back a block. They presented the same appearance that the big buildings down-town had presented—humanity
everywhere, even on the chimneys. Canal Street itself seemed to be
a mass of colors. Flags were flying from every window in the buildings, and all appeared to be decorated. Above Canal Street are the
piers of the Atlantic Transport Company and the French Line.
Two steamships were in each of them. The ships, like all the other
ships along the line were filled; the piers were crowded.

The Admiral stood, taking in the scene and evidently deeply
affected by it. Finally he left the bridge and climbed over on the
superstructure and up on the platform, where the signal boy stands
when he wigwags the signals. There he was above everything. His
was the most conspicuous figure on the ship. He stood there with
nothing to interrupt the view either of himself or of the multitude

alongshore and in the boats who were looking at him. With his glasses he swept the river. To say that the scene at this time was inspiring is putting it mildly. No man could look at it without becoming intensely enthusiastic himself. It was only natural that the Admiral should be impressed to a degree that made it impossible for him even to speak. He stayed up there on this superstructure for several minutes and then he climbed back on the bridge, and for a season paced up and down.

Twenty-third Street was reached, still there was no let up in the crowds, and the everlasting noise of the whistles, instead of diminishing, seemed to grow louder and more earsplitting. Loud and awful as it was, it was almost redoubled a few blocks further on, where are the piers of the New York Central Railroad and where the Central has its yard. The Central Railroad piers are equipped with railroad tracks and the railroad men had run down on them all the locomotives they could command. A locomotive has a sharper and more piercing whistle than the average boat. Every one of these engines started going at once and at the same time the sirens in the fleet, that had been comparatively silent since the start of the parade, joined them. It was confusion worse confounded. There are railroads on the other side of the river at that point, too, and the engines over there joined in the uproar.

Admiral Dewey walked up and down the bridge ; he tried to speak a dozen times, but he might as well have remained silent, for, speak as loud as he would, his voice could not be heard a foot from his face.

Near Forty-second Street one of the West Shore boats got a ducking from the stream of water sent out by the fireboats. There are coal pockets near Forty-second Street, and these bore a heavier weight of humanity than of coal.

As the fleet proceeded up the river beyond this the boats alongside the *Olympia* grew thicker. Many tugboats, excursion boats and yachts had not gone down the bay at all to join in the procession, but had lain in wait up here for it to come along. They were responsible in a large measure for mix-ups in divisions, want of order and all that, that necessarily marked the celebration. They fell into the line anywhere and everywhere after the warships had passed. The police

kept them out until that time. While the police boats could keep
them out of the course they could not keep them out of the line between the shore and the parading ships. They cut off the view of
thousands of those who had gathered along the shore hoping to have
a good look at the *Olympia*. The Admiral saw this and he remarked
that it was a shame that these people who were undergoing such discomfort as they were, should by such a fluke be disappointed. He
sent word to the *Patrol* and asked if something could not be done,
but it was impossible to do anything because there were so many of
the boats.

It was only a little further uptown, however, that the ground
began to get higher and these waiting disobedient boats no longer
interfered with the view. There was more open ground, too, and the
Admiral had a better chance to see crowds gathered in spots wherever there was a vacant lot. Wherever there was a place on the bluff
that did not hold a building, there was a crowd.

"Look at it," said the Admiral. He turned then and saw the
rising ground of the Jersey side and there the story was the same.
Up and up, almost from the water's edge, the people sat in great
tiers.

A little further on, Riverside Drive with its countless thousands
of spectators came in view, and in the distance Grant's Tomb loomed
up. Along here was a yacht anchorage, and every owner was waiting
to salute the *Olympia* when she came along. So again there began
the roaring of the cannons and the popping of the guns and revolvers
on the little yachts. Each new sort of noise that came along started
up all the old noises again, or rather gave them new vigor, for they
never stopped, and so it was that on the way up by Riverside Drive
the earsplitting features of the celebration did not die out. There
must have been not less than one hundred yachts that saluted the
Admiral and his flagship in this trip before the stakeboat was
reached.

It was twenty-three minutes after two o'clock when Grant's
Tomb came in sight. Before this the line of the parade had been
near to the New York shore. Now there was a turn and the boats
headed over as close into the Jersey shore as it was possible for them
to get for safety. Captain Lamberton himself was on the bridge of

the *Olympia* commanding his ship, and he kept men throwing the lead to make certain of his depth of water. The floats were the next thing that attracted attention. The one representing Victory had an incomplete appearance because of an accident that happened to it on Thursday night, when the government boat *Wompatuck* was towing it. The float representing Peace was all right. Admiral Dewey was greatly interested in these floats, but it was the people that attracted him most. Never before in his life had he seen such a gathering, and it was all in his honor and in honor of the men who sailed with him.

As the flagship turned the stakeboat word was given to fire the salute in honor of the memory of General Grant, and the *Olympia's* guns spoke out. The river at this point is between very high land on both sides and the roars of the cannon were echoed and re-echoed from the Palisades and from the Drive. Every one of the seventeen guns seemed four or five separate guns, so distinct and so loud was this echo.

It was twenty-five minutes to three when the stakeboat was turned, and on the Admiral's order signals were run up directing each of the other warships in the fleet to fire the same salute for General Grant as they turned. The *Olympia* started back down the line on the New York side. As she passed warship after warship the jackies were drawn up along the rail. The bands on nearly all the boats played the "Star-Spangled Banner," and the *Olympia's* band itself joined in, playing it over again and again, and then starting off on other airs. As the *Chicago* came by, the Admiral commented on her neat appearance, and called the attention of everybody around to it.

The *Olympia* went on down the river to a point about opposite 115th Street, when the bells in the engine room stopped ringing and the order was given to let go the anchor. From this position Admiral Dewey said he would review the paraders.

Never before was such a crush of boats seen in these waters. The shores on either side of the river were filled with people, shores that from the river bed appeared to be mountains. There they sat, tier upon tier. They were all the colors of the rainbow. The American flag everywhere. At a little distance Grant's Tomb towered. Up

the river, down the river, on either side as far as the eye could reach
without, so far as could be seen, a single break was a mass of human
faces ; and then on the river itself from shore to shore were boats
without end, and each in itself a mound of human beings. No matter
what way you looked, on the water or off the water, you saw a struggling, shouting crowd. The boats from down the river seemed all
to be coming head-on to the *Olympia*, and so with the boats from up
the river, all making directly at her, crowded so closely together
that it seemed as if they must hit each other. And there was the
deafening noise, the noise of a thousand whistles, the noise of a hundred bands playing at once, and the noise of ten thousand voices all
within hearing distance. Such was the scene of nearly two hours
and a half without a single break, without a let-up of any kind.
Again and again the thunder of cannon was heard, and again and
again the crew of the *Olympia* was called upon to respond to the
cheering multitude.

As the warships came by on their return trip they passed very
close by the *Olympia* on the New York side. The officers in every
case were drawn up on the bridge. The marine guard was drawn up
on the quarter and the jackies lined the side.

There they all stood at an attitude of salute, and as the officers
doffed their hats in salute, the Admiral in each case returned the
salute in the same manner and the band of the *Olympia* played the
national air.

The only thing that grew really monotonous about this reviewing stand was the everlasting and infernal din, and for this the police
boats were chiefly responsible. For when there was any sign of letting up they would start it afresh. Time and time again they did
this until it was provoking to a degree. After the passage of the
warships, Admiral Dewey left the bridge for the first time since he
had gone on at the beginning of the parade.

Going below he was not gone more than five minutes when he
returned to the bridge and for a little time more steam was put on
the uproar.

After the warships there was no order at all in the procession
as it passed in review. The one thing that was particularly noticeable was that it was in all ways the day of the common people. The

14 D.D.

common people were on the older boats in the fleet, and the captains of the older boats were not so particular about getting a bump or a torn rail, and they took all sorts of chances to get the inside track, with the result that they cut out the view of many of the yacht owners who were in the parade and many of the people who traveled on the higher priced boats whose captains were more care ful. Another thing that was particularly noticeable was that the signs, or banners, rather, that were carried by the various excursion boats were almost always the same. They bore the words " Wel come Dewey."

All the afternoon the Admiral remained on the bridge, per sonally returning the enthusiastic salutes that were given in the only way that he could do—by bowing and lifting his hat. He was particu larly interested in every one of the big excursion boats. There was the *Glen Island*, the *Slocum*, the *St. John's*, the *Claremont*, the *Rosedale*, the *Grand Republic*, the *Middletown*, and every other boat about, that makes a business of carrying excursionists out of New York or out of any port near here. Towering above them all was the great *Puritan*. How many thousand persons she had on board nobody but the officers of the steamboat line that owns her will ever tell. She was a sight to behold. She was a sight that attracted the Admiral's attention, and that held it, and for fully five minutes, while she was slowly, almost drifting by, he stood there now bowing and waving his hat, now looking through his glasses searching for the face of some one he knew. When he turned away from her he said : " It is wonderful, isn't it ? Wonderful ! "

He was also particularly interested in the show that was made by the Naval Militia. The Naval Militia were on the big tugboats *H. B. Moore*, the *Rochester*, the *Transfer No. 11* and *Transfer No. 12*. These boats got excellent positions and the Militia made a splendid show. They passed on the port side of the *Olympiu* and were all drawn up on their various boats on the starboard side, the line on each boat extending from stem to stern. They stood with their hands touching the visors of their caps and while they were so standing the Admiral stood on the bridge with his hand raised in salute in exactly the same manner.

On one of the big excursion boats as it passed a woman's voice shrieked, " Hail to Dewey !" and that cry was taken up and passed along the line. Thereafter every boat that came along for a while bore a crowd that shouted, " Hail to Dewey !" And the salute always got a reply from the Admiral.

The Admiral was anxious to see the yachts and it was a considerable disappointment to him that so many of them were unable, owing to the danger of getting into the mob, to get close enough to the *Olympia* to greet him and receive his greeting. Of those who did there was the beautiful *Corsair*, Mr. J. Pierpont Morgan's yacht. In the early part of the parade before the formation was spoiled by the interlopers who stayed up the river and stole in the moment the warships were by the *Corsair* was the leader of the fleet of yachts. There was really no fleet of yachts at the time the review began. The *Corsair* came along, however, close enough to salute the Admiral. There was a big party on her bridge and it was just as enthusiastic a party as was found on any of the excursion boats and just as demonstrative. After the *Corsair* came Oliver H. Payne's yacht, the *Aphrodite*. She was by far the best dressed yacht that was seen during the day. She was a mass of dress flags and they were arranged in the most tasteful and harmonious manner.

Altogether, perhaps twenty out of all the yachts that took part in the parade got a fair chance at the *Olympia* and the Admiral. The others that passed stayed outside the jam of boats. It was never safe for them to get in it.

The tail end of the procession was made up of excursion boats almost entirely and they were even more crowded than those that had gone before. The *Idlewild* sat so low in the water that it washed over her guard-rail and sometimes washed into the gangway where, on ordinary days, she takes in freight. She was only one of twenty that were as bad. As these boats passed the flagship, of course, the crowd insisted on getting over to the side nearest the ship, with' the result that they careened at most dangerous angles. In some cases there was really momentary expectancy on board the flagship that the boats would tip over, and it was always with a sigh of relief that the salutation to the people on those boats was finished.

25

Admiral Dewey stuck to the bridge until the last of the boats had passed. It was probably as hard a day's work as he had ever done in his life. He said :

" There never was anything like it ! It is magnificent ! It is astounding ! Just see the people ! Just see them ! There never was anything like it."

" And there probably never will be anything like it again," suggested a listener, laughingly. The Admiral smiled too. Later, through one of his staff, he requested that it be printed that he could not in person answer or acknowledge all of the good wishes and all of the congratulations and pleasant remembrances that he has received since he came to the city. He asked that this public acknowledgment be made of it.

It was half-past five o'clock when the Admiral left the bridge. The sun had gone down and the day ended with that most impressive of all ceremonies on shipboard, the salute to the flag. The band was drawn up on the superstructure, every man on shipboard stood at attention facing the ensign, and the band played the Star Spangled Banner. Not a soul stirred until the piece was ended, and as it was the ensign came down and every man raising his right hand to his forehead, saluted with a bow.

The day's celebration ended at night in a blaze of fireworks, such as threw all previous Fourths of July into the shade. Everywhere it was pop, bang, sizz and dazzling splendor. The East River celebration was made tremendously impressive, by the burning up of the two floats bearing the main supply of fireworks for the parade in that waterway. This took place at the foot of Fifty-ninth Street, and for a quarter of an hour the glare for blocks was more vivid than at noonday.

The most enormous crowds and the most stupendous displays of fireworks were off the Battery on floats and on Governor's Island, Bedlow's and Ellis Islands ; but the sky-scrapers, the parks, and the city itself were wrapped seemingly in one overpowering glare and glow in which all the colors of the rainbow blazed forth with bewildering splendor.

It was half-past nine when the celebration opened with a salute of 101 aerial bombs. A vast flight of rockets burst into drifting clouds of iridescent globes, which rose over Governor's Island, and while still climbing the sky, and bursting and spreading, the whole island broke into a flame of red, white and blue lights. Grim old Castle Williams loomed out of the darkness, and was crowned with a similar glare ; then Bedlow's Island flashed up, and the statue of Liberty was encircled by a halo of changing color. Ellis Island burst forth, and the whole bay looked as if it were on fire. The sun, moon and stars, could they have shone at the same time, would have hidden their diminished heads. Accompanying all this were the explosion of bombs, the shrieking of whistles, and the hurrahing of the enthusiastic hundreds of thousands.

In the midst of the indescribable racket, a vast portrait of Admiral Dewey appeared to the east of Castle Williams in outlines of white fire. It set the people wild and the roar, the shouts, the hurrahs and the bedlam of the whole day seemed condensed into the succeeding few minutes. Then the rain began falling and the people scampered to cover.

The setting sun at Riverside Drive revealed the warships at anchor in the North River, the *Olympia* at the head of the line, which extended from opposite Grant's Tomb as far down as Sixtieth Street. Then when night had fully come, there flamed out the most gorgeous and beautiful picture the Hudson has ever seen. A row of brilliant points of light marked the deck line of the *Olympia ;* three other lines joined the mastheads and descended in graceful curves to prow and stern ; a searchlight illuminated the American flag floating from the peak, and making the four stars in the Admiral's pennant shine like the real ones in the vault of heaven. Behind her were the *New York*, the *Chicago*, the *Indiana*, the *Texas*, the *Brooklyn* and the *Massachusetts*, resembling and yet differing as one star differs from another in glory.

The wonderfully fine weather, which began on Wednesday, continued through Saturday the last day of the official reception. The din and noise was less than on Friday, for the steam whistles, sirens and cannon were silent, hundreds of thousands of human voices taking their places, and shaking with their cheers, the metropolis of the New World from centre to circumference. Nothing of the kind was ever before seen in the history of the city. Business, as on

Friday, was suspended and all that was done and thought of was how to give the hero of Manila a rip roaring, overwhelming, resistless and all-surpassing welcome to his native land.

"Isn't it wonderful!" exclaimed the Admiral. "I never dreamed of anything like this. To think of this great city shutting down for two days to show its patriotism, for it is that. Leave me out altogether; they are honoring themselves."

Knowing that a hard day was before him, the Admiral was up at half-past five, having been notified by the Reception Committee who had him in charge that they would call for him at half-past seven. The officers had attended to every detail, and at the hour named the Admiral went to the *Patrol* with the committee, and she started down the river for the Battery.

The opening of the day's programme was to be the presentation of a loving cup to the Admiral by the Mayor. Clad in the full uniform of his exalted rank, and as usual somewhat ahead of time, he and a number of distinguished friends, stepped on the pier, where the waiting crowds broke into cheers, which swept up Broadway like a great wave, keeping pace with the Admiral's carriage, and mingling with the chimes of Trinity, as the party hurried to the City Hall, nearly a quarter of an hour ahead of time. The Mayor hustled off for the platform where the gold loving cup, thirteen inches tall, was to be presented to the Admiral. Among those who accompanied the Mayor were Governor Roosevelt, Rear Admiral Schley, Rear Admiral Philip and Rear Admiral Higginson. In addition, there were the six captains of Dewey's squadron, Captain Lamberton of the *Olympia;* Captain Dyer of the *Baltimore;* Captain Coghlan of the *Raleigh;* Captain Wildes of the *Boston;* Captain Walker of the *Concord*, and Captain Wood of the *Petrel*. Besides there were General Miles and his aide; Governor Richards of Wyoming; Governor Tunnell of Delaware; Governor Dyer of Rhode Island, and a number of the relatives of the Admiral.

When the preliminaries were finally arranged, the Mayor read from manuscript the following speech:

"The true dignity of manhood can never be over-estimated in the study of the influences which build up or preserve a State. Hero worship, if it be merely a manifestation of a full recognition and appreciation of such manhood in the individual leader's performance of duty to State, either in war or in peace, is most commendable. It holds up his high standard to be emulated by the living as well as the unborn millions to be. To such a hero death itself bows, for he lives in memory for all time. In this spirit I shall not hesitate in this presence to freely express America's estimate of your character and achievements. The nation would gladly have its dominion extended over the face of the globe in order that admiring millions of additional fellow-citizens might be here to-day to pay homage to you and welcome you back.

"Your countrymen are interested in and know every detail of your life. Your joys and your sorrows are theirs. They have traced your ancestry and your character and deeds from the cradle rocked by a fond mother to the *Olympia* rocked by the rolling waves of the mighty deep. They listen with delight to the story of the fighting Deweys bravely doing their duty in every war of their country for two hundred and fifty years; of your pointing out, when a mere child, to your father the pictures in the clouds of ships and battles, including the battle of Lake Erie and the form of Perry saving his country's flag from the disabled ship; of the devotional impress stamped upon your character by a loving mother; of your struggle with the schoolmaster, which taught the necessity of discipline in the affairs of life; of your inherited love for children and music; of your alert, bright and vivacious boyhood, mingled with the mischievous, but never with the malicious; of your deferential respect for those of your mother's sex; of the romance of your courtship and happy marriage; of your service under Admiral Farragut in the Gulf Squadron as the executive officer of the *Mississippi*, when you plunged iron shot and shell through the armor of the Confederate ram *Manassas;* of the sturdy and fearless manner in which you defended your ship against the guns of Port Hudson, and the quiet and orderly manner in which you abandoned her when she sunk, calling for special commendation of your superiors in their report; of the circumstance that between wars Farragut forty-eight years and you for thirty-seven years devoted yourselves to the study of your professions, and both at the end of a long peace were found fully equipped and ready to give their country splendid service and to raise themselves to the highest place of fame and renown.

"The romance of sea warfare has charmed and enchanted the imagination of man as no other theme has ever done, arousing in him the sentiment of patriotism and inspiring the poet with songs of his country and her heroes. This has always been so, whether in the times when Neptune with trident rode the sea in shell-shaped boat drawn by dolphins, or when the Vikings roved the North main carrying all before them, or when the sea kings with the modern navy were stationed upon the ocean to guard and protect the equal rights of civilized governments and their commerce upon the highways of the sea.

"The world stood enthralled and then broke out in loud huzzas which can never be silenced, when the electric spark flashed the news over the globe that on the first day of May, 1898, your fleet had destroyed in Manila Bay the Spanish navy, silencing the forts and taking the Philippine Islands, thus stripping the East of every vestige of Spanish domination. Spain was that moment conquered. The Pacific Ocean was that instant cleared of hostile forces, leaving to the remainder of our naval and land forces the task of sweeping clean the Atlantic Ocean and her islands of the depressed, half-famished and scattered bands of Spanish stragglers.

"This all was accomplished in a naval battle of less than seven hours, including the coolly ordered intermission for breakfast. Not an American killed, but two hundred Spaniards laid low, seven hundred wounded, the Spanish navy destroyed, and an empire lost to her forever. History records no achievement of such superb completeness as the battle in Manila Bay.

"This demonstration is no mere tribute to a personal friend, a fellow-citizen. It is a simple and deserved recognition of the debt due the public servant who has proved himself grandly and efficiently faithful to his country's welfare and honor. You are called a man of destiny. You are—but it is the destiny of merit and worth—the conscientious obedience to duty of one skilled in his art and judgment.

"Our Republic has no reason to fear a comparison of her seafighters with those of other nations. The birth of the Republic gave her Paul Jones; the war for freedom of ocean highways gave her

Perry, and the war for her moral and physical integrity gave her Farragut. She points with pride to any one of this trinity and says to all nations, match him if you can. The war against Spain, waged for common humanity's sake in behalf of her island neighbors, gave her Dewey, who can safely be proclaimed chief among the naval heroes of the world.

"The route of these idolized nautical sons of the Republic is well marked. Their exploits go resounding through time, partaking of the vast and overwhelming character of the ocean upon which they rode, lived, acted and attained their great achievements, which are the pride of all Americans.

"From your entry to your departure from Manila Bay you were a history-maker, and if the old style prevailed of naming the period after him who bore the most illustrious name of any living man, this would be known as the Dewey age. Solitary in the grandeur of your achievements, you are lifted above all those who have gone before you.

"To the Mayor has been assigned the personally pleasant duty of presenting to you in the name of the city of New York, the metropolis of our country, this loving cup, a keepsake, to remind you from time to time of her love for you and her special pride in your deeds of valor, which she believes will for ages to come insure full respect of all nations and people for our starry flag, whether flung to the breeze over the man-of-war or the ship of commerce."

To this somewhat lengthy speech the Admiral responded:

"It would be impossible, Mr. Mayor, for me to express in words how deeply I am moved by this—all these honors you have heaped upon me, one after the other, that beautiful cup, the freedom of the city, this great, magnificent reception. I cannot say what I want to, but, speaking for myself and the gallant squadron I had the honor to command at Manila, I thank you from the bottom of my heart.'

The loving cup which the Mayor gave to Admiral Dewey on behalf of the city is made of gold, eighteen carats fine. It is thirteen inches in height and will hold four and a half quarts. The form of the cup is Roman. The handles are three green gold dolphins. They divide the cup into three panels. The front panel is decorated with a relief portrait of the Admiral, framed in an oak wreath. The frame rests on the outstretched wings of an eagle. Under this panel on the band that runs around the foot of the cup are the letters "G. D., U. S. N." Between the next two handles is a half relief picture of the flagship *Olympia*. Under it is a shield bearing the four stars that denote the rank of the Admiral. The commemorative inscription, with the names of the Mayor, the members of the Municipal Assembly, and the Plan and Scope Committee, is on this panel. Beneath are the coat of arms of the city of New York. About the upper circumference of the cup is a row of forty-five stars. Around the foot are anchors, small dolphins, seaweed, knotted ropes and other nautical devices. The cup cost $5,000.

The Admiral was now escorted to the foot of Warren Street, where the steamship *Sandy Hook* was waiting to bear him and other distinguished guests and the city officials up to One-hundred-and-thirty-third Street to take the post of honor in the land parade. When the carriages were drawn up in two lines, the arrangement was as follows:

In the first were Admiral Dewey and Mayor Van Wyck, next came the six captains of the warships that had taken part in the battle at Manila Bay, two to a carriage. The fifth and sixth carriages were occupied by the personal staff of Admiral Dewey; in the seventh was Rear-Admiral Howison with President Guggenheimer of the Municipal Council. In the eighth were the three members of the personal staff of Rear-Admiral Howison; Rear-Admiral Sampson and President Wood of the Board of Aldermen occupied the ninth; the personal staff of Admiral Sampson and the commanding officers of the North Atlantic Station, eight in number, occupied the next two carriages. Rear-Admiral Philip with his aides, and St. Clair McKelway were in the twelfth. The thirteenth, fourteenth, fifteenth, sixteenth, seventeenth and eighteenth were occupied by the other naval officers of the North Atlantic Station. The twentieth was occupied by Governor Stone, of Pennsylvania, and his Adjutant-General and their escorts. The nineteenth by Governor E. W. Tunnell with his Adjutant-General, and ex-Mayor Boody, of Brooklyn, and Vernon M. Davis. Governor Voorhees, of New Jersey, and his Adjutant-General and his escort, one of whom was United States Senator William J. Sewell, occupied the twenty-first; the Governor of South Carolina and his escort, the twenty-second; Governor Russell and his escort, of North Carolina, the twenty-third; Governor Dyer, of Rhode Island and his escort, the twenty-fourth; Governor Smith, of Vermont, and his escort, the twenty-fifth; Governor McMillin, of Tennessee, and his escort, the twenth-sixth; Governor Bushnell, of Ohio, and his escort, the twenty-seventh; Adjutant-General Jumel, of Louisiana, and his escort, the twenty-eighth; Adjutant-General Henry, of Mississippi, and his escort, the twenty-ninth; Governor Atkinson, of West Virginia, and his escort, the thirtieth; Governor Richards, of Wyoming, and his escort, the thirty-first; Governor Wells, of Utah, and his escort, the thirty-second; Major-General Miles and his aide, with ex-Governor Levi P. Morton and Edward Lauterbach, the thirty-third; Major-General Merritt, his aide and his escort, the thirty-fourth; Rear-Admiral Miller, Rear-Admiral Schley and Vice-Chairman Berri, the thirty-fifth; Senator Depew, Richard Croker and William McAdoo, the thirty-sixth, thirty-seventh and thirty-eighth, and the Aldermen who were on the committee occupied four carriages. There were forty-two carriages altogether.

The bugle sounded a few minutes after eleven o'clock, and the parade started with the police in advance, six mounted officers riding on either side of the street in single file. Then followed half of the mounted force in wedge formation and next two files stretching all the way across the street. The battalion of sailors from the *Olympia*, after saluting the occupants of the carriages, had passed ahead and taken a position immediately behind Sousa's Band. Thus they were the first organization in the line of march. Uniformed in blue, with the name of their ship on their hats, they were recognized at once, and the moment they came in sight, the cheering began.

Directly behind the battalion came the carriage of Admiral Dewey, at sight of which the thousands lining the sidewalks, crowding the windows and roofs roared their applause again and again. It may be said that hundreds of thousands did nothing but wave hats, flags, parasols, and handkerchiefs, and dance, and cheer themselves hoarse, many of the women becoming frantic in their enthusiasm. The Admiral was kept continually bowing his ackowledgments until he must have grown weary.

Wheeling east, the line passed into Seventy-second Street, where the wild scenes were repeated. As the head of the parade passed under the elevated railway, it came upon one of the most beautiful stands of the whole review, being that of the school children. They were all dressed either in white or blue, and were so arranged that those in blue formed a field and those in white spelled the word "Dewey" in immense letters. The children broke into song, dancing and clapping their hands, but preserving the distinct formation of the word "Dewey." When the Admiral saw the sight, and heard the children singing "See the Conquering Hero Comes," he stood up in his carriage and tears filled his eyes. He ordered the carriage to stop opposite the stand, and for a full minute he stood facing the stand too much overcome to speak a word. Then he bowed, his chapeau in hand, and his smiling, glowing face showing his happiness.

Resuming the advance, Eighth Avenue from Seventy-second Street all the way to Fifty-ninth, where the next turn was made, was packed with the cheering, delighted throngs, who broke into irrestrainable enthusiasm the moment the *Olympia's* sailors came in sight, the climax being reached when sight was caught of the Admiral.

It was the same story throught the whole length of the parade until the reviewing stand was reached, where the Admiral and Mayor took their places, standing at the front, while the other members of the party retained their seats.

The *Olympia's* pioneers, fourteen in number, came first, marching ahead of the band and making a fine appearance, followed by the signal men and then the battalion of sailors. In the rear of the column was wheeled a rapid fire gun taken from one of the fighting tops. It was mounted on wheels and drawn by means of a rope in the hands of twenty-four sailors.

Now came the Naval Brigade of the North Atlantic Fleet, with a battalion of United States Marines at the head. They numbered four companies and marched evenly and yelled vociferously. They were followed by the sailors of the *New York*, the *Texas*, the *Indiana*, the *Massachusetts*, the *Brooklyn*, the *Lancaster* and the *Dolphin*.

The next division of the parade was from the regular army, and directly after them was the battalion of West Point Cadets, who never made a finer showing, their marching being perfection. The similarity of their uniform to that of the New York Seventh caused many of the spectators to mistake them for the body of men who did not go to war, and because of this error, they received a number of hisses.

Behind the cadets marched a battalion of Engineers, and after them two battalions of the Fifth Artillery; then a battalion of the Seventh, including a siege battery, whose huge guns were drawn by eight horses each. This was the first time these siege guns were ever seen in parade in New York.

The artillery had hardly passed the stand, when Governor Roosevelt appeared in civilian dress, riding a coal black charger. He received many cheers, and, in response to his salute, Admiral Dewey bowed several times to him. Squadron A was the escort of the Governor, and, being home troops, they were generally applauded. They were followed by the rest of the National Guard, of the State of New York, the Brooklyn soldiers having the place of honor, with the Naval Militia sandwiched among them, and the Old Guard bringing up the rear.

The Tenth Pennsylvania, a veteran regiment of the Filipino war, with Governor Stone riding at their head, received an enthusiastic welcome, which they heartily deserved, the Admiral standing with head uncovered until all had passed under the arch.

The Jerseymen, looking spick and span, followed, marching well, with Georgia next in line, every man showing himself a true soldier. The Governor's First Guards, of Connecticut, in their brilliant Continental uniforms, and a company of horse guards were next in order. To the strains of "Maryland, My Maryland," the troops of that State swung into view, and won applause for their elegance of uniform and the perfection of their marching. The "Dandy Fifth," of Baltimore, received a specially warm welcome. The regiment of South Carolinans looked like veterans, and were followed in quick succession by New Hampshire and North Carolina.

Governor Bushnell, at the head of the Ohio militia, was roundly cheered, the Gatling Gun Battery from Cincinnati attracting the most admiration. The horses of the Indianapolis Light Artillery plunged through the arch at a brisk trot ; the Mississippi Rifles followed ; then the Maine Signal Corps, followed by the Florida men ; the Corsican Rifles from Texas, and the District of Columbia's troops, which had been assigned the last place in the line.

The veterans now appeared, with General O. O. Howard at the head of the division. He saluted the Admiral, who returned it and then leaned forward. The General wheeled his horse to the right, and, taking the lines in his teeth, reached his one hand to Dewey, who warmly clasped it. The incident caused a renewal of cheering, which was repeated as the Duryea Zouaves, the Loyal Legion men and the other veterans of the Civil War marched past. Last of all were the veterans of the Spanish-American War, under Major-General Keifer. They included the Astor Battery, and a body of young veterans, bearing a large American flag inscribed, " The First American Flag to Wave over Morro Castle." Admiral Dewey uncovered and clapped his hands, all the spectators doing the same.

Re-entering the carriage with the Mayor, and escorted by Squadron A, and preceded by a squad of mounted police, the Admiral was driven rapidly up Fifth Avenue to the Waldorf, where he attended a dinner at which the guests were his officers and the officers of the ships which took part in the battle of May 1, 1898. It was purely a naval family affair and nobody else was present. Thus closed a demonstration which, in many respects, has never been equalled in America.

Admiral Dewey rested quietly over Sunday at his hotel, seeing only his relatives and immediate friends, and on Monday left in a special car for Washington over the Pennsylvania Railroad. Thousands were gathered at the different stations, in the hope of catching a glimpse of him as the train thundered past. At Princeton the students literally compelled a halt, and would not leave the track until the Admiral showed himself, when he was received with thunderous cheers. The Admiral, who was accompanied by his son, referred to him as a graduate of Princeton University, and to the fact that that institution had lately conferred the degree of LL.D. upon himself, at which there was more cheering.

The Admiral, who had made several attempts to sleep, was compelled to give it up, for it may be said that the whole journey to Washington was a continual ovation. . As usual, he arrived at the national capital sooner than he was expected, but he was quickly recognized and the multitudes cheered him to the echo. It need hardly be said that his reception by President McKinley was of the most cordial nature, and the long confidential chat was characterized by the utmost good feeling on both sides. The Admiral was closely questioned by the President regarding the Philippines, and the confidence in his judgment was shown by the government adopting his suggestions without delay. A strong additional naval force was ordered to Manila, a more rigid blockade was determined upon, and it was decided, in accordance with the Admiral's advice, to send reinforcements to General Otis at the earliest possible moment.

At the official reception the Admiral was presented to the members of the Cabinet, and to Mrs. McKinley, and he charmed all by his vivacity, good nature and modesty.

Tuesday, October 3d, was a perfect autumn day, cool and crisp, but sunshiny. Having secured a good night's rest, the Admiral rose refreshed and in high spirits. He left the home of Mrs. Washington McLean, where he was staying, amid the cheering of the thousands who had gathered. Escorted by a strong force of police, his handsome carriage was drawn by four dark horses, two of them ridden by postillions in livery. The carriage arrived at the Executive Mansion at half-past ten, followed by the victorious captains of his fleet, in carriages. Colonel Bingham, the army engineer officer, acting as Superintendent of Public Buildings and Grounds, escorted the Admiral from the carriage into the White House and up the stairs to the Cabinet Room, where the President and the members of his official family were awaiting the arrival of the Admiral. Salutations were exchanged all around, and in a few minutes Admiral Dewey, the President and the Cabinet came down the stairs.

The Admiral, at the request of the President, entered his carriage and was seated on his left, the members of the Cabinet following by twos in carriages. There was tremendous cheering all the way to the Capitol, and the President compelled the Admiral to do all the acknowledging.

All this was preliminary to the presentation of a sword to Admiral Dewey. The stand on which the ceremony took place projected some thirty feet beyond the steps of the eastern front of the Capitol building, and in front of this and between the large stand and the crowd was the platform on which the Marine Band was stationed.

At half-past eleven the President, Admiral and the Cabinet party arrived, and close behind them were the fleet captains who fought with Dewey at Manila Bay. The party was conducted to the Senate Chamber, where they waited until noon the hour appointed for the ceremony. Then the captains of the Manila Fleet led the way, followed by the members of the Cabinet, Supreme Court Justices, and the leading axecutive officers of the government.

The first cheer was given when Admiral Sampson arrived, followed by hearty applause for Admiral Schley, and other well-known officers of the Army and Navy. Major-General Miles, attended by his staff and a troop of cavalry, rode well up to the right of the stand, while the members of the local committee, all mounted, took a position to the left.

The head of the procession; of which the President or Admiral were a part, were greeted with cheers as they emerged from the great bronze doorway. The Admiral was kept bowing for some minutes, and then, at the suggestion of the President, he sat down in a chair on the left of the balcony that projected beyond the platform proper.

SECRETARY LONG'S SPEECH.

When an invocation had been offered and the confusion had partly subsided, Secretary Long read the Congressional resolution, authorizing the presentation of a sword to Admiral Dewey, and said :

"It was by this solemn sentiment, approved by the President, that the people of the United States made provision for putting in material form one expression of their appreciation of your valor as an officer of their navy, and of your great achievement as their representative in opening the door to a new era in the civilization of the world. The victory at Manila Bay gave you rank with the most distinguished naval heroes of all times. Nor was your merit most in the brilliant victory which you achieved in a battle fought with the utmost gallantry and skill, waged without

error, and crowned with overwhelming success. It was still more in
the nerve with which you sailed from Hong Kong to Manila harbor,
in the spirit of your conception of attack ; in your high commanding
confidence as a leader who had weighed every risk and prepared for
every emergency, and who also had that unfaltering determination
to win, and that utter freedom from the thought or possibility of
swerving from his purpose, which are the very assurance of victory.
No Captain ever faced a more cruicial test than when on that morning, bearing the fate and the honor of your country in your hand,
thousands of miles from home, with every foreign port in the world
shut to you, nothing between you and annihilation but the thin sheathing of your ships, your cannon and your devoted officers and men, you
moved upon the enemy's batteries on shore and on sea with unflinching faith and nerve, and before the sun was half way up the heavens
had silenced the guns of the foe, sunk the hostile fleet, demonstrated
the supremacy of the American sea power, and transferred to the
United States an empire of the Islands of the Pacific. Later by
your display of large powers of administration, by your poise and
prudence, and by your great discretion, not only in act, but also in
word, which is almost more important, you proved yourself a great
representative citizen of the United States, as well as now its great
naval hero. The lustre of the American Navy was gloriously bright
before and you have added to it a new lustre. Its constellation of
stars was glorious before, and you have added to it another star of
the first magnitude. And, yet, many of your grateful countrymen
feel that, in the time to come, it may be your still greater honor that
you struck the first blow, under the providence of God, in the enfran-
chisement of those beautiful islands which make that great empire of
the sea ; in relieving them from the bondage and oppression of
centuries ; and in putting them on their way, under the protecting
shield of your country's guidance, to take their place in the civilization, the arts, the industries, the liberties and all the good things of
the most enlightened and happy nations of the world, so that generations hence your name shall be to them a household word, en-
shrined in their history and in their hearts.

" By authorizing the presentation of this sword to you as the
mark of its approval, your country has recognized, therefore, not

15 D.D.

only the great rich fruits which, even before your returning from victory, you have poured into her lap, but also her own responsibility to discharge the great trust which is thus put upon her, and fulfil the destiny of her own growth and of the empire that is now her charge. It is a new demand upon all the resources of her conscience, wisdom and courage. It is a work in the speedy and beneficent consummation of which she is entitled to the cordial help, sympathy and uplift of all her citizens, not the faint-hearted doubts and teasing cavils of any of them. It is a work on which she has entered in the interest of early peace in these new lands, their stable government, the establishment in them of law and order, the security of life and property and the American standards of prosperity and home. Let those who fear, remember that though her children, guided by you, took the wings of the morning and dwelt in the uttermost parts of the sea, even there the hands of our fathers' God shall lead them and His right hand shall hold them. In this work, in view of the great part you have taken in the sudden development of her sovereignty, your full knowledge of the situation, and the just hold you have on the hearts of all her people, she looks for your continued service and listens for your counsel, in the high hope and purpose that the triumph of her peace shall be even greater than her triumph in war.

"It is my good fortune, under the terms of the enactment of Congress, to have the honor of presenting to you this beautiful sword. If during the many coming years, which I trust will be yours, of useful service to your country, it shall remain sheathed in peace, as God grant it may, that fact will perhaps be due more than to anything else, to the thoroughness with which you have already done its work. I congratulate you on your return across the sea in full health of mind and body to receive it here; here in the National capitol; here on these consecrated steps where Lincoln stood; here standing between the statue of the first President of the United States and him who is its living President to-day; here in this beautiful city adorned with the statues of its statesmen and heroes, the number incomplete until your own is added, here amid this throng of citizens who are only a type of the millions and millions more who are all animated by the same spirit of affectionate and grateful welcome. I cannot doubt that it is one of the proudest days of your life and I know that it is one of the happiest in the hearts of each of your fellow countrymen wherever they are, whether on the continent or on the far-off islands of the sea.

"Now, following the authorization of Congress, I present this sword of honor which I hold in my hand—my hand rather let it go to you through the hand of one who in his youth also perilled his life and fought for his country in battle, and who to-day is the Commander-in-Chief of all our armies and navies, the President of the United States."

Secretary Long did a graceful thing by handing the sword to the President, who in turn handed it to Admiral Dewey. The President's voice was loud and clear, and when he said to the Admiral: "There was no flaw in your victory; there will be no falter in maintaining it," men and women, all of whom caught the true significance of the words, broke into cheering. Admiral Dewey was greatly affected and had difficulty in uttering his few words of thanks, as the President handed him the magnificent sword. The ceremony closed with appropriate tributes, and the Admiral returned to the handsome residence of Mrs. McLean, which had been placed entirely at his disposal.

The Congressional appropriation for the sword was $10,000. Except its steel blade and the body metal of its scabbard, the sword is 22-carat gold. On the pommel is carved the name "*Olympia*," and the zodiacal sign for December, in which month Dewey was born. Circling these is a closely woven wreath of oak leaves. Below these the pommel is embraced by a gold collar, on the front of which are the arms of the United States, with the blue field of the shield in enamel. Below them are the arms of Vermont, Dewey's native State, with the motto, "Freedom and Unity," and the colors of the shield in enamel. The plain part of the gold collar is decorated with stars, and a graceful finish is given to it by a narrow band of oak leaves. The sword blade is damascened, with the inscription: "This gift of the Nation to Rear-Admiral George Dewey, U. S. N., in memory of the victory at Manila Bay, May 1, 1898."

The sword grip is covered with fine shark skin, bound with gold wire and inlaid with gold stars. The guard is an eagle terminating in a claw, which grips the top in which the blade is set. The eagle's outstretched wings form the guard proper. The scabbard is of thin steel, damascened in gold, with sprays of a delicate sea plant—the *ros marinus*. These sprays are interlaced ; stars fill the inner spaces, dolphins the outer spaces.

Sprays of oak leaves and acorns secure the rings and trappings of the scabbard. Above these, on the front of the scabbard, is a raised monogram in diamonds entwining the letters " G, D.," and immediately under them are the letters " U. S. N." surrounded by sprays of the sea plant. The ferrule, or lower end of the scabbard, terminates in entwined gold dolphins.

The sword box is of white oak, inlaid with black velvet, and at the centre of the cover has a gold shield surmounted by an eagle and inscribed with a single star, and the words, " Rear Admiral George Dewey, U. S. N."